NO GOOD DEED

BOOK ONE IN THE MARK TAYLOR SERIES

BY
M.P. MCDONALD

This book is a work of fiction. People, places, events, and situations are the product of the author's imagination. Any resemblance to actual persons, living or dead, or historical events, is purely coincidental.

Dedicated to my husband Robert, and my three children, Brian, Tim, and Maggie.

Books in the Mark Taylor Series:

Mark Taylor: Genesis (Prequel)

No Good Deed: Book One

March Into Hell: Book Two

Deeds of Mercy: Book Three

March Into Madness: Book Four

CHAPTER ONE

The baby floated face down in the tub. The image hadn't changed, not that Mark Taylor expected it to. Not yet anyway. He tucked the photo in his back pocket and trotted down the steps from the 'L' platform. With any luck at all, the next time he looked, the baby would be fine. He skirted around an old lady tottering in his path and glanced at his watch.

All he had to do was find the apartment, convince the mom that he wasn't a nut case, or worse—a peeping tom—just because he knew that her phone would ring and distract her from bathing her daughter. Yep. Nothing complicated. Just get in, alert the mom, and get out. Five minutes. Tops. Mark jogged, cursing under his breath at the rush of people heading towards the train station. The crowd thinned, and he broke into a sprint, his breath exploding out in a cloud of white.

Cars blocked the crosswalk, trapped there when the light turned red. *Shit.* He paced left, then right, willing the light to change. To hell with it. He darted into the street, ignoring the blasting horns. It wasn't like the cars could advance anyway. He stumbled when one bumped his thigh, or he bumped it. He wasn't sure which and didn't have time to find out. Limping, he raced on.

Mid-block, he slowed to read the address numbers set above the entrance of an apartment building. This was the one. He pivoted and took the short flight of concrete steps two at a time and tugged at the door. Locked. *Of course.*

Bracing his hands on the door, he panted. *Think.* There had to be a way in. He wouldn't fail. Not this time.

He swiped his hand down a panel of numbered call buttons, not caring who answered as long as someone let him in. "Come on…*come on.*"

"Who is it?"

"Hey buddy, I forgot my key." It was the first thing that came to him and it didn't work. The next lie didn't either. Unable to think up a plausible story, he resorted to the truth on the fourth response. "It's an emergency! Life or death."

Maybe his voice sounded as desperate as he felt, or maybe the person didn't give a damn—whatever the reason, the guy let him in. He blinked as his eyes adjusted to the dimness. It was the second floor. He was sure of that. The dream played in his head like a movie, showing him the silver number twenty-two nailed to the door.

There was an elevator, but it was on the fifth floor. He spotted the stairs and flew up them, grabbing the railing to make the tight turn up to the second flight. It occurred to him that the door to the hallway might be locked, but luck was on his side this time, and it opened. Bent in a runner's stance, hands on knees, he huffed and glanced at the number on the door nearest him. Twenty-three. He guessed left and turned in that direction. He raised his hand to knock, but froze when an anguished scream raised the hairs on the back of his neck.

"*Christy!*"

Startled, he stumbled back, bumping against the wall opposite the door. He was too late. He spun and slammed the side of his fist against the wall, a curse ready to explode off his tongue, when he heard fumbling at the door behind him.

6

"Help me! Someone!"

At the desperate plea, he lunged to the closed door. "Hello? You okay?" He knew it was a stupid question. Of course things weren't okay.

The door cracked open before a young women clutching a limp, gray baby, elbowed it wide." My baby." Wild, desperate eyes met Mark's. "Please..."

Mark swallowed the acid in his throat and instinctively reached for the infant. "What happened?" He couldn't let on that he already knew. That led to questions he couldn't answer.

"I forgot her in the tub!" She clutched the baby and gave her a shake. "Oh god! Christy! She's not breathing!"

"I know CPR—give her to me." His sharp tone sliced through the mother's shock and she released her daughter with a wail of grief.

Mark positioned the baby with her head in his hand, her bottom in the crook of his arm.

The mother keened with her hands balled in front of her mouth. "Help her!"

The poor woman was teetering on the edge of hysteria, not that Mark could blame her. He was toeing the line himself, but he couldn't cross it. Not if there was a chance of saving the baby. With his free hand, he caught the mother's arm and gave it a firm squeeze. "I'm gonna help her, but you gotta listen to me. You need to call 9-1-1. Got it?"

She tore her gaze from her daughter, nodded, and raced back into her apartment. Mark wracked his brain, searching for a scrap of CPR knowledge that he knew was there. He cringed at the baby's glassy stare and blue-tinged lips. Her legs dangled lifelessly over his arm.

ABCs. That was it. Airway, breathing and circulation. He didn't see any water in her mouth, so her airway seemed okay. He covered her miniature nose and mouth with his own, feeling like a big clumsy oaf. Her scent filled his nose—so clean and innocent. Like baby shampoo and powder. A damp, silky tuft of her hair tickled his cheek. If she died, it'd be his fault. He could have prevented this. He blew again. There wasn't time to worry about guilt now.

Her chest rose with the breaths and he felt it move against his arm. Out of the corner of his eye, he saw doors down the hall opening, and a small crowd gathered around him. Some shouted instructions, and a deep voice ordered someone to the lobby to let the paramedics in when they arrived.

There was no change in Christy's color. *Shit.* Those paramedics better get here pronto. Why didn't someone else step forward to do the CPR? Hell, there had to be someone more qualified. There was supposed to be a pulse point near the elbow, but damned if he could find it. It wasn't like he'd ever searched for one on a healthy kid before let alone one who might not have one. Was that it? He prodded the inside of her arm, but between his shaking hands and the pudgy cushion at the bend of her elbow, he couldn't feel a beat.

Go to the source. He put his ear to her chest. Nothing. He swallowed hard as he placed two fingers on her breastbone and pushed down. The feel of her tiny chest caving in with each compression made his stomach churn.

He lost count of the cycles of breaths and compressions. It seemed like forever before someone suggested he stop and check for a pulse again. The mom had returned to his side at some point, but his vision had narrowed to Christy's little body cradled in his arms. Mom stroked Christy's forehead and pleaded with her to breathe.

8

Listen to your mama, sweetie. *Breathe, dammit.* Wait...was she pinker? Or was it wishful thinking? He paused the compressions, but gave another breath.

As he lifted her to listen for a heartbeat, Christy blinked.

Startled, he jerked his head back and glanced at the mom to see if she'd noticed it too. Her eyes full of anguish and fear, lit with a spark of hope as she met his look. It hadn't been his imagination.

Christy shuddered, and then coughed. Mark sat her up as she gagged, worried she was choking. She rewarded his efforts by puking sour milk down the front of him. She cried then, the sound as soft as a newborn kitten's. Impulsively, he kissed the top of her head.

A cheer rose in the hallway, and Mark glanced around, astonished to see so many people. A grin tugged at the corners of his mouth. The mother took her daughter from Mark, but planted a kiss on his cheek. The elevator at the far end of the hall opened, and paramedics stepped out.

Sure. Now they show up. Mark laughed, unable to suppress the giddiness. He took a deep breath, and leaned against the wall, his knees wobbling like Jello. He swiped his arm across his forehead. It was like a damn sauna in here. People crowded around, slapping Mark's shoulders and pumping his hand. Someone handed him a towel and he used it to mop up the mess on the front of his leather jacket, but there wasn't much he could do for the bit that leaked inside.

"Good job, man!" The speaker looked to be early to mid-thirties, close to Mark's own age. "That was awesome!"

"Thanks." Mark opened his mouth to ask if he could use a bathroom to wash up, when his stomach lurched and the bitter taste of bile filled his mouth. Panic surged through him and he rushed into the nearest apartment with an open door. He spotted a hallway and found the bathroom just in time for his lunch to make a return visit.

Spitting out the vile taste, he flushed the toilet and moved to the sink to wash, scooping some water into his mouth and swished it around. He dried his hands on a towel hanging over the shower curtain. He reached for the door-knob, but stopped and pulled the photo out of his back pocket, just to make sure. The picture had only one similarity with the one he'd put in his pocket only minutes before. The baby was still Christy, but now, she was grinning at the camera, showing off two pearly white bottom teeth. It was official. He'd erased another photo.

There was a knock on the door a second before Mark opened it.

"You okay?" It was the guy from the hall. He leaned against the doorway, arms crossed.

Mark nodded and motioned towards the toilet "Yeah. Just feeling the nerves. Sorry for barging in."

The man laughed and stuck out a hand. "No problem. I'm Jason."

"Mark." He clasped the man's hand and gave it a shake.

Jason gave Mark a speculative look. "A few minutes before that happened," he pointed his chin towards the hall, "someone buzzed my apartment, saying they had to get in—that it was an emergency."

Mark tried to play it cool as he edged towards the hallway. "Yeah?"

"That was you, wasn't it?" It was a statement.

"I...uh—"

Jason waved a hand and cut him off. "No worries, dude. I was just curious. I had a grandfather who used to get premonitions. It was spooky. Never thought I'd meet someone else like that. Glad I let you in."

Rattled and still shaking from the flood of adrenaline, Mark could only nod. He breathed a sigh of relief when Jason motioned for him to go first as they went out to the hall.

They watched as the paramedics started an IV on the protesting Christy, and he winced at the blood oozing around the IV site. Poor little thing. He felt a tap on his shoulder and turned to find a Chicago police officer behind him.

"Sir, can I ask you a few questions?"

Mark shoved his hands into his pockets to hide the shaking and shrugged. "Sure."

He asked Mark's name and for some ID. After speaking some cop code into his shoulder radio, he glanced at Mark's driver's license. "You don't live here, so why were you in the building?"

Mark pulled at the collar of his shirt under his coat. Necessity forced him to lie in these situations and he hated it, but the truth was far too complicated. Experience allowed his story to slip easily off his tongue. "I intended to visit a friend, and when I got to the building, someone was coming out, so rather than buzz, I just caught the door. When I got up here, I realized I had the wrong building." He forced a laugh. "My buddy's building looks a lot like this one and I guess I got them mixed up." Mark shook his head and rubbed the back of his neck. He was rambling and decided to cut the explanation short. "It's about time my faulty memory came in handy."

Luck was with him and the officer chuckled. "It sure did. You did a great job."

Mark dipped his head as heat rushed up his cheeks. "Thanks."

The cop's radio squawked, and in the midst of indecipherable code, Mark heard his own name.

The officer cocked his head, his gaze fixed on Mark as he reached up to key the mic. "10-9?"

The message was repeated and the officer tensed, his eyes cold as he acknowledged it and requested back-up. With one hand hovering over his weapon, he pointed at Mark with the other. "Turn around and place your hands on the wall."

Confused, Mark hesitated. "What...why?"

"Hands on the wall. Now!"

The commanding tone jolted Mark into action and he nearly tripped in his haste to comply. "Listen, sir, can I just ask—"

"We can do this the easy way or the hard way. The officer grabbed Mark's arm. "I've been told to bring you in for questioning."

"Who wants to talk to me? Why?"

The few people still milling in the hallway fell silent.

The cop glanced at the watching crowd and hesitated. "Unpaid parking tickets."

Parking tickets? Since when did they go to this much trouble for parking tickets? What the hell was going on? He twisted to see the cop's face. "I don't owe on any tickets. What's this really about?"

Jason stepped forward and pulled out his wallet. "Look, officer, the dude just saved a baby. What does he owe? I'll pay it."

"Step aside; this isn't any of your affair."

"Come on, man, don't be a hard-ass." Jason smiled at the cop, and gestured towards Mark. "I mean, this guy doesn't exactly look like Charles Manson."

Jason's attempt at humor backfired when the cop offered to let Jason accompany Mark.

Jason glared at the cop before casting an apologetic look at Mark. "Sorry. I tried."

Mark nodded. His face burned as the bystanders — the same people who'd cheered him just a few minutes before — now pointed fingers, and whispered to each other.

The cop's fingers dug into Mark's bicep. "Come on. You got some people waiting to meet you."

"Who?" This was going way too far for a few tickets that he couldn't even remember getting. "You sure you got the right Mark Taylor?"

The fingers tightened again as the cop frog-marched him towards the elevator. Mark balked. This was crazy. When the cop pressed him forward, he didn't think, he just reacted, jerking his arm free. "Quit pushing me!" The second the words left his mouth, he wanted to suck them back in.

"Get down! Right now. On your knees." The cop pulled his baton and prodded Mark with it.

"Whoa! Calm down. I just want to know the truth. I have that right, don't I?"

"I'm not going to tell you again." The radio blasted a sharp tone, and Mark started at the sudden noise.

The cop mistook Mark's reflex and swung the baton. Mark ducked his head and the blow landed with a thud against his shoulder. Pain rocketed down his arm like he'd touched a live wire. He sank to his knees. Two more blows landed on his back. He bit his lip to keep from crying out as he fell face-down on the floor, his nose buried in the dank, musty carpet.

13

The bystanders yelled at the cop while the cop shouted for them to shut up. Without pausing, the officer ordered Mark to lie down. Confused, Mark attempted to lift his face away from the nasty floor to tell him he was already lying down, but a sudden sharp pressure in the middle of his back pinned him to the floor.

He fought to breathe as his arms were wrenched behind him and cuffed. He managed to turn his head, the skin on his face pulling painfully taut as he sucked in air.

The door from the stairwell burst open and three more officers ran towards them, pulling their batons as they charged down the hall. Two men in suits followed, their manner and attitude exuded an aura of power and authority.

The first to reach Mark flashed a badge at him, but Mark couldn't get a clear look from his angle on the floor.

"I'm Special Agent Johnson and this is Special Agent Monroe. We have a warrant for your arrest as material witness to terrorist acts against the United States."

CHAPTER TWO

Jessie looked up at the knock on her door jamb. "Hey, Dan. What's up?"

"Lieutenant wants to talk to you." Her partner avoided her questioning gaze and before she could ask him what it was about, he turned away and rushed down the hall to the men's room. Figures he'd hideout in the one place she couldn't follow him. Whatever. She grabbed her jacket and shrugged it on and strode to her boss's office.

"Excuse me, sir? You want to see me?" She glanced at the file he held in his hands.

Lieutenant O'Hanrahan glanced up from a paper he was reading. The desktop was covered with more papers. "Yes, Detective Bishop, I do. Have a seat." He gestured to the chair on her side of the desk. He put the paper on top of the others, and straightened the mess into a neat stack, before slipping them into a folder.

Jessie waited, but his obvious stalling made her nervous. "So...?"

"Detective Bishop, I've heard from various sources, that you're dating a man named Mark Taylor?"

Jessie straightened, squaring her shoulders. Is that all this was about? She'd already talked to Internal Affairs about this. "Yes, I am, but it's okay, sir. I discussed it with IA and made sure that I wasn't breaking any regulations. Mark had a few scrapes with us before, but he was cleared every time."

O'Hanrahan nodded. "Yes, I'm aware of that, but I'm afraid this is different. Your...boyfriend is in custody right now—"

"What? Why?" Jessie scooted to the edge of her seat. What had Mark gotten into this time? It had only been, what? Four months since the last time he'd been questioned when he interfered with an investigation. He promised it wouldn't happen again. She gripped the sides of the chair. He'd better hope they locked him up, because if not, she was going to kill him.

"Hear me out, I wasn't finished. It's not us who have him—it's the Feds. Taylor had a run in with one of our guys, and when it came over the radio, the Feds called and said they want him. It seems they were preparing to arrest him, when lo and behold, his name pops up on the scanners."

All thoughts of murder flew from her mind. "The FBI? What do they want with Mark?" Her pulse quickened.

"It has to do with September 11th. They want to question him about it." He held up a hand when Jessie opened her mouth to ask more questions. "Hold it, that's all I know. I just thought I'd give you a heads-up."

It took Jessie a few seconds to realize that O'Hanrahan was done. "Sir, would I be able to talk to him?"

Her lieutenant regarded her with a mixture of pity and regret. "I can send the request up the chain, but it's doubtful. At least, not right away. I do have the name of the special agent in charge. It's Johnson. "

"Thank you." At least it was a place to start. She stood, amazed that her legs held her. "Did they take him to the Metropolitan Correctional Center?"

O'Hanrahan nodded. "I expect FBI will have some questions for you as well."

That hadn't occurred to her, but she'd welcome the interview. Mark had some peculiarities, but she had no doubt he was a good guy.

* * *

A bead of sweat raced down Mark's back, and he could feel more gathering on his brow. The room stank of stale cigarettes and body odor. He picked at a cigarette burn on the scarred table. How long were they going to keep him waiting? It had to have been at least an hour, but there were no clocks in the room so he didn't know for sure. The window on his right reflected only the inside of the room and he knew it had to be a two-way mirror.

The door opened and Mark's heart tripled its rate. Even though he wanted to straighten the mess out and had wished someone would come talk to him, a shiver of fear shook his body. Johnson led a new group of agents into the room. He carried a folder and set it on the table across from Mark.

The agent sat and took out a pair of glasses, perching them on the end of his nose. Mark hunched over the table, keenly aware of the two remaining Feds flanking him.

Johnson tapped the folder with one index finger. "I have some very disturbing information about you, Mr. Taylor. Especially in light of recent events."

"There's an explanation. This is all just a misunderstanding." Mark's head ached and he rubbed his temples.

"Do you admit that you made a series of phone calls on the morning of September 11th to various government agencies?" He opened the folder and sorted through several documents. Running a finger down a line of print, he added, "Calls that began a full three hours before the planes hit?"

"Well, yeah. Of course I admit that. I left my name."

"How did you come by your information?" Johnson leaned towards Mark and said, "And I must caution you that withholding important details will only make it go worse for you."

"It's gonna sound crazy, but hear me out." He tried to laugh, but it fell flat. "See, the thing is, I have this camera and when I take pictures, the photos sometimes come out much differently than..." He hesitated. How could he explain this in a way that would make sense?

Johnson cut in, "Get on with it."

Mark swallowed. "Sorry." He wiped his hands on his thighs and darted a look at the other agents. "The photos—they show up in my dreams, only with more detail. And my dreams...they come true." Johnson narrowed his eyes and Mark rushed on, "It's the truth and because I see what happens before it happens, I can change it...sometimes."

He closed his eyes as the visions of the planes hitting the towers played in his mind. "Only, it didn't work on September eleventh. There wasn't enough time. That dream...well, I've had some bad ones before, but..." He shuddered and opened his eyes, but couldn't get the images out of his head. He ground the heel of his hand against his brow as if he could erase them.

"Stop!" Johnson slapped his hand down on the table top.

Mark jumped, and then froze.

"I don't have time for this crap. We have tapes of your calls. We have records that you traveled to Afghanistan two years ago. We know that you associated with Mohommad Aziz, a suspected terrorist."

Mo? A terrorist? Mark didn't buy it. He had known the guy for years. He was no more a terrorist than Fred Flintstone.

Johnson took a sheet of paper out of the folder, grabbed pen from his shirt pocket and shoved them both across the table. "Please write down everything you did and the names of the people you met in Afghanistan."

Anger simmered inside of him and Mark tried to shove it down. He eased the paper back towards Johnson. "I already admitted I made the calls. You have the tapes." Glancing at the two agents beside him, and then back to Johnson, he shrugged. "Yeah, I did go to Afghanistan. It was work related. Mo Aziz is a free-lance photojournalist I've known for about five years now."

Agent Johnson's eyes narrowed. "Oh really? How interesting." He jotted something on a note pad.

"Listen, would ya? He's no terrorist. He's a good guy. He wanted to do a story on women's rights, or lack of them, actually, in that country. Mo had some connections there, so we were able to go places where outsiders aren't normally welcome. He interviewed the people and I took the photos. It was a hell of a book and I was proud to help with the photos."

Johnson nodded, his pen scratching across the paper. "Good. Where can I find a copy of this book? So we can verify your story."

Mark sighed. "Unfortunately, it was never published. Nobody was interested in the plight of the women of Afghanistan at the time." He scratched the back of his neck. "Last I talked to Mo, he was still shopping it around."

"So, you have no proof that this book exists?"

"I have my negatives," Mark said. "You're welcome to see them." Should he have offered them? Maybe he should ask for a lawyer. His hope that this would all be quickly sorted out, faded.

"Believe me, we will. In fact, a search warrant on your home has already been executed." Head bent, the agent continued writing.

"Oh." Shit. He didn't have anything to hide, but hated the idea of strangers going through his things.

"That make you nervous?" Johnson raised his eyes and smiled for the first time. Mark wanted to punch the smug look right off his face.

"No." His voice shook with anger so he cleared his throat. It wouldn't help matters to lose his temper.

Johnson motioned to the agent on the left. "Why don't you get Mr. Taylor something to drink?" He looked at Mark. "You have any preference? Coffee? Soda?"

He wanted to refuse, but fear and anxiety had caused his mouth to feel like cotton. "Water's fine."

Mark tapped his foot on the floor, his arms crossed as Johnson thumbed through a stack of papers in the folder. What could they have in there about him? He started to lean forward, hoping to get a glimpse, but Johnson glared at him.

The agent returned with a bottle of water and set it in front of Mark. Before he could take a drink, Johnson said, "So, why don't we start over. I'm willing to pretend that this conversation has just begun. What do you say, Mr. Taylor?"

Mark put the bottle down untouched. "I don't have anything to say that I haven't already said." Should he tell them about his other dreams? They could go question some of the people who had been in them. People he had saved. There were dozens of them. Mark didn't know all of their names, but he remembered some. They would vouch for him. "If you've done all this fact-digging on me, then you'll know about other times I've had dreams that came true. The Chicago P.D. knows. Have you talked to them?"

Johnson chuckled. "They know you all right. Let's see, Detective Cruz says that you spoiled three months' worth of work when you tackled him just as he was about to make an undercover buy. They could have arrested a dozen gang members in that one."

"Cruz was going to be shot. Did he mention that?" It should have been part of the file. The guy Hanson was buying from had been killed when a rival gang sped past spraying bullets as they went.

"That's just one of a very long list of incidents you've been in with the police, so I don't think you're high on their list of favorite Chicago citizens."

Mark's leg bounced and he swallowed. "You make it sound like I'm a criminal...or a terrorist." He folded his arms around the back of his head. The headache had reached migraine level and the bright lights stabbed into his brain. He pinched the bridge of his nose. "Look, I need to talk to a lawyer."

CHAPTER THREE

Mark ground the heel of his hand against his forehead. How many days had he been here already? A court-appointed lawyer had been in to see him, but the legal mumbo-jumbo had gone in one ear and out the other. All he knew was that his calls on the day of the attacks and his trip to Afghanistan two years earlier had caused enough suspicion to get him locked up.

He slumped on the edge of the hard bed and buried his head in his hands. The questions they'd asked made no sense. Mark's eyes shot to the door as a key scraped in the lock. His lawyer said he wouldn't be back for several days. As far as Mark knew, nobody else was aware that he was here. A guard entered, a length of chain held loose in his hands. Instead of taking Mark out of the room, he snapped a cuff around Mark's ankle and attached it to metal ring embedded in the floor. He was no better than a dog.

The guard left only to return a few minutes later with Jessie trailing behind him. Mark tucked his tethered foot behind his other one, but the chain rattled and he didn't miss the shock in Jessie's eyes when her gaze followed the sound.

"Jessie." He tried to smile and pretend he hadn't noticed her hesitation, but heat flooded his cheeks. How much did she know? After the initial shock, her face had frozen into a neutral expression.

"Mark." She stopped a few feet away, crossed her arms and ran her hands up to her shoulders a few times, as though warding off a chill. "How are you doing?"

The concern in her voice drove his emotions to the surface, and he blinked hard, looking away with a shrug. He cleared his throat. "Guess I've been better."

"That's the understatement of the century."

Startled at the flippant tone, Mark stared at her.

She surveyed the stark cell and then bent her head, giving it a shake. "I'm sorry. That was a cruel comment." Tears swam in her eyes when she finally looked at him again. "I'm confused. When I get stressed, I say dumb things. Do you realize I had to call in every marker I had just to find out where you were?"

"No, it's okay. I'm just glad to see you." Despite his shame at having her see him like this, he felt a thrill that she was here. Why hadn't he confided in her before? He should have shown her the camera. It wasn't like there hadn't been plenty of opportunities. If he'd shown her from day one, when he'd first contacted her in an attempt to change the outcome of a photo, maybe none of this would be happening. Maybe he wouldn't be stuck in this damn jail cell. He hung his head. Hell, maybe three thousand people would still be alive. It was a huge maybe, but he couldn't help wondering.

"Mark, I only have a few minutes. It's only because my partner knows some of the Feds that I was even able to get in here at all."

Her gaze swept him, and he rubbed his chin self-consciously, the bristles prickling his palms. He looked like crap—like the terrorist they were labeling him. Did she see him that way?

How much credibility and trust had they built up in the two years since they'd met? Maybe if they'd started dating right away, he'd have told her his secret, but their romantic relationship was less than three months along. There hadn't been much time to tell her about the camera and dreams. It was a poor excuse and he knew it. He wished he'd given her a chance to understand, but he hadn't. He'd never given anyone a chance.

He'd convinced himself he couldn't divulge the secret of the camera and dreams to anyone. It was too risky. What if the camera fell into the wrong hands? It was a legitimate worry, but not the whole truth. A part of him had relished the cloak of mystery; the feeling of being a real-life superhero.

Jessie tucked her hair behind her ear and took a deep breath. "Talk to me, Mark. What have they got on you?" Her voice shook.

Mark searched her face. Would she believe him now? He had no proof. "I thought I could help stop the attacks. That's all I was trying to do." The words came out in a harsh rasp. His leg bounced with pent-up nerves and the chain clanked, drawing her eye once again. Trapping the chain under his foot, he willed his leg to still. Eyes closed, he leaned forward, hands clasped behind his neck. Most times, he could wake from the nightmares, reason out how to change them—could make things right.

The planes hitting the buildings, the fall of the towers, the terror on the faces of the people fleeing—it had been too catastrophic. There was no way to fix it, even as he had called the authorities to warn them, part of him had realized that. He was only one man.

Jessie paced, her heels clicking on the cement and echoing in the cell. Her black boots crossed in front of his vision as he opened his eyes.

"How could you think you could stop the attacks? Unless...were you part of it?"

Even though he'd worried, hearing her voice her doubt felt like a kick to the chest. "You really think that?" Did she know him at all?

She bit her lip, but her eyes didn't waver. "What the hell am I supposed to think, Mark? In the two years I've known you; you have never leveled with me! Not once! At first I overlooked it because you had good information and were pretty harmless. Then I overlooked it because..."

Jessie turned away and crossed her arms. When she spoke again, her voice cracked, "I overlooked it because I'd come to care for you." Facing him, she swiped tears off her cheek with a brusque motion, her eyes accusing. "You want my trust? Well, why the hell didn't *you* trust *me*?"

He had blown his chance. Mark sagged back against the cinder-blocks. "I should have. But I was an idiot."

She paced again, her arms tight across her chest. "You've been running around Chicago sticking your nose into situations where it doesn't belong. Turning up at bank robberies, or at the scene of a drive by shooting, only you just manage to get yourself and bystanders out of the line of fire." She paused her pacing long enough to level a look at his leg. "Usually, anyway."

Mark dropped his hand to his left thigh, rubbing the scar. He could feel the ridge of it through the coveralls they had made him wear.

"So, you've never once told me who your sources were. Do you understand how that makes you look now?"

"Yeah." He drew in a ragged breath and bent his head. The remains of a cockroach stained the cement between his feet. He nudged it with his toe.

Kneeling beside the bed, she looked up into his face. "Listen, Mark. You helped me out a few times with tips on cases. I appreciated that, even if my boss gave me grief over how I'd acquired my information. So, now, I want to help you. Will you let me?" Her voice softened and her eyes bore into his.

"I already told them the truth. What more can I do?" Mark held her gaze. Whatever it took, he'd do it. He had to clear his name. Even if that put the camera in the wrong hands. He grimaced. Not that there was much chance of that. The authorities had ridiculed that explanation.

"You need to lay all your sources out for them. Names, dates, places. If you fully cooperate, your lawyer will push for leniency."

A roar built in his ears as his hope plummeted. "I can't do that." She asked the impossible.

She shook his leg, her voice rising, "You have to do it. You have no choice in the matter."

"You don't understand. I can't do that because I don't have any 'sources'!" He raked a hand through his hair. "I have..." Oh God, this was hard. "I have a camera. Those times when I showed up...the robberies...the shooting...I-I have a camera and when I use it, the photos that come out...they aren't anything I photographed. There are pictures of those things happening."

Her eyes widened in shock and disbelief.

He licked his lips and rushed on, "I don't know where they come from, or...or how they end up on my film, but they do. Then at night, after looking at the photos, the images come to life in my dreams. Like a movie—" He shook his head with a mirthless laugh. "The next day, they come true...unless I do something to stop it."

The look on her face had gone from disbelief to pity.

He reached for her hand. "Please, you gotta believe me, Jessie. You've seen me stop things. How else would I know what I know?"

26

She pulled free and backed to the cell door. She turned, her shoulders slumped as she rested her head against the steel. For a long minute, she remained that way before facing him. "You realize how that sounds?"

Mark nodded. What more could he say? He picked at an orange thread on his sleeve. It sounded insane. He knew that. Flicking the thread from his fingers, he watched it float to the floor and rest beside the cockroach. "They think I'm crazy don't they? You think I'm crazy."

She threw her arms wide. "What do you expect? You give them this bizarre story and then wonder why they don't believe you?" She stood in front of him, hands on her hips. "Come on, Mark."

"Jessie, listen, *please*." He willed her to believe him. "I was only trying to help—I did help. You know that!"

He saw doubt as she looked away. She thought he was crazy. Or guilty. *Oh God*. His gut twisted and pain ripped through him. Why had he tried to stop it? It wasn't something isolated, like most of the things he'd changed. It had been bigger than himself. He should have realized that. This ability that he had to see the future in his dreams had never been meant for something this big.

"Right now, I'm the only one even willing to listen to you. The guys in charge," she flicked her hand towards the hallway, "they're done listening. They're talking about enemy combatant status now."

Her words seemed to come from a distance as his mind slowed. Nobody believed him.

"An enemy combatant, Mark. Do you have any idea what that means?"

He jumped as Jessie lifted his chin to meet her eyes. "No." His voice cracked and he cleared his throat.

"It means no lawyers, no trials, and you leave your rights outside the door. It's just you and them."

Mark's fear gave way to anger and it burned through him. What did they want from him? Did they expect him to confess to something that he didn't do? "I dreamed the whole thing, Jessie. The whole damn thing." He blinked sudden moisture from his eyes, embarrassed. "Why won't anyone listen? Instead, they chained me up like I'm a god-damn animal!"

"That story won't work, Mark." She stepped back, putting distance between them.

Ignoring her comment, he cradled his head in his hands. The dream of 9/11 replayed in his mind like a horror movie. "I saw the planes hitting the buildings, Jessie. I saw them collapse. Hell, I even saw the damn hijackers. I told them all that." Fists balled, he leaned towards her, his voice low and hard, "They could have stopped it if they'd listened. They could have stopped the attacks."

Mark stepped towards Jessie, barely catching himself when the chain brought him up short and the metal cuff bit into his ankle. With a cry of frustration and rage, he yanked his foot, ignoring the cut of the metal against his leg.

"Stop, you're hurting yourself! Are you crazy?" She moved as if to stop him, but paused, fear flashing in her eyes.

It was gone in an instant, but he saw it and staggered back at the realization that she was truly afraid of him.

"Crazy?" He spread his arms wide. "Look around you, Jessie. I guess…I guess I am…crazy." He choked out the last word, wanting only to crawl into a corner and curl up with his shame and humiliation.

The guard burst into the room and shouted at him to sit down. Mark took a step backwards to sit, but saw the fear and alarm splashed across Jessie's face. Ashamed of his outburst, he reached towards her, intending to apologize. He never got the chance. The guard slammed him against the wall, and Mark's cheek and forehead cracked against the cinder blocks. His vision flickered and he tasted the salty tang of blood in his mouth. More guards filled the room and his hands were yanked behind his back and cuffed. The door clanked shut and Jessie was gone.

CHAPTER FOUR

A half dozen guards circled him. Dressed in riot gear, the men looked ready to battle an army. One held chains, another clutched darkened goggles and some kind of earphones. Still another had a pair of thick mitts tucked under his arm. Mark took a step back in confusion. What the hell?

One guard, empty handed, moved behind Mark and undid the cuffs, only to re-secure them in front. "Raise your arms."

He lifted his arms. "Where am I going?"

The guard wrapped a chain around Mark's waist and let the end drop towards the floor. He spoke in a cold voice, "I have no idea and even if I did, I wouldn't tell you."

Shocked, Mark ignored the snide tone. "What about the hearing the lawyer said I'd get?"

The guard shrugged and adjusted a pair of goggles.

Before Mark could ask another question, the guard placed the goggles over Mark's eyes. Every last spark of light cut off. Earphones settled over his ears and all sound disappeared as well.

Disoriented, he shook his head to dislodge the equipment. His hands were caught in a paralyzing grip and the mitts forced on. Anger overcame his shock. The moment the men released him, he doubled over and tried to rip at the goggles, but the chains thwarted his attempts. Rationality abandoned him as terror and the survival instinct kicked in to high gear. Mark knew it was useless to fight, but he couldn't help it. Self-preservation demanded that he try. He yanked his hands, but dizzy in the black, soundless void, he stumbled. His right shoulder smashed against the concrete. He barely felt the impact as terror consumed him. His efforts to get free of the gear were futile and he was hauled to his feet.

He hunched in a half- crouch, his body quivering. The chain around his waist tightened and tugged him forward. It was either fall again, or give in. Gasping, he took a step and slid the other foot up to meet the first. The length of chain shortened his steps, and he had to manage a jogging shuffle to keep pace with the guards.

When he would slow, the hands on his biceps squeezed, forcing him to quicken his pace. Would they drag him if he fell?

Mark's toe caught on something and the floor changed from smooth concrete to something rougher. Asphalt? A hand went to his head while the two on his arms lifted. Confused, he balked, but was pushed from behind. The chain around his waist went taut, and off balance, he stumbled, banging his shin on something. He swore at the sharp pain, then realized that he was supposed to step into a vehicle. It took a few attempts for him to find the edge with his foot, and then he climbed in. He sat on the first seat he bumped against. The chains tightened with a little jolt, and he guessed they had secured the ends somehow.

His heart pounded from the exertion and he panted. It felt like he had run a mile instead of what was probably just a short distance through the jail hallways. What was the point of all the security measures? Wouldn't this transport have been easier on everyone if he could at least see where he was going?

The vehicle started and stopped several times and turned a few corners. Stop lights and traffic. He could almost see it. After that, there was a stretch of unbroken motion with a few bumps. They had left the city and its pot-holes behind. When the vehicle stopped, the chains went tight before loosening, and he realized someone had unclipped him from the seat. Responding to the pull of the chains, he twisted on the seat, and took a leap of faith that the ground would meet his foot as he stepped out.

Wind tore at his clothes and he hunched his shoulders against it. The air smelled of exhaust and gasoline...no... An airport. Where the hell were they taking him? He trembled from more than just the icy blasts of air.

The chains pulled him forward and he resumed his shuffle. His foot rammed into something and he tripped onto an incline. The guards saved him from hitting too hard, but they were none too gentle as they righted him. He felt in front of him with his toe. A ramp. Mark balked. No way was he going to get on a plane until he knew where they were taking him. He turned his head to where he thought the guard was standing. "Wait. Please. I just need to know where I'm going." Unable to hear his own voice, he wasn't even sure he spoke out loud.

Despite the cold, he broke out in a sweat. It stung his eyes. More hands joined the ones on his arms, and he was shoved up the ramp. Finally, the chain went slack and the hands pushed down on his shoulders, urging him to sit. The trembling ceased as exhaustion stole his energy.

Hours seemed to crawl by, but he had no real clue to the passage of time. His ears popped, so he knew that the plane was in the air. His stomach rumbled. When was the last time he'd eaten? Breakfast must have been hours ago.

To add to his misery, nature came calling. He squirmed, trying to ease the discomfort of a full bladder. Just when he thought he'd embarrass himself, hands yanked him to his feet and led him twenty steps away. He didn't know why he began counting the steps, but it gave him a feeling of control to have some measure of space.

His hands were freed of the mitts and the earphones lifted.

"If you gotta take a leak, now's the time."

Mark's face burned, but he hastened to relieve himself.

Afterwards, someone squirted what smelled like hand sanitizer into his palm. How thoughtful. At least they were being hygienic. Then his hands were wrapped around a cold object. Startled, he almost dropped it before realizing it was a cup. Wary of what it might contain, he felt for the rim and raised it, taking a tiny sip. Water. Cold, blessed water. He guzzled, afraid it would be taken away before he finished. When no more poured into his mouth, he lowered the cup and hoped in vain for more.

It was twenty steps back to his seat. He didn't remember falling asleep, but he woke up with a start. His heart thundered in his ears.

The vibration from the plane had ceased. They must have landed. Fear of the unknown rose in him. It was bad in the FBI lock-up, but he had a feeling that where he was going would be infinitely worse.

Mark put one foot in front of the other. He didn't bother counting the steps this time. It wouldn't matter. The walk wasn't long, and soon he sat in what he assumed, from the vibrations, to be another vehicle. After a time the vibrating stopped and he was once again forced to walk, this time for longer. He shuffled along and stopped when the hands on his arms tightened and tugged. Fingers brushed the sides of his head, as the earphones were removed.

The rush of air on his eardrums and the sudden return of sound almost hurt. Wherever he was, it was quiet, and from the echo of the guards' shoes on the floor, it sounded like another cell.

The goggles came off, and Mark squinted, blinking at the harsh light. It took a few seconds for his eyes to adjust. It was a cell, but one even smaller and more stark than the previous one. Three guards stood in the room with him. Two others remained just outside the cell door. One took the mitts off Mark's hands, and then removed the chains and shackles on his legs. Another took Mark's shoes.

"Stand here until the door shuts, and then put your hands through the slot," said the guard who had taken his shoes, as he pointed towards the door. "Then, put on those clothes over there, and put the other clothes through the slot as well." The man looked Mark in the eye. "You have three minutes. Don't make us come in to help you."

Mark nodded. The guards left the room, and the door clanked shut. He shuddered at the sound, then went to the slot and put his hands through. The cuffs came off and his hands began to tingle as blood flow increased. He hadn't realized how tight the manacles had been until they were gone. As quickly as he could, he changed into the orange t-shirt and baggy pants. A number was stenciled across his chest. His number.

Gathering the dirty clothes, he shoved them through the opening. Nobody came in to help him, so he must have met the time requirements. The bed jutted out from a wall, if it could be called a bed. A thin mattress covered a simple metal shelf; at the foot of the bed was a folded blanket.

He sat on the shelf and rubbed his wrists. So, this was it. He glanced at the steel toilet and tiny sink. Other than the bed, that's all there was.

Shivering, he took the rough blanket and pulled it around his shoulders. What would happen to him now? Thirst hit him but his body felt paralyzed and he remained on the edge of the bed.

He didn't know how long he sat. Nothing in the cell changed, the light stayed just as bright, and no sounds penetrated the thick walls. If they kept him here too long, he would lose his mind. He needed color. The photographer in him already missed framing shots in his mind. It was second nature to him, even when he didn't carry a camera. But here, there was nothing. No shadows, no colors. Just white walls, a dirty gray floor, and dull steel fixtures. Only the orange of his clothing broke up the monotony.

After a while, his stomach growled, and his thirst became over-powering. He shook off his lethargy, got up, and drank from the faucet. Finished, he splashed his face and worked the water up into his hair. He felt grimy and scrubbed his fingers into his scalp and across the back of his neck. The water wasn't warm but it still felt good. Since he had no towel, he swiped his face along his shoulder and pulled his shirt up, using it to dry off.

Afterwards, he felt a little more human, but the beginnings of a headache tightened the muscles down his neck. Mark groaned and curled up on the bed, pulling the blanket over his shoulders. Numb with fatigue and overwhelmed with the situation, he simply stared at the wall.

The clink of the slot opening woke him some time later. A foam tray slid into the room. Mark swung his feet off the bed and hurried to it. The plate held a casserole of some sort. A thick sauce held bits of chicken, peas, and egg noodles together in clumps. He sniffed, but it gave off very little scent. A carton of milk, lukewarm, a dry biscuit and rubbery gelatin completed the meal. It wasn't haute cuisine, but it was edible and he was hungry.

Not long after he had finished, the slot opened and a voice commanded that he send the tray back out. He obeyed and then sat again on the bed, at a loss as to what to do next.

When he was a kid and did something wrong, he'd be sent to his room. It was the worst punishment imaginable. No freedom to play outside. No running through fields or catching frogs. Just four walls. At least he'd had windows and books, and his parents usually relented after an hour or two. Especially his mom. He caught his breath at the sharp ache the memory caused. It spread from his chest to his throat and formed a lump. His lawyer had promised to contact them and fill them in on what was going on. This would kill them. He had hoped to make his dad proud of him. Instead, he was stuck in prison.

Mark tried to swallow the lump but it hurt too much. His dad had been right. If he had never picked up a camera, he wouldn't be in this mess now. He shook his head. It wasn't just any camera though. It was the antique one. If only he hadn't spotted the camera in the bazaar. The pain in his chest intensified and he closed his eyes and took slow, deep breaths. If only he had passed that stall. If only he had ignored the vendor, he would be home right this minute. If only.

He lay back and clasped his hands behind his head, focusing on the ceiling, but seeing the dusty marketplace at the base of an ancient citadel. Mark had taken some shots of the impressive structure, and after the light faded, he'd wandered into the bazaar and bought some fruit. As he ate, he browsed the stalls. One sold gorgeous scarves and Mark purchased one for his mom. Another vendor had tables laden with intricately carved wooden items and so for his dad, he bought an ingenious collapsible wooden bowl. His father liked working with wood and would appreciate the craftsmanship. Mark almost bypassed the vendor selling the cameras; it was getting late and his arms were already full.

At first glance, he'd dismissed the cameras as pure junk. Most were so old, he doubted that they worked any more, but one caught his eye. As he held it, he felt a shock in his hands, as if he'd touched a live wire. He jumped, nearly dropping the camera as he thrust it away. Mark backpedaled a few steps. His fingers tingled and he wiped them on his jeans, but he couldn't leave the camera alone. He had to pick it up again. This time, instead of a shock, it warmed his palms and gave a charged hum.

Turning to the vendor, he asked if it worked, but the vendor just shrugged. Mark didn't know if that meant the man wasn't sure if it worked, or he just didn't understand the question. Mark fiddled with the camera, held it up and framed a shot in the viewfinder. The hum felt good in his hands. Even if it didn't work, cleaned up a bit, it would look good in his studio. He had to have it. Curious about its history, he tried to find out how the vendor had acquired it, but the man only smiled and shook his head. The price was steeper than he expected, but Mark had paid without even trying to barter.

Restless, Mark sat up and paced the cell. It was five steps lengthwise, and when he stood in the middle of the cell, and stretched his arms out at his sides, he could touch each wall with his fingertips. He remembered reading that a person's arm span correlated with their height. He was six-foot two, so he guessed that the width was about six feet.

A smothering sensation clawed at his throat, and he tugged his t-shirt collar as he eyed the walls. Flat and white with no shadows, they seemed to close in, ready to crush him.

He closed his eyes and tried to quell the rising panic. Leaning against the cold wall, he slid down until he sat with his knees bent; elbows propped against his thighs and cradled his head. Swallowing rising nausea, he fought to get a grip.

The silence was absolute and deafening. He hummed, not sure what song it was and not caring. It broke the stillness. Mark let his head droop and intertwined his fingers on the back of his neck. The memories of the days after he returned home from Afghanistan flowed into the vacuum created by the isolation.

He hadn't trusted anyone else to clean out the camera, so he had done it himself, making sure that no grains of sand remained in the body. Mark massaged the muscles of his neck and smiled when he recalled his excitement of loading the camera with film for the first time. He had spent the whole day down at the lake front shooting pictures. Nothing was safe from his shutter. He snapped skaters, dogs catching Frisbees, sun-bathers, the skyline and dozens of other things.

Mark sighed. What a great day that had been. If he closed his eyes, he could almost smell the fresh cut grass mixed with car exhaust and topped with a faint fishy odor from the damp sand. He remembered lying down and taking a picture straight up into a tree. The sun had shone through the branches creating a great light and dark contrast on the rough bark.

That night he had developed his film, eager to see how the camera performed. Most of the shots were junk, but a few came out well and he had been happy. One shot had puzzled him though. He couldn't recall taking that picture and he would certainly have remembered if he had. A small child lay on the sand, her hair plastered to her head. A man bent over her blowing into her mouth and a woman appeared to be doing chest compressions.

He shrugged it off as being some kind of test picture on the film. That night, he'd dreamed of a child drowning, dying on a beach. The child in the photo. It had been so vivid, so real, he had recalled even the smallest details. The dream had stayed with him all that next day, and he stared at the picture, wondering about the little girl. Mark was sure it had to have been a still from an old movie. But no matter how hard he had tried, he could not erase the stark scene from his mind. Even the scent of the beach had lingered in the morning. He felt silly, but after doing two photo shoots that day, he had gone back to the same beach from the day before. Somehow, he knew it was that beach.

Picture in hand, he had walked the beach and even thought about asking the lifeguards if they had been involved in a rescue of the child, but they were busy watching the swimmers. Mark would always recall the feeling he'd had at that moment. It was a feeling of anxiety and foreboding. Uneasy, he had paced the packed sand at the edge of the beach, sidestepping toddlers and darting children. He had searched the waves, not really knowing what he searched for but feeling compelled to continue. For a half hour, he walked the shore. He had ignored the glares from some parents even though he knew his behavior was making them nervous. He was helpless to stop.

Then, it happened. He heard a woman scream, and whirling, he saw lifeguards rush towards the shore and long minutes later, the little girl was hauled in, limp and blue. Mark had backed away while every hair on the back of his neck stood on end. On the way to his Jeep, he had sunk to his knees and vomited on a sand dune.

Mark had ignored the camera after that, but curiosity picked at his resolve, and two weeks later, he took it down from the shelf in his studio. After a thorough examination, which showed nothing but normal wear and tear on a fifty-year old camera, he held it to his eye. Just to prove that it had been nothing but a coincidence, he pointed towards a church across the street, and snapped a few pictures. Then he shot a couple of cars rolling to a stop at the corner of his street. He finished off the roll of film with other random, boring shots.

When he had developed the film, the one that should have been a truck double-parked in front of his building, had changed to a horrific traffic accident. Mark had flung the print away.

That night, like before, he had dreamed the details. The next day, he found the street, saw the car that would be involved in the accident, and he let the air out of one of the tires. He had never done anything like that before, but it had been like he was possessed. The owner had come out of nearby bar and shouted, but Mark was too fast for him.

When he went home, the picture had changed. Instead of the accident, he had a print of a guy changing a tire on the car.

The slot on Mark's door opened with a screech and ripped him from his memories. He tensed, his hands braced on the floor at his sides.

"Approach the door and lie with your feet through the slot," said a disembodied voice from a speaker set somewhere in the ceiling.

Mark didn't take the time to look for the source. He followed the directions, flinching when the hated shackles

40

snapped around his ankles. He repeated the process with his hands. The voice then told him to stand in the middle of the room with his back to the door.

He took a deep breath, trying to will his muscles to relax, but the stress and fear overcame him and the chains on his shackles rattled with every wave of fear. If only he had a clue what was going to come next.

The door creaked open, and guards entered. The web of chains again circled his waist and attached his hands and feet to a central chain. He dared to look at the guards surrounding him, relieved that none held the other gear. He felt he could face whatever was coming as long as he could see and hear.

The guards took him down a half dozen hallways, through locked doors and into an elevator. He realized it didn't matter that he could see. He became so turned around and confused, he had no idea where he was. None of the guards spoke and the halls were quiet. If there were other inmates, Mark didn't see or hear them.

The group arrived at a door that looked no different than the dozen that they had passed en route. The guard in the lead opened the door and held it open, locking it behind them.

Mark's apprehension escalated when he noticed some odd features in the room. Eye rings jutted up from the floor and the cement sloped down towards a rusty drain. A wood table with six chairs took up the far wall. Five of the chairs looked like they had been pulled from offices. One was straight-backed and wooden. He had no doubt which one was meant for him.

The lead guard pulled that chair into the middle of the room and motioned for Mark to sit. He did as he was told and waited. The guards remained, none speaking. Mark wondered what they would do if he spoke to them. He could ask the one in charge if he wanted to go have a beer with him after work. Go shoot the breeze.

Of course, he wouldn't do that. Even if he had tried, it wouldn't have worked because when he attempted to make eye contact with them, one by one, they looked right through him. It was like he was invisible. Only one, a younger guy, made eye contact, and the flash of knowledge and pity, in the guy's eyes an instant before he looked away, sent Mark's heart racing. That guard knew what was coming and whatever it was, wouldn't be pleasant.

Time passed, but how much, Mark had no way of knowing. His hands became numb from the cuffs and the position in which he had to hold them. When a key rattled in the door, a bolt of pure fear pinned his back to the chair. His vision narrowed to the entrance and his heart thumped so hard, it threatened to punch a hole through his chest.

CHAPTER FIVE

Five men entered. Three sat at the table, facing Mark. Two of them had pads of paper and pencils and almost immediately began writing. The third sat back and raised one ankle to rest on his other knee and tilted a bottle of water, taking a long drink.

Mark didn't like the way the man seemed to be settling in and making himself comfortable. It was as though he expected to be there a long time.

The other two men spoke quietly in the corner for a few minutes. One had dark hair cut short and he moved with a military bearing. The other sported a shaved head, and appeared to be trying to convince the first of something. The dark haired man shook his head, his jaw set.

Mark strained to hear what they said but couldn't make out the words. After a few minutes of looking through a folder, they appeared to come to some agreement and turned towards Mark. The shaved one ambled up to Mark, halting just in front of him.

"Hello. I'm Bill and this is Jim." He jabbed his thumb in the direction of the other man. "This group behind me will be observing and taking notes. How it works is like this—we ask you some simple questions, and you answer them. If the answers are satisfactory, then we'll all have a pleasant session." He spread his hands and smiled. "We all like when a session is easy, don't we, Jim?"

Jim grunted and glared at Mark, his arms crossed. "Let's just get on with it."

Mark squirmed under the scrutiny. What more could he tell them that he hadn't already told the FBI? What was this Jim guy so pissed about?

Bill shrugged. "Okay. You go first, Jim. I'll just go sit over here."

Jim directed a glare at the guard on Mark's right. "Why is he sitting in a chair? This isn't a goddamn social call."

"Sorry, sir."

The guard yanked Mark up by the arm and Mark staggered as the chains connecting his ankles and hands pulled his arms down. He didn't know why he felt guilty, like he had done something wrong. The guards had told him to sit, so he had, but Jim aimed his annoyance at Mark, not the guard.

He stood as straight as he could and tried to meet Jim's stare without flinching. The shackles tugged on his arms and kept his shoulders hunched. Instinct told him to stand straight and tall, but it was physically impossible. To compensate, he refused to look away from Jim's glare.

"What are you looking at?" Jim approached Mark, stopping when their faces were less than a foot apart. "You have something you want to say?"

That did it. Mark broke eye contact for an instant.

"I didn't hear you." Now Jim's nose almost touched Mark's.

Mark flinched, drawing back, but the guard poked him in the spine with something hard.

He struggled not to wince and licked his lips, the desert in his mouth making speech difficult. "Yes. I do have something to say. I want to state that I'm innocent." Out of the corner of his eye, he saw the men with the paper scribbling and hoped they noted his declaration.

Jim's expression didn't change and he spoke as if Mark hadn't said anything. "You are to address me as sir, understand?" He never raised his voice, but threat laced every syllable of the sentence.

Mark nodded. "Yes, sir." His face burned with humiliation. It must be easy being a tough guy when your adversary was trussed up like a Thanksgiving turkey.

"Now, I have some simple questions. I just want the facts." Jim stepped back and opened the folder. "It says here that your name is Mark Andrew Taylor. You're thirty-five years old, never married and you live in Chicago. Is that all true?"

Mark nodded.

Jim cocked his head. "I didn't hear you."

"Yes, sir. That's all true," Mark said. The menace in Jim's voice sent shivers shooting through him.

Jim asked some more questions, verifying the names of Mark's parents, where he grew up, the college he had attended. Mark knew all that information had to be in his file and tried to determine the motive for asking it all again. The questions moved on to Mark's photography and despite the circumstances, Mark felt his enthusiasm for discussing his craft begin to surface.

"What kind of photography do you do?" Jim's voice sounded almost friendly, as if he and Mark were chatting at a party.

"I do portraits and commercial photography in the studio in my loft."

Jim didn't reply, just nodded and waited, so Mark continued, "Commercial jobs are for magazines and advertisements, mostly. Portraits are anything from family and group shots to head-shots for actors and models."

"Is that all you do?"

Mark shook his head and just in time, remembered to add the sir to his next reply. "No, sir. Those jobs pay the bills, but what I love to do is take candid photos of people and try to capture their...their spirit." He knew it sounded hokey, but he didn't know how else to explain it. When he caught someone on film with that unguarded expression that invited the camera in, it was like hitting a home run.

"What kind of photography did you do in Afghanistan a few years ago?" Jim's voice had an edge to it. "I don't expect there are a lot of actors looking for head-shots in Kandahar or Kabul."

"Um, no sir. I was there to do photos for a friend's book."

Jim paced in front of him and then halted and quirked an eyebrow at Mark. "And did that pay the bills?" Sarcasm dripped from the words.

Sensing that Jim was zeroing in on key questions, Mark considered his reply carefully. "No, sir. Mo offered a partnership of sorts. He paid for the trip, but I would get a percentage from the sale of the book."

"How much did that turn out to be?"

"Nothing, sir. He is still shopping the book around, the last I heard."

"So you're telling me that you went there out of the goodness of your heart to help out a friend?"

"I thought it could be a good opportunity. It was a chance I took."

Jim shook his head, as though Mark had been cheated. "So, Mo was your friend for how long?"

Mark counted back to the time he'd met Mo at a red carpet event they were both covering. "About five years. He helped me out with some photo shoots when I needed another photographer. Sometimes, he even waited for payment until I was actually paid for the shoot. Photography is a small world and we try to help each other out when we can."

Jim chuckled. "Oh, really?"

Mark remained silent, not sure if Jim asked a question or was just commenting. The look on the other man's face frightened him. He had seen a cat play with a mouse before, swiping at it with his paw, letting it crawl away, only to pounce in for the kill when the mouse was only a few inches from the safety of its hole. Jim looked like that cat.

Flipping to another page in the file, Jim smiled. "You might consider Mohommad a friend, but he sure doesn't feel the same about you. Do you know what he told us?"

Mark shook his head. His stomach twisted. He hadn't spoken to Mohammad for six months. Every time he called him, he got voice mail.

"He said that you were at an al-Qaeda training camp. That you and he trained there and agreed to take pictures of targets in the U.S. Your area was Chicago."

Confused, he had no idea how to reply. Had Mo really said that? Why would he lie? "That's not true, sir. I don't know why he would say those things. I only took pictures of the subjects for Mo's book. I never saw any training camps. And I definitely never agreed to take pictures of targets in any city, let alone Chicago."

Jim shrugged, his head tilting. "Hey, he's *your* friend."

He let that statement hang in the air, and the men sitting at the table bent their heads, the scratch of their pens the only sound in the room. Fear coursed through him—a desperate fear that they would judge Mark guilty by association.

Jim turned to Bill. "I've finished with my questions for the moment."

Bill stood and stretched. "So, let me make sure I have this correct?" He put his hands behind his back and, head down, approached Mark. "You went to Afghanistan with a confirmed member of al-Qaeda, but you deny any involvement?"

Desperation rose up and spilled out. "I never heard of al-Qaeda until the attacks. I swear to God. I never talked to anyone."

Bill sighed. "I wish we could believe you. Really. I do."

"The FBI guys in Chicago took all my negatives, all my photos—check them out. You'll see. This is all a big mistake." Mark looked from Bill to Jim, willing them to believe him. Sweat drenched his body and he could smell the acrid scent of his own fear.

"Oh, we will. Preliminary reports state some photographs of the Sears Tower were found amongst your files."

Mark searched his memory. He took thousands of pictures a year. It's likely at some point he had taken some pictures of the building. Who in Chicago hadn't?

Before he could reply, Bill motioned to the guards. "Set him up for position three."

Position three? What the hell was that? A guard circled in front of him and released Mark's hands from the chain that connected to the one between his ankles. The guard attached a longer chain on the end and passed the end over Mark's shoulder to another guard behind him. The wooden chair scraped across the floor, and Mark turned to see the guard behind him stand on the chair and pass the end of the chain through an eye bolt jutting out of the ceiling. Dread flooded him and he looked to the men seated at the table. The two writing had set their pens down and the other one sat back with his arms folded. Were they just going to sit there and watch?

Seconds later, Mark's arms jerked as the chain tightened until his arms were pulled up and behind his head. In front of him, the first guard secured a short chain to a bolt in the floor. His shoulders began to ache almost immediately and when he tried to step back to ease the tension, the chain connected on the floor pulled tight, and he had the sensation of falling backwards. A knife-like kind of pain shot across his shoulders as they bore all of his weight for those few seconds. The position forced him to keep his feet forward while his arms pulled him back. It didn't take long before the ache turned to an unrelenting burning.

Mark hung with only the balls of his feet touching the floor. If he pushed with his toes, it relieved the pressure in his shoulders a tiny bit, but created a new pain in his calves.

They didn't need to do this. His breaths scraped out, harsh and loud. Sweat dripped, stinging his eyes. He tried to swipe his face on one of his shoulders, but they were pulled too far back. A groan escaped him and Jim looked up from the file, his face impassive.

Mark looked at Bill. Maybe he would show some mercy. He licked his lips, ready to plead with the man, when without warning, a hood descended, cutting off Mark's vision. He shook his head, knowing it was futile but the pain and sense of suffocation forced him to react.

His hands went numb even as his shoulders and legs shot bolts of agony though his limbs. He tried to stay quiet- tried not to let them hear how much it hurt. He didn't want to give the bastards the satisfaction. Despite his resolve, his head sagged forward and every gasping breath ended in a moan. He couldn't help it. His eyes watered and he was almost glad for the hood. At least that shame was hidden.

Occasionally, sounds in the room would register as the men spoke to each other, or a chair creaked, but for the most part, he was lost in his own little world of pain.

A long time later, the chain holding his arms went slack. Mark groaned and collapsed, his legs unable to hold him. He lay on his side and his muscles quivered uncontrollably. The floor felt cool against his body. He grit his teeth at the needles of feeling that returned to his limbs. Nobody touched him, and exhausted, he lay limp. He didn't think he could move at that moment even if they held a gun to his head. The thought that might actually be their next tactic crossed his mind. He wouldn't put it past them, so when the footsteps approached, he tried to muster his energy to stand.

"Get the hood off him." Mark recognized Jim's voice. He hoped the tears had dried.

When the hood was lifted, Mark took a deep breath. In all his other misery, the suffocating heat in the hood had been the least of his worries, but now that it was gone, he sucked in the fresh air. It felt wonderful. His hair was plastered to his head, and with a groan, he swiped his forehead on his shoulder, but it did no good as every part of his body was soaked with sweat.

Jim leaned over him, his face unreadable. "Stand."

Mark turned and pushed up from the floor. His legs wobbled, but he made it to a standing position. His chest heaved with the effort.

Jim paced in front of him, and then circled Mark, his nose wrinkled in disgust. "Next time we ask for answers, I hope you'll be more forthcoming."

Mark couldn't reply. His throat was raw hamburger, but he shook his head. How much more could he say? What did they want him to say? If only he could figure it out. They demanded a confession and it was the one thing Mark couldn't give them.

* * *

He collapsed on his bed. He should splash water on his face and get at least some of the sweat off his body, but before the thought could fully form in his mind, he slept.

The light was still just as bright when he woke up and a tray of food sat on the floor. He swung his legs over the side and grunted at the stiffness in his body. He felt like someone had taken a bat to his shoulders, and his calves cramped when he attempted to stand. Mark sucked in a breath and bit his lip as he slowly straightened.

The food beckoned and he shuffled over and took it back to bed to eat. It was an odd combination of eggs and chicken, canned fruit, a slice of bread and tomato juice. He hated tomato juice, but drank it anyway, washing it down with the juice in the fruit cup. After finishing the rest of the meal, he filled the juice cup up with water from his sink and guzzled it.

The water and food revived him a bit and after shoving the tray back out into the hall; he did his best to wash up in the sink. He didn't have a towel and had to use his blanket to dry off. He even rinsed his t-shirt and wrung it out, hoping it would dry before he had to go on any other excursions.

Mark lay curled on his side with the blanket wrapped around him. The time in the interrogation played over in his mind. Until then, he had believed that they would realize their mistake and that he would be released. The brutal treatment shoved that notion out of his head. He shivered, and pulled the blanket tighter.

The thing that shocked him most was Mo's statement that implicated him. They had been friends. Maybe they weren't best friends, but Mark had felt nothing but pride in the book Mo had written. Pride that he had been a part of something that tried to bring an injustice to light. Now, he doubted that there had ever been a book. Why had Mo dragged him along? Just as a cover?

The more he thought back on that trip, the more things he had shrugged off began to make sense. The two days Mo had left him at the hotel to go meet with a family. Mo had told him that the family didn't want their pictures in the book, and that he was going to use an alias for them. Mark could remain at the hotel. It had made sense at the time. That was when he had gone exploring the city and found the bazaar. If only he had known what a turning point his life would take after that trip.

He rubbed his eyes and wished that they would turn off the damn lights. The constant glare made his head hurt. Mark swung his legs off the bed and stood, dropping the blanket in a heap. His shoulders ached and he knew that his legs would be sore in the morning. Or evening. Or whenever the hell it was.

A window high in the wall teased him with its blacked out rectangle. At first, he thought it was nighttime, then he studied it, noting that the small rectangle of plexiglass had been covered on the outside with something black. He balled his fists in fury as he recognized how intent they were on breaking him. Even daylight was forbidden.

Mark stalked to the door and pressed his face to the window, angling his head to look to the right. If there was a window at the end of the hall, he might see sunlight stream-

52

ing through it. Nothing. Just dim artificial light. Frustrated, he pounded on the door a half dozen times. The side of his hand stung, but the door was so solid, it didn't even yield a satisfying thunk when he hit it. *Shit!*

With no way to vent, his anger built, and he braced his hands against the door. Gritting his teeth, he tried to rein in the violence threatening to explode out of him. It would do no good. He leaned against the door, taking deep breaths until he regained control. Fight or flight responses denied, he sank to the floor in defeat.

The cold metal felt good on his shoulders and was probably the closest thing to an ice pack he would get in here. He tilted his head back and stared at the dull white ceiling. A black plastic bubble poked out of a corner. A camera. He almost laughed at the irony.

Hours passed and as the metal warmed, his bare shoulders stuck to it, but he didn't bother moving. He had nothing to do, and even with his constant anxiety about what the future held, boredom set in. How long would they hold him like this?

His life, especially since he bought the old camera, had been a whirlwind. If he didn't have a future picture to make right, he had photo shoots scheduled or clients to meet. Even on the rare days when he had nothing scheduled, he rode his bike, jogged, or just hiked around town, his camera a constant companion. He missed the weight of it around his neck. Reaching up, he felt the roughened skin on the side of his neck where the strap always chafed. How many times had he been teased because it looked like a hickey?

Mark stared at the opposite wall, smiling at the memory of Jessie Bishop raising an eyebrow at the sight of the permanent abrasion. He took a deep shaky breath. What he wouldn't give to talk to her right now. Hell, to talk to anyone.

His throat constricted, the ache building until he was sure it would choke him. What if they kept him in here for months? He would go crazy.

Once, he had been on Lower Wacker Drive just trying to get some shots of something different. A homeless man had staggered into him, and Mark would never forget the chill he had felt when he had looked the man in the face. The man's expression held no emotion. After stumbling away from Mark, he had pulled a dirty bakery bag out of his coat and dug out bits of donuts, shoving them in his mouth. It was like the man ate only to exist. Mark shuddered. Would he become like that poor fellow—just a shell of a person, more animal than human?

CHAPTER SIX

Jessie tapped her pencil eraser against the desktop as she surveyed the files stacked in the out-box and felt a surge of satisfaction. She was finally caught up. It had taken two months, but every case file that held something that might interest the FBI had been identified and the information forwarded to the Chicago bureau. It was out of her hands now.

She glanced out the window at the bleak gray sky. The few leaves, brown and curled, clung to a maple outside her building and twisted in the wind. Jessie wondered how a few always managed to cling all winter despite the abuse. How come the rest of the leaves couldn't hang on? She shook her head at the idle thought. Yawning, she opened the bottom desk drawer and withdrew her purse, digging into it for her lip balm. A knock at her doorway made her look up.

Balm poised in front of her mouth, she said, "Yes, can I help you?" to a man standing in the threshold.

His off-the-rack suit couldn't quite conceal a slight paunch and the button on his jacket strained. Short, dark hair, graying at the temples should have lent him a dignified air, but his sallow complexion detracted from it. A briefcase completed the picture of a middle management government employee.

"Jessica Bishop?"

Capping the balm and tossing it back in her bag, Jessie nodded. "Who wants to know?"

The man reached into his suit-coat breast pocket and pulled out identification. "Sean Daly, CIA. Is there a place we can talk?"

A sliver of dread coiled in her stomach as she dropped her purse back into the drawer. Jessie stood and motioned to the chair on the other side of her desk. If she had to speak to the CIA, it would be on her home turf. "Have a seat. We can talk right here."

He stepped in and shut the door. Any objections he might have had to doing the questions here, didn't show in his expression. Jessie sat and scooted her chair closer to the desk then folded her hands and waited. Hopefully, Dan wouldn't walk in right now. He had gone down to talk to the desk sergeant about practice for the precinct basketball league. She had a feeling this was going to be about Mark, and Dan had already tried to grill her about Mark's arrest a few months back. He'd have a field day with this. It wasn't every day a police detective's boyfriend was arrested as a terrorist.

Daly glanced around the cramped office and then lifted his briefcase onto his lap and withdrew a pad of paper, a tape recorder and a file folder. Jessie narrowed her eyes at the recorder. So, this was going to be official. He set the case on the floor and then arranged the other things on Jessie's desk, raising his eyes in question when he began to move a photo of her niece. Jessie shrugged. She was determined not to make this any easier for him.

He clicked the button on the recorder and said, "This is Officer Sean Daly. For the purpose of accuracy and records, please state your name."

Jessie spoke in a clear voice, "Jessica Bishop."

"Do you know Mark Taylor?"

"Yes."

Daly looked like he expected her to say more and he waited a few seconds. She was familiar with the tactic. People liked to fill silences and he thought she would jump in

56

with more information without being asked. She quirked an eyebrow. Nice try.

"When did you first meet the subject?"

Jessie thought for a moment. There was a file in the cabinet with the information, but unless he asked, she wasn't going to mention it. "I don't have the exact date right now, but it was approximately two years ago."

Once again, he waited and when she didn't elaborate, a trace of a smile played around his lips. "And under what circumstances did you meet?"

"I was working a case and he called the precinct with some information pertinent to my case. I agreed to meet with him."

He didn't wait this time, but just jumped in with another question. "What was your first impression of the man?"

Jessie looked towards the window, recalling how nervous Taylor had appeared. The meeting took place at a fast food restaurant in the River North area. He had given her a general description of himself and what he was wearing so she spotted him before he saw her. He had been standing at one end of the front counter, a cup of coffee in front of him and a couple of open creamers. Her first impression was that he was taller than she expected. Her next impression had to do with how well his jeans fit.

Jessie glanced at Daly and hoped she wasn't blushing. Taylor had been too modest when describing his looks. Brown hair and a bit over six feet tall made him sound average. But more than his looks, she had been struck by how expressive his face had been. She recalled thinking he would be terrible at poker. "My first impression was the guy couldn't lie his way out of a parking ticket."

Daly tilted his head and leaned forward. "What made you think that?"

Smiling, Jessie looked down at the desktop before raising her head to meet the agent's eyes. "Have you met Mark Taylor? If you had, you wouldn't have to ask. Every emotion he feels zips across his face."

"No, I've never met the man." His tone hinted that he never wanted to.

Jessie's smile hardened. "Well, it's your loss." The words surprised her even as she spoke them, but she realized it was the truth. "He's a bit different, I'll grant you that, but I no more believe him capable of helping al-Qaeda than he is of flying to Mars by flapping his arms."

"What do you mean about different?" Daly picked up the note pad and pen. He finally looked interested.

Jessie wanted to bite her tongue. Despite her best efforts, she had done just what she had vowed not to do. She had offered more than was necessary to answer the question. "I mean that he would call me with information. Like he had heard a mini-mart was going to be robbed. He thought one of the robbers had a gun he might use. When I would ask how he came by the information, he gave vague answers."

His pen flew across the paper and without looking up, he asked, "And, was he right?"

"That's the thing. He usually was." It still bugged her that Mark never told her the truth about his sources. One look at his face and she knew he was lying, and he knew that she knew. He had always squirmed and looked embarrassed, but even so, he never came clean.

"Taylor tipped the police to criminal activities and was evasive on how he came by his information. Didn't that make you suspicious?" Daly shook his head, as though talking to an idiot.

Jessie leaned forward, no longer concerned with keeping her mouth shut. This guy just pissed her off. "Do you take me for some wet-behind-the-ears rookie?" She didn't wait for him to answer. "Of course it made me suspicious and I questioned him and looked into his background. There was absolutely nothing that raised red flags. No known criminal contacts, no drugs, no arrests, no priors period, unless you count some parking tickets in college. He was a successful photographer with dozens of professional references." Leaning back, she crossed her arms. "But you should know that already."

Daly's lips thinned and his face flushed as he narrowed his eyes. "You better believe we've checked his business contacts." He moved to the edge of his seat and smirked. "Now we're checking his personal contacts. Which led us to you, Ms. Bishop."

She played it cool. "Really?" She arched an eyebrow at him.

He ignored her comment and flipped through some papers in the file. "Our investigation turned up that you and Taylor had a relationship. Is that correct?"

Jessie chuckled and stood. Crossing her arms, she moved to the window and sat against the ledge. "Wow, you guys certainly do your homework."

"We're very thorough." He threw her a smug look and then fiddled with the tape recorder. Jessie knew moving around would make the recording come out less clear, but she didn't care.

She countered his look with one of her own. "I would hardly count a few months as a relationship." Jessie plucked a dead leaf off of a plant on the ledge beside her. No matter how hard she tried, the plant never thrived.

"You've only been seeing each other for a few months?" He sounded surprised and Jessie felt a measure of satisfaction. She knew the agent was only doing his job, but being the subject of an investigation was new to her, and she didn't like the idea of someone going around questioning her friends behind her back. The irony that she did the same thing when she investigated a case didn't make it any easier to accept.

"Yes. And I'm surprised we even made it that far because the first date was pretty much a disaster." Except for the kiss. Jessie didn't think Daly needed to know that detail. Before Mark had rushed off, he had dropped a kiss on her lips. It had been unexpected, but not unwelcome. "We saw each other several times afterwards, but it wasn't serious." Not yet anyway. There hadn't been enough time. She cleared the lump in her throat.

"At any point when you were with him, did he mention going to Afghanistan in August of 1999?"

Jessie moved back to her chair and sat. "Yes." She leaned to the side and tossed the dead leaf into the trash can beside her desk.

Daly didn't even try to hide his irritation this time. He motioned with his hand, circling it in a keep going motion. "And..."

She shrugged. "He showed me some pictures he took. They were amazing." Jessie recalled the poverty in the photographs and even more, the stark despair in the women's eyes. That was all she could see of them, covered head to toe in their garments.

Daly leaned forward. "Did you see any pictures of what might have been training camps?"

Confused, she leaned back in her chair. "No. Just shacks with women and children. There were some landscapes too. Those were stunning also, but Mark won't admit this, or maybe he doesn't know, but what he does best is candid photos." Jessie bit her lip. She didn't have a creative bone in her body, but even she had realized how mesmerizing the photos were. It was as if the women were allowing a brief glimpse into their souls. They had trusted Mark enough to lower their defenses.

"Candid photos? Like snapshots?"

Jessie rolled her eyes. This guy knew even less about photography than she did. "Well, sure. I guess you could call them snapshots. Just like you could call the Mona Lisa 'some painting'. What Mark did was art."

"Oh, excuse me. I can see I hit a nerve with you." Daly smiled, but it didn't reach his eyes. He stopped the recorder and flipped the tape over.

"Listen, Mark Taylor and I had only been seeing each for a short while, but I knew him for several years before. Yeah, he drove me nuts with his premonitions, but even so, I couldn't help liking the man. He's a good guy." She raised her chin in defiance when he snorted. Jessie rolled her chair up tight against her desk. "And now, he's just disappeared." She snapped her fingers. "Just like that. And nobody has any clue where he is. Even his lawyer is in the dark."

Daly's face closed down and she got the impression he knew something and it didn't bode well for Mark. "I'm not at liberty to tell you where he is, but I can tell you that he's been transferred to a more secure location."

"Secure?" Wasn't a federal prison secure enough? "Why?" Jessie glared at the man until he began to squirm. As satisfying as that was, she knew it was pointless. This man was low-level CIA; he probably didn't have a clue where Mark was being held. She sighed and dropped the tough act. Her voice softened, "He has family and friends that are worried about him. No matter what you think he might have done, his parents, at least, deserve to know where their son is." The anguish in his mother's voice the time she had called looking for information was something she never wanted to hear again.

Daly sighed. "I'm not sure about the location myself, and even if I knew, I couldn't tell you. You realize the President has declared him an enemy combatant?"

She'd been right. The guy had been bluffing before, but it didn't matter. Since seeing Mark in custody, she had done some research on enemy combatant status. The designation was reserved for those deemed significant threats to the country. "I didn't know it was official." When she had mentioned it to Mark in the holding cell, she had been trying to scare him into talking. Never had it entered her mind it would actually happen.

* * *

Eggs. Again. At least they were better than the oatmeal. Mark poked the spork into the yellow, rubbery mass. He ate every morsel and used his finger to wipe up the tiny pieces left on the plate. As unappetizing as the meals were, they were the highlight of his day. The only problem was, he never knew when they would arrive. He had already been awake for hours.

Some mornings, breakfast would be waiting for him as soon as he opened his eyes, others, he would work out for almost two hours before a clink at the slot would announce its arrival. The length of time between the meals varied too. On occasion he had barely shoved out his lunch tray when dinner arrived, but often he became light-headed before the next meal slid through the flap. It was hard to stay calm when that happened. He couldn't help wondering if he had been forgotten.

Once, in an effort to stem the panic, he'd tried to save some of the food by stashing a piece of bread under his blanket. They immediately demanded that he send the bread out. The loss of the food had bothered him almost as much as finding out they were constantly monitoring him. Sure, he knew the dark bubble on the ceiling concealed a camera, but knowing for certain that he never had a moment of privacy made it more intimidating. His next meal hadn't come for a very long time. He never tried to hoard food again, and he ate every bite of whatever came in on the plate, even if it tasted terrible.

It didn't take long for him to realize he would go mad confined to his cell with nothing to do but stare at the walls. He set himself a routine, a margin of control. When he awoke, he considered it 'morning' and did as much of a normal bathroom routine as he could manage under the cir- cumstances. Then he began his exercise program. Despite the cell's tiny dimensions, he was able to do crunches, push-ups, lunges and squats. He made sure every movement was pre- cise, the intense focus kept his mind sharp. Counting out each exercise and holding the positions for a set amount of seconds, gave him a rough estimate of the passage of time.

He worked especially hard on his stretching. His ses- sions with Jim and his team had taken a nasty turn. Not sat- isfied with the endlessly same answers to the endlessly same questions they had decided he would think of more interest- ing things to say if they chained him to the floor or the walls of the interrogation room and made him bend his body into 'positions'. Muscles stretched or cramped, joints twisted, bearing weight they were never designed for and if he broke the position they would make him 'start over', but he never knew what measure of time they were using. More than once he'd had to lean on a guard to steady himself for the walk back to his cell. The stretches helped. A little.

Mark downed the milk and sent the tray out. It had been a late one today and he had already completed his workout. He sat on the floor, legs crossed. If nobody came to take him away for questioning, he spent the time between breakfast and the next meal doing imaginary photo shoots. Today, his model was a top cover girl. Her picture graced the pages of swimsuit issues, high fashion magazines and she had her own line of clothing. Every detail of the photo-shoot played in his head. The lighting, the camera angles, and the location. Sometimes, he even allowed some bad frames to tarnish the proof-sheet. On a good day, those mistakes made him smile.

He had just tested the light meter in the imaginary shoot, when the tinny voice came over the speaker commanding him to put his hands through the slot. The photo-shoot dissolved in his mind, and his heart thumped against his ribs. Even with all of his exercises and stretches, the positions caused him agony. It just took longer for the pain to hit.

There was a tiny part of him that welcomed the excursions. As horrible as they were, at least he had someone to talk to. Pain was the price he paid for company. Pain he could deal with because it wasn't permanent. There was an end to it, and then it was gone with nothing to show for it. No scars or disabilities. It could be worse. He could be in a pit with rats and fed maggot infested rice. Compared to that, this was nothing. Mark took a deep breath and rolled his shoulders. He winced as the left one grated in its socket. Maybe just a little bit of disability.

Five minutes later, he stood in the familiar room. The three usual spectators sat at their table, quietly chatting as he entered. He listened as hard as he could. Sometimes, he caught bits of sports scores or traffic reports. As mundane as it was, he relished every scrap of it. He felt less isolated when he knew the Knicks beat the Lakers or that there was a ten car pile-up on the freeway. There was still a world going on outside his walls and he clung to that fact like a tick to a dog.

Jim strode into the room and Bill tagged along behind him blowing on a cup of coffee. Mark's mouth watered at the scent. They ignored him while Jim sorted through some papers and Bill told an off-color joke to the other three. Mark filed the joke away for later, when he could smile in private.

Finally selecting a sheet of paper, Jim closed the file. It was Mark's. He knew it. Every time he was brought here, it was a little thicker.

Jim approached him, his face grim and not in sync with his greeting. "Good afternoon."

Mark filed that information away too. So, it wasn't even morning although he had eaten breakfast less than an hour ago. He would try to go to sleep earlier today and see if he could get his nights and days back on track.

"Good afternoon." He didn't mean to emphasize the afternoon part, but Jim caught it, and gave him a sharp look. Mark knew somehow he had blundered.

"I have some questions to ask you, but you probably already knew that."

"Yes, sir." There, he had spoken. It felt good, even if it was to Jim.

"You're looking rather smug today." Jim quirked his mouth, as though trying to figure out what Mark was up to. "What's going on?"

Mark raised his chin a notch. He would never admit coming here was better than sitting in his cell waiting for the walls to close in on him. "Nothing, sir." His stomach churned. It was their mission to make his life a complete hell. It wasn't enough that they stole every last shred of pleasure from his life, now even a pleasant thought was forbidden.

"We'll see if you're feeling so pleased with yourself after today."

Mark swallowed and dropped his gaze to the floor. Maybe the cell was better.

Jim paced, his measured steps in cadence with his words. "Okay, first, I'll give you the opportunity, as always, to be forthcoming and admit to your crimes. Give us the information we've been asking of you." He stopped directly in front of Mark. "We can end this session on a good note for once. How about it?"

Mark lifted his gaze, not fooled by the hopeful look in the other man's eyes. The men at the table behind Jim sat straight, more alert than he had ever seen them. One drummed his fingers. Mark's stomach went from churning to a whirling mass of acid.

"I...I don't have anything to confess." He almost wished he did. He would do nearly anything for all of this to be over. More than once, he'd considered making up a confession. If only he had details. Plausible details. But he didn't.

Jim sighed. "I didn't want to have to do this." Regret flashed over his face and it looked genuine. Then he nodded to the guards stationed behind Mark.

They unlocked his ankle shackles from the floor and grabbed each arm, dragging him to a corner and ordered him lie down on a hard board. His arms were stretched over his head and secured so tightly, his own arms restrained his head from moving. The chains on his ankles tightened, and he heard the clink as the guard clipped his feet to something. His heart skipped a beat when the foot of the board was raised. Blood rushed to his head, and he tried to control his trembling. What were they going to do to him?

There was a shuffling and the scrape of chairs on the floor. Jim stood to the right of Mark's head. He couldn't turn his head far enough to see, but it sounded like the men in the room had come closer. The door to the room opened, sending a slight breeze over him and he shivered.

Jim stepped away from Mark, his footsteps headed towards the door. "Thanks for joining us, Dr. Solomon. We're almost ready to begin, so please, just have a seat."

A doctor? What the hell did they need a doctor for? Mark pulled against the restraints as his stomach twisted into a tight knot of fear.

"I can't say I'm glad to be here, but it's good to see you again, Jim." Out of the corner of his eye, Mark caught a glimpse of a white coat and heard a rustle. The doctor was going to just sit and watch while they did whatever the hell it was they planned to do?

The guard spoke to Jim and pulled Mark's attention away from the doctor. "Sir? How do you want me to do this?"

The uncertainty in the man's voice terrified him. Was there a hint of reluctance too? The man had never been reluctant to restrain him before. What was different this time?

Jim returned to the spot near Mark's head. "Use the cloth. Put it over his nose and mouth. That usually works best."

Did they plan on smothering him? His breath rasped out in ragged pants as he tugged again on the chains. "I don't have anything to confess. Please."

He met the guard's eyes, but whatever reluctance had flashed earlier, was gone, and the guard let his gaze slide away from Mark's. The other man's expression a blank mask, he draped a cloth across the lower part of Mark's face. It felt too light to smother him. The guard disappeared from his vision, but Mark's fear escalated when water splashed nearby. The hair on the back of his neck prickled as a chill swept through him.

The guard returned with a large pitcher in his hand. It was like the one Mark's mother used to mix Kool-Aid when he was a child. The guard looked up as though waiting for a signal from someone. Mark riveted his eyes on the man's face and held his breath waiting for...what? If only the guard would look at him again. His eyes would show if it was going to be bad. If he knew for sure, he could brace himself. Mark froze when the guard took a deep breath and nodded to someone out of Mark's field of vision. The signal had been given.

The cloth fluttered against his lips with every ragged breath. Mark locked onto the pitcher in the guard's hand. He held it over Mark's head and wouldn't look him in the eye. The water flashed in the light an instant before it hit his face. For a few seconds, Mark sputtered, too ticked off about the iciness of the water to recognize the real threat. With every breath, water flooded his nose and mouth. His body spasmed in an effort to get rid of it. The water kept coming and coming. He coughed and gagged, sucking in even more liquid. It ran into his nose and his sinuses burned as they flooded. He fought, bucking against the shackles and arched his back in an attempt to move his head. That only made the stinging in his sinuses worse and increased the pressure behind his eyes.

This was it. He was going to drown. Above the roar in his ears, Mark heard Jim ask if he'd had enough. If he just talked, the torment would cease. He opened his mouth to say yes, just to get them to stop—whatever it took, but the water filled his throat. Without enough breath to even cough, his vision narrowed and his strength ebbed.

CHAPTER SEVEN

Mark coughed and felt his body turning until he was lying on his side. He panted and discovered the cloth was gone and he was no longer chained to the board. His arms remained shackled in front of him, but when he curled his legs to his chest, there was no resistance. His stomach churned and he barely made it up on one elbow before he vomited eggs and water all over the floor. His throat felt raw and his chest ached as he retched until nothing more came up.

Each cough tore through him like he was being turned inside out, but finally, the spasms died down. He hung his head, exhausted and his chest heaved as he sucked in air. Spent, he sagged onto his side. He was vaguely aware of the voices around him. Someone kept asking him if he was okay. It was the dumbest question he had ever heard. There was a splash nearby, and in blind panic, he rolled back to a half-sitting position and used his elbow and feet to scramble away from the sound. The guards were there in an instant, grabbing the chains and shackles.

Jim leaned over him. "Maybe next time, you'll talk." He straightened. "Get him out of here."

* * *

The walk back to his cell was a blur as Mark stumbled along between the guards. It was all he could do to put his hands and feet through the slots to have his shackles removed before he crawled onto the bed, wrapping the blanket around his shoulders. He couldn't stop shaking and his teeth chattered. He clenched his jaw until it ached. It was only a matter of time now, he was convinced of that. No longer was it a matter of if, but a matter of when. They would kill him and there was nothing he could do to stop them.

His stomach rumbled and he staggered to the toilet, but he was reduced to dry heaves. Afterward, he leaned on the sink and scooped water to rinse his mouth, but as soon as it touched his lips, the nausea came roaring back and he gagged. Exhausted, he sank to the floor and curled up in the blanket. His shadowy reflection on the outside of the stainless steel toilet bowl looked sinister, his eyes just dark smudges in his chalky face.

There was no hope. As far as he could tell, he had been here months already. Mark tried to track the seasons by the weather when he was allowed out in the courtyard every few days. Spring had come to wherever he was, and since he had been here, he had seen only the gang of interrogators. Even his request for his lawyer was ignored. How could they do that? He had watched plenty of cop shows. The bad guys always got lawyers. How come he hadn't been able to talk to his?

Jessie had mentioned the term "enemy combatant", but he hadn't had time to ask her exactly what that meant. Now he knew. It meant they could do anything they wanted to him. Anything at all.

His shivering abated, but his energy didn't return. He coughed, his whole body shuddering and he groaned at the ache in his ribs. He felt like he had been beaten with a bat. Wrung out emotionally and physically, he slept.

The clink of the slot woke him. They were back. He scuttled under the bed, banging his head against the metal in his haste. If they tried to take him, he'd fight. It would be better to die fighting right now. Backing into the farthest corner, he strained to hear over the sound of his own breathing. A soft scrape reached him and then the creak of the slot closing. Mark remained under the bed for a long time, ears attuned for any other sounds. Slowly...carefully, he inched his way out and spotted his meal tray.

Eyes glued to the door, he retrieved it and set it on his bed. The sandwich looked safe enough. He sniffed it. Turkey. It was dry, and after a bite, he reached for the purple juice that didn't taste at all like grape juice. The liquid hit his mouth and it was all he could do to keep the small bite of sandwich from coming back up.

After two more attempts to eat it, he gave up. His stomach couldn't handle the food and what little he had managed to swallow came back up moments later. When the slot opened for him to push the tray out, he shoved it as hard as he could, and the curse of the guard on the other side almost made him smile.

Days passed and they didn't come to take him to be interrogated. Every time a meal arrived, he jumped at the sound at the door, terrified they were coming for him. The constant stress made eating impossible and his hunger diminished. At first, he tried to eat everything, but when he puked more often than not, he quit trying. What difference did it make anyway? Starving or drowning, the end result was still dead. At least he controlled one.

He abandoned his exercise routine. There was no point. Time didn't matter and he sat in the cell staring at the wall. They took away his blanket after he shoved out a meal a second time, and he was sure they cranked the air conditioning on to its lowest setting. He shivered and lay on the bed. Mostly, he slept.

His dreams no longer held future events, instead, he dreamed of the past. Christmas, summer vacations, sitting in school. The settings didn't always look like he remembered, but somehow he always knew where he was in them. And he was always safe.

Delivery of meals became an annoyance that took him from his dreams and forced him to get up to push the tray back out. At last there came a time when he couldn't get up. He tried, but his head spun and he sat back down. Three times, he tried to stand. They would be mad at him. He knew it, so he lurched to his feet. His head swam and the floor raced up to meet him, slowed only by the thud of his head as it hit the toilet.

He lay stunned, watching with mild interest as blood flowed across the floor. His blood. At least he had added some color to the room. The puddle spread and felt sticky and warm beneath his ear. He raised his head a fraction and tried to swipe at it, but his arm was too heavy to move. With a wet squelch, his head sank back to the floor. It felt like ice against his cheek. Mark shuddered and closed his eyes. He was so tired.

Voices, urgent and angry, penetrated his consciousness. They were angry at him—he could tell. They were probably mad that he had made a mess in his room. If they just gave him a minute, he'd get up and clean it. If he could just get his body to cooperate. He had to get up.

The command from his brain died on its way to his limbs. Shiny black boots halted a few feet away and a blur of pink became a face. It was speaking to him, but Mark couldn't process what it was saying and gave up when the effort sent a bolt of pain through his head.

He couldn't remember closing his eyes, but he felt something prying them open one at a time, and groaned when a bright light flashed in them. He tried to close his eyes and turn his head but hands held him still and tore at his shirt. Something tight went around his neck. Fear that they were going to strangle him entered his mind, but he couldn't summon enough energy to open his eyes. It wasn't until he felt a hard board at his back, and his body rolled onto it, that the panic set in. He tried to scramble off the board, but his arms and legs had been strapped down. It was no use. He was trapped. The voices dimmed and became distant. Then they were gone and everything went black.

* * *

"Open your eyes!"

A hand shook his shoulder and Mark blinked awake with a start. He squinted at a greenish curtain dangling from the ceiling. Where the hell was he? The room wasn't the same as the interrogation room and he was in a bed. A real bed. With a real pillow and he smoothed his hand against the mattress. Sheets. Scratchy ones, but they felt heavenly to him. Blankets covered him up to his chest. He wanted to close his eyes and burrow into them, but the hand shook him again.

The voice came again, "Oh no you don't. No going back to sleep." While still commanding, it wasn't threatening.

"What?" Mark tried again when his first attempt came out as a croak, and he sought out the speaker. Jim.

Mark jerked and tried to scoot to the far side of the bed. A clip on his finger fell to the floor and he nearly tore his hand off when the handcuff attached to the bed pulled him up short. What did Jim want? He blinked, and rubbed his eyes against the top of his shoulder, feeling dizzy. A loud beeping began, adding to the confusion.

"Christ! Lie down before you pass out again." Jim put a hand on Mark's arm, urging him back against the bed. "Stick your finger out. You knocked this thing off."

Mark complied, but never took his eyes off the other man as Jim put the clip back on Mark's finger. At least the annoying beeping stopped. He licked his lips; they felt dry and cracked.

Jim looked over to a guard by the door. "Free one of his hands, would you?" When the guard had done so and moved back to his post, Jim picked up a pitcher on the rolling table and poured some water into a cup.

Eyes wide, Mark watched, an alarm from some monitor barely audible over the sound of his heart beating in his ears.

"Here." Jim thrust the cup at him.

Mark recoiled, batting it away. It sailed into the curtain, splashing water across the bed and onto the floor.

Jim looked from the cup, still rolling on the floor, to Mark. "What the hell did you do that for?"

Mark didn't cower, but he couldn't look Jim in the eye. He took a deep breath and forced an answer. Remaining silent would only make it worse. "I'm not thirsty, sir." It was a lie, but the truth, that shoving a container of water in his face sent his pulse racing, was too embarrassing to admit.

"Bullshit." Jim glared at him and then said, "And I suppose you aren't hungry either."

"No, sir." That was true. He couldn't recall the last time he had eaten, but he was beyond hunger.

"Well, you're going to buy yourself a feeding tube. We aren't in the practice of starving inmates to death."

"No, sir. Drowning is quicker." Mark flinched at the dark look on Jim's face. What made him say that out loud? Fear pounded through his veins, only one beat ahead of the hate and shame.

The man stepped closer, face stiff with anger. "They'll be in shortly to insert the tube. I heard it's not pleasant." Jim turned to leave, motioning to a guard on the other side of the curtain to come and sit in the room with Mark.

The thought of a feeding tube scared the hell out of him. He couldn't handle that someone would be shoving food into his stomach. It was just one more thing beyond his control. "Wait...sir."

Jim held the curtain with one hand and turned back. "Did you decide you were hungry after all?"

Mark nodded. "Yes, sir." He went limp against the pillow. They had won again. He expected Jim to leave then, and was surprised when the man came back and stood beside the bed. He studied him until Mark began to squirm.

"The doc here says you've lost twenty pounds since you came here. How is that possible? We're very careful about supplying enough calories."

Mark shrugged.

"Did you go on a hunger strike?" Jim's voice was quiet. Almost like he cared.

"No, sir. My stomach just couldn't handle food after...after the last time you questioned me." Mark stared at the foot of the bed. Chains snaked out from under the covers, attaching to steel loops on the foot board. He moved his leg, feeling the scrape of the shackle against his ankle. "After awhile, I wasn't hungry any more. There didn't seem much point in eating."

Jim tilted his head, his tone sarcastic, "No point in eating?"

Anger shot through Mark. It felt good after days of feeling nothing but fear. "Yeah. No point. You guys are going to kill me anyway. What do you care? Am I taking the fun out of it if I kill myself?"

"If you would just come clean—"

"I didn't *do* anything!" Mark glared at Jim, his rage bolstering his courage. "I'd rather die than confess to something I didn't do."

Jim turned on his heel and stalked out of the room.

* * *

Jim brushed past a guard at the door. "Have them get him a tray of something decent to eat if the doctor okays it."

"Yes, sir."

I'd rather die. Taylor's answer rang in Jim's ears. Maybe the guy didn't start out trying to kill himself, but he sure as hell didn't seem to care if he ended up dead. Jim made the long trek from the naval hospital to the brig across the base. He could have driven, but it was just close enough to make him feel guilty for not walking. He hated laziness in others, and held himself to a higher standard.

How could Taylor have not eaten for a week and nobody had told him? Jim swore under his breath and wished he hadn't traveled to Washington, but it wasn't his choice. At least he'd been able to see his son, so it was worth it except in the two days he'd been back, nobody had mentioned Taylor's food strike. If the guy died in custody, the press would have a field day. Already, there had been a few articles from the left calling for Taylor's release, but so far, there hadn't been much public outcry. Jim intended to keep it that way— even if it came down to force feeding.

Jim strode past his own office and went straight to Bill's. He entered without bothering to knock.

Bill looked up from his computer. "How is he?" Before Jim could answer, Bill went back to typing.

"He'll live...for now, even if he doesn't want to." Jim paced the confines of the office. "He thinks we're going to kill him, so he figures he might as well control how he dies."

The typing stopped and Bill swiveled his chair to face Jim. "He said that?"

Jim shrugged and shoved his hands into his pockets. "Basically. He's given up."

"I thought we were getting close to cracking him."

Jim sank onto a chair. "Oh, he's cracking all right. Just not like we had hoped."

Bill grunted and leaned back into his chair. "Is he salvageable?"

He knew what Bill meant. Had Taylor been so broken that he was useless as a source of information? Taylor's burst of anger at the end convinced Jim the man wasn't quite there yet. "Did you ever think maybe this guy is innocent?"

"Nope." Bill flipped through his desk drawer and pulled out a pack of gum, popping a stick in his mouth before holding the pack out to Jim, who waved him off. "The guy was fingered by a confirmed member of al Qaeda. He went to Afghanistan-we have proof of that. We also have the tapes of the calls he made just a few hours before the attacks took place. How else would he have known about the attacks?" Bill shook his head, his jaw working the gum like he had something personal against it.

Jim looked out the window, a few cherry trees bloomed, their color brilliant against the blue sky. Bill had a point. Taylor had to be guilty. He took a deep breath and brought both hands down on the arms of the chair, levering himself up. "Yeah. I guess so." He began to leave, but turned back, adding. "I just hope we get some good information before he goes completely over the edge. He's teetering."

"So, we give him a little break. Question him a few times without any physical persuasion." Bill grinned and wiggled his eyebrows. "Then, when he's relaxed, bring him in again and twist the thumb screws."

"I think you enjoy the interrogations just a bit too much. You scare me, you know that?" Jim was only half-kidding.

"Hey, these guys are getting what they deserve. Every time I see pictures of that mass of rubble in New York, I get pissed and you should too." He shoved another stick of gum in, his usually pleasant expression darkened with anger.

"I know. I get angry too, believe me, I just want to make sure I'm getting angry at the right people. That's all."

"Don't worry. You are."

Jim nodded and left. He wished he was as confident of Taylor's guilt. It would make his job a whole lot easier.

* * *

Jim spent the rest of the afternoon finishing some paperwork and then headed home. His stomach rumbled, and he recalled he had skipped lunch when he got the call that Taylor had been taken to the base hospital. A mental inventory of the contents of his cupboards and fridge revealed his meal choices would be limited to a can of soup and some leftover Chinese, week-old leftover Chinese at that.

There was a little diner just outside the base he could go to. He had eaten there a few times and the meatloaf was good. And maybe that pretty waitress would be working tonight. He cracked a smile and turned on the radio. It was the best idea he'd had all day.

Thirty minutes later, he dug into a thick slice of meatloaf smothered in a mushroom gravy. The waitress hadn't been there, but as he ate a forkful of mashed potatoes, he decided he had still made a wise decision. Even the milk was good here, ice cold and plenty of it.

"Wow, you look like you're starving," his waitress joked when she stopped to inquire if everything was okay. "Don't worry, nobody's gonna snatch the plate away from ya, hon."

The bite he had in his mouth lodged in his throat and he had to take another gulp of milk to wash it down. "Excuse me?"

The waitress grinned. "Nothing, I'm just teasin' you. I like to see a man with a healthy appetite." She patted him on the shoulder and moved on down to ask a family across the room how they were doing.

Jim's appetite shriveled at her words, and he set his fork down, pushing away the plate. He had acted like he was starving, but he had no clue what it was really like to have missed more than one meal. He always knew if he skipped one, he could make up for it at the next meal. Taylor's gaunt face popped into his mind and it contrasted sharply with the image he held of the man he had first questioned months ago. That guy had been tanned, healthy. He had been the picture of a man in the prime of his life. Now, he was pale and thin with his green eyes dulled by apathy and despair. A man who would rather starve.

Jim recalled Bill's anger about what had happened on September eleventh. He set his jaw and picked his fork up. Bill was right. The bastard deserved it. He stabbed the last bite of meatloaf and crammed it in his mouth. Yep, he deserved it. Probably.

CHAPTER EIGHT

Jessie shivered in her leather coat and wished her car would warm up. She fiddled with the heater settings in an attempt to coax more warmth out of the vehicle. The morning had started out in the high forties, but a stiff breeze from the north had made the early spring day feel like January. Stomach rumbling, she headed for the hot dog place and out of habit, glanced down Mark's street as she stopped at the intersection on the corner.

What in the world? The front lawn of the building was full of furniture and other items. It looked like someone was getting evicted. She began driving past, feeling vaguely sorry for whoever it was, when it dawned on her Taylor could be in that situation soon. Slamming on the brake, she stopped, as a horrified thought hit her. What if those were Mark's belongings? She ignored the glare of the driver who passed her on the right. If it was, all of his things would disappear within hours. She stomped on the gas and did a U-turn, pulling up in front of Mark's building just as a group of teens began pawing through boxes.

Jessie jumped out of the car and flashed her badge. Judging by all the photography equipment tossed haphazardly into boxes, it had to belong to Mark. "Step away, please." The youths looked at her and the badge. One protested, "Hey! We're not breaking the law. We always get to take what we want from evictions."

She strode up to him, stopping close enough to count his eyelashes. "I'm sure you do, but some of these items might be important in an ongoing government investigation.

The landlord should have cleared it with the FBI first." In all likelihood the landlord had been given permission, but the teens didn't know that.

The kids gave a token protest and grumbled, but left. Jessie, hands on her hips, gazed around at all the boxes. She would take what she could. If nothing else, she could send it to Mark's parents. Thirty minutes later, her car was packed with boxes. She had decided to try to get as much of the photography equipment as she could stuff into her car. When Mark came back, he would want that.

After unloading the car at her apartment that evening, she decided to swing by his place again to see if she could salvage anything more. What she saw made her jaw drop. A lamp lay broken, its shade missing, a box of papers that appeared to be the contents of a junk drawer, and some clothing, dirty and trampled, was all that remained. Sickened, she reached into the papers and pulled out a piece of junk mail. It was addressed to Mark Taylor. She let the mail flutter back into the box.

That evening, she sat at her kitchen table and examined the cameras. All of them hung open with the film compartments empty. She was sure any undeveloped film had been confiscated, but the equipment itself was of no use to the Feds.

She picked one up that had a cracked lens. She didn't know much about cameras, but that couldn't be good. Setting it aside, she reached in and pulled out an older camera. Its solid black body was textured, and the lens ring looked to be made of brass instead of plastic. Her grandfather had owned a camera that looked similar, but probably wasn't nearly as old as this one. It was certainly an antique, and maybe an heirloom? Turning it in her hands, she marveled at its simplicity compared to all the gizmos on modern cameras. She wondered if it took regular thirty-five millimeter film. Unlike the others, this one held film. She thought it odd until she saw the counter was set at one. Perhaps they hadn't bothered because the film was still unused? Or maybe they had overlooked it since the camera was obviously old. Did it even work?

Jessie returned all the other equipment to the box and stashed it in her hall closet. She wanted to go over the antique camera a bit more, but it had been a long day and she was exhausted so she left it on the table. It could wait until tomorrow.

The next morning was a Saturday, and she dashed around town doing errands. Her car needed an oil change, her fridge was almost bare, and if she didn't get her hair trimmed, she knew she would end up taking scissors to it herself, a situation that never ended well.

Later that afternoon, she collapsed on the sofa. The pantry was stocked, the car now good for another three thousand miles and, she ran a hand through her now neatly trimmed locks and smiled; her hair was safe from the kitchen shears. She started to doze, then remembered her niece's dance recital and groaned. It wasn't that she didn't want to go, she loved watching Maggie dance, but she couldn't help wishing that it wasn't this Saturday. Not that next Saturday would be any better. There never seemed to be enough time on the weekend to get everything done.

Glancing at her clock, she saw that if she was going to make it to the ballet recital, she'd have to hurry. Thirty minutes later, she had her hand on the doorknob when her phone rang.

"Hello?" She tucked the phone against her shoulder as she fished her keys out of her pocket.

"Hey, Jess." It was her sister, Barb. In the background, Jessie heard a multitude of excited little girl voices. The recital was going to start in twenty minutes. She'd be cutting it close, and figured her sister was checking to see if she was coming or not.

"I'm on my way—save me a seat, okay?"

"Of course, but I'm glad I caught you. I forgot my camera. Can you bring yours?"

Jessie tried to remember where she had stashed hers. She hardly ever used it. Well, it had to be here somewhere. "Sure." It took her ten minutes to find it, and when she did, she discovered she had no film. Damn. Already, she would be lucky to get there before the first class did their routine. Her gaze fell on the old camera still sitting on her table. It had film. She didn't think Mark would mind, besides, he'd probably never know. She grabbed it and hurried out the door.

* * *

Sweat dripped into his eyes and Mark swiped it with his shoulder as he finished his last two push-ups. He sat on the floor, his back against the edge of his bed, and reached over to grab his shirt. He felt too sweaty to put it on right away, and held it loosely in his fist until he cooled down. Since returning from the hospital, he had renewed his exercise routine, but not with the same precision. Mostly, he did it out of boredom. There had been no more interrogations, which he was thankful for, but he hadn't been out of his cell since returning from the hospital ward except for showers.

Once more he had lost the ability to track the passing of time. He tried counting meals, because for awhile, they came at regular intervals, but once he regained some of the weight, the meals became unpredictable again. His stomach rumbled even as he thought of food. He couldn't be sure, but his trays had a tad more food on them since he had returned, but even so, he never felt full.

Time passed in mind-numbing boredom. Mark tried to envision photo shoots, but had difficulty focusing. The silence ate at him. Heavy and oppressive, it saturated the cell. Maybe his mind was trying to fill that silence, because he swore he heard people talking to him. Not all the time, but enough that it scared the hell out of him. Was he losing his mind? Were they screwing with him and playing voices over the speakers?

Except the voices belonged to people he knew. Once, he heard his mother calling him to dinner. Another time, Jessie's voice came to him and said that she liked mustard on her hot dog. In fact, when he thought about it, the voices always spoke about something related to food, so he figured it was all in his head.

Mark stood and ran some water on his hand, then patted his face. When he had first started exercising again, he had, without thinking, splashed water on his face in his usual fashion. The simple act caused him to hyper-ventilate until he became so dizzy, he had so sit with his head between his knees. Now he made do with the least amount of water possible.

He had just finished swiping the remainder on his chest when the key turned in the lock. He held his breath until he saw it was the doctor. At last, another person to talk to, even if it was only for a few minutes. Mark ignored the guards who stood ready at the door.

"Hey, Doc." Mark wanted to shake the man's hand, but he'd learned that wasn't acceptable, so he settled for nodding.

"Hello, Mark." The man wasn't chock full of warmth, but at least he wasn't the one who attended Mark's near drowning. "I see you're keeping in shape. You could stand to gain a few pounds."

Looking down at his washboard belly, Mark patted it and smiled. "I always wanted a six-pack. Guess I can thank the government for finally attaining one."

"Yes, I guess you can." There was no humor in the doctor's voice. "Have a seat please."

Mark's smile faltered. He should have learned by now that the man would do no more than he had to do. No joking, no small talk. Nothing that would give Mark the impression that the doc regarded him as anything other than a job to do.

After a quick exam, the doctor made a couple of notes on a small pad of paper. "You're looking good. Your shoulders are doing better?"

"Yeah." Mark rotated them to prove it. "I've been given some time off."

"Right. Well, until next time I come by, just keep doing what you've been doing. The exercise routine is a good idea, but don't overdo it. That might be what's keeping your weight down." The doctor walked over to the door and without another word, left the cell.

Mark slumped onto his bed and lay down. Maybe the chaplain would come soon. Once in awhile he visited. He was nicer. While he didn't stay long, he did ask Mark if he had any requests. The last time, Mark had asked for some books. The chaplain said he would pass on the request. It had been awhile now.

There was nothing to fill his time. He could sleep, but that brought pain. Not the kind inflicted by an interrogation. No, this was worse. It was pain born of loss and frustration. Despite the risk, he still craved the dreams sleep brought. He'd dream of food. Dreams so vivid, he'd wake to find his mouth watering. He'd lie still and try to fall back into the dreams, and sometimes, he succeeded.

It wasn't just the food, it was the good times and happy memories surrounding the meals. Pancakes dripping with maple syrup at Boy Scout breakfasts. Fried chicken on Sunday afternoon after church. Lazy summer afternoons eating watermelon on the front porch while his mom hung laundry to dry. His dad waving away smoke as he manned the grill while Uncle Larry and Mark played a game of catch on the Fourth of July. The smell of the hot dogs, brats and burgers had tantalized them. Mark swallowed. Afterwards, they'd feast on apple pie topped with homemade ice cream. His mom would smile at him as he tucked into his dessert. It was his favorite and she'd made it especially for him.

Then the dreams changed. The smile on his mother's face would turn to confusion, and she'd look at him blankly, without recognition. It was the lies she'd been told by the authorities; he'd never been allowed to call and explain. The dream would go on, with his dad holding out a plate piled high with Thanksgiving favorites, only he'd withdraw the offering as Mark reached for it. Then Jessie would appear and just as he bent to kiss her, she'd push him away with the look of fear he'd seen back in the holding cell.

He'd awaken with a gnawing in his gut. A hollow ache. She hadn't believed him. No one believed him. Had his shame been made public? Did anyone know where he was? Had they even tried to contact him? Or had they forgotten him and gone on with their lives? Did they hate him that much? Even his mother?

The scrape of his meal tray sliding across the floor pulled him from his thoughts. What would it be this time?

He was sure it wouldn't be apple pie. He squashed his disappointment when he saw grits. Pancakes would have been nice. Out of habit, he stepped to the sink and washed his hands, not that anyone would care if he ate without doing so, but his mother had ingrained the action. Cupping some water, he patted some onto his cheeks and neck. It made his skin crawl to splash the water on his face, but he forced himself to deal with it on shower days. It was either that, or never shower again. Right at the moment, he needed one. He sniffed down by his underarm. Badly. When he rubbed his hand across his jaw, the stubble felt prickly, almost beard length. A shave would be nice too.

After washing, he sat cross-legged on the floor, tray balanced on his lap. He grimaced. Grits. Well, it was food and it would fill his belly. Out of necessity, he ate quickly, lest they demand the tray back before he was done. Sometimes, that meant shoveling the food in without using any utensils. Today, he did his best to eat in the manner his mother had taught him. He even imagined eating breakfast with his parents. His dad asked him how the photography business was going, but Mark knew what he really meant was, had he come to his senses yet and taken a real job.

His mother would brag about some photo Mark had done, pointing out how talented he was. Then she would ask him if he was seeing anyone special. It was no secret that she longed for grandchildren. His folks drove him nuts with their nagging. A lump rose in his throat. He stared at the empty bowl and swiped a finger along the rim, snagging a few bits he'd missed. He popped the finger into his mouth and tried to swallow the lump with the little bit of food.

What he wouldn't give to be in his mom's sunny kitchen right this minute. She could nag him about girlfriends and grandchildren to her heart's content, and he would just smile. He wouldn't even mind his dad yammering on about respectable jobs. Hell, he might even go get one, if he ever got the chance again.

The order to send the tray out came, along with the demand that he put his hands and feet through the slots for shackles. His hands shook as put them through the opening. Were they going to interrogate him again?

His fears died down to their usual level when he only went down the hall to the shower room. They didn't allow much time, but that was okay. He didn't like spending much time in the spray, but he did love the clean feeling afterwards. He shaved and dressed in clean prison garb. Done, he waited to be taken back to his cell, but instead, they took him towards the yard. Mark began trembling again, but this time in anticipation. It had been so long since the last time he had been outside.

Mark stepped into brilliant sunshine and closed his eyes, feeling the heat on his face. A soft breeze ruffled his still wet hair and sent a pleasant shiver through him. He looked around in wonder. The last time he had been out, it was overcast and blustery. He had still enjoyed it, but today was perfect.

The guards released his leg shackles and Mark was very conscious of their guns held casually at the ready, but there was nowhere for him to run. Ignoring them the best that he could, he ambled into the center of the small yard. The scent of flowers carried to him on the breeze and he smiled. It was one thing they couldn't control. He laid on the concrete, not caring how hard it was. It warmed his back, and he closed his eyes.

In the distance, he heard leaves rustling and birds singing. An ant tickled a path across the back of his hand. He could have fallen asleep right then and he'd dream that he was on North Avenue beach. His limbs grew heavy and he almost dozed, but shook his head to rouse himself. He didn't want to waste a precious second outdoors in slumber. Sitting up, he draped his arms over his bent knees. Soft pink petals from some tree fluttered in the air like fragrant snowflakes. The sky beyond the walls supplied the ultimate blue backdrop.

The sun shone almost directly overhead and his hair dried. He wanted to soak in the sunshine and save it up for later. Who knew when he would see it again? This week? Next? Never?

Too soon, his time was up and he blinked as his eyes adjusted to the dimness of the hall. The prison stank of sweat, floor wax and stale cooking odors. He resented those smells taking up residence in his nose and replacing the scent of cherry blossoms and springtime.

It was one of the few times when he had an idea of night and day. It had been near midday when he had been outside, and he did his best to gauge the time when he returned to his cell. When he deemed it night, he laid down on the thin mattress and pulled the blanket over his head. Between that and draping his arm over his eyes, he achieved some darkness. He missed the blackness of night.

Mark thought of nighttime in Chicago. It was never truly dark. Some nights he would go to the roof of his building and look south towards the Loop. He never tired of the gorgeous skyline. It killed him to think that people thought he wanted to destroy something so beautiful. He curled on his side, facing the wall. Sleep came more easily than usual. The little bit of fresh air had done its magic, and with his head turned in to his bicep to block the light, he caught the faint scent of spring on his skin.

"We've tried to give you a break. Did you notice the extra food? The time outside? Those perks don't come for free. Now you have to pay for them. You have to give up some information."

"I can't, sir." Why did they keep asking him the same questions? Frustration welled and Mark clenched his teeth as he tried to slow his breathing down. He leaned against the wall, his arms spread wide, only his fingertips holding him away from it. His legs angled behind him as though he was doing a push-up against the wall. Only he had to hold the position. For hours. The white cinder-block an inch from his face blurred into a vision of faint gray craters and white ridges. A black scuff mark marred the wall. His arms burned and when they gave him permission to use his forehead to help hold his weight, the relief only lasted a few minutes.

"I bet your friend Mo didn't hold out this long before pointing the finger at you. Why are you protecting him and the others?" Jim tapped him on the shoulder with a pen or pencil. Mark wasn't sure, but even the light tap hurt his quivering muscles.

The clank of the door slot awakened Mark and he bolted up in bed. What the hell? Instead of the interrogation room, he was still in his cell. His body was slick with sweat and he swiped it off his face. It had been so real. It was like one of his camera induced dreams. How could that be? Shaking, he got up and began pacing the cell.

CHAPTER NINE

"Jeez, lady. I almost called the police when I developed these photos." The owner of the photo developing shop grimaced and shook his head as he rang up her total. "Including the new film, that will be ten dollars and sixty-six cents."

Jessie cocked her head. "Excuse me?" She handed him her money. "I'm afraid I don't know what you're talking about."

He held up his hands and looked to the side briefly. "Hey, whatever you're into is your business, but I'd prefer it if you didn't bring your film here anymore. At least, not if it has pictures like those on it."

Confused and embarrassed but not sure why, Jessie took the envelope of pictures and left. She sat in her car in the parking lot and pulled out the prints. Her niece grinned at her, not the least bit bashful about the two missing teeth. More pictures of the recital, and one of her sister and Maggie. She held one up to get a better look. Maggie had leaned towards her at the last minute and instead of a head and shoulders shot, it was an extreme close up of Maggie's nose and eyes. It looked kind of cool, even if she did say so herself. Grinning, she flipped through the rest.

The last few should have been group photos of Maggie with her ballet class, but instead, one was a side view of a man facing a concrete block wall. His body leaned forward, arms spread wide with only his fingertips and forehead holding the weight of his body off the wall. Where in the world had that photo come from? Shaking her head, she set it aside. There must have been a mistake at the processing lab. The guy at the camera place should have been paying better attention to his work instead of looking askance at her. She focused on the very last picture, hoping to get at least one group shot.

She gasped at the image on the paper. It wasn't a group shot. A man sat on a bare concrete floor with his hands shackled to his ankles, his face screwed into a mask of pain. On the edges of the photo were booted feet with camouflage pants tucked into the top. She noted a chain that ran from the man's shackled ankles, to a ring anchored in the floor. The poor guy. His face, eyes open but glazed with exhaustion, angled towards the camera. A shiver of recognition shot through her. Her hand shook as she took a closer look. With a shocked cry, she flung the picture on to the dashboard.

It was Mark.

* * *

All morning, Mark waited. He knew it was inevitable. They would come for him today. He tried to eat breakfast, but it came up as his stomach churned. The day dragged on, and the muscles at the back of his neck tightened, sending waves of pain shooting through his skull. Alternating pacing with sitting against the wall massaging his neck, he tried to put the dream out of his mind. Maybe it was just a regular dream. A very vivid regular dream .Lunch came and went untouched. When the command came to present his hands for the shackles, it was almost a relief. The waiting was over.

Mark stood motionless as the team assembled in the interrogation room. Head down, he didn't bother trying to listen for idle chatter this time. What good would it do?

Bill approached. Mark could tell by the sound of his footsteps. They were slower, less measured than Jim's. "Did you enjoy your nice little break?"

Mark clenched his fists, and then took a slow deep breath forcing his fingers to relax. Anger would do no good here. What could he reply to that? Yes? That he'd had a grand old time? Better to remain silent. He didn't think he would be able to control his sarcasm if he spoke.

"Say again? I didn't hear you. Look at me when I speak to you," Bill snapped.

Even though he was the 'good' one, Mark doubted that Bill had a speck of sympathy for him. "I had a great time...sir." Mark tried not to glare and averted his eyes, focusing on the wall across the room. He made sure he looked above the group, including Jim, seated at the table watching him.

Bill leaned into Mark's field of vision, his eyes narrowed. "You know what? Just to get this show on the road, what do you say we start out with a little stretching exercise?" He motioned to the guards. "Get him in the rowing position." He turned back to Mark. "You ever rowed a boat?"

Mark hesitated, looking past Bill to Jim at the table. Did he look annoyed with the suggestion? It was hard to tell. "Uh, yes sir. A few times."

"Well then this should bring back some memories."

The position they put him in did bring to mind rowing a boat, but only if he remained in the coiled position without ever pushing with his legs and straightening his body. The shackles bit into his wrists and his back muscles jerked. They left him like that while they went to get lunch. The guards remained, but neither spoke to him. What was the purpose of this? Mark tried to come up with something he could tell them. Had something happened in Afghanistan that they would want to know about? He straightened his knees as much as he could to ease the pulling on his shoulders. That worked for about a minute, and then his hamstrings burned. Mark bit his lip to keep from moaning. His thighs ached as though red hot pokers were being jammed into them.

Sweat ran in rivulets down his face, the itching causing its own torment. He wiped his cheek against his arm, then left his head there, blocking out the bright lights.

In a small town outside Kabul, he had witnessed a woman being beaten by a crowd. He'd wanted to rush over to help, but Mo had stopped him with the warning that the crowd would turn on them if they did anything. It was the custom there, and there wasn't anything they could do. Horrified, Mark had turned away, but not before using his long lens to get some shots of the atrocity.

That night, Mo had gone off alone, telling Mark he was just going to visit some old friends. Mark hadn't felt like socializing after seeing the scene in the town square and had been happy that Mo had dropped him off at the hotel in Kabul. What if Mo's visiting had been something more sinister? Mark groaned with both physical and mental anguish. How could he prove that he had been at the hotel and not off hatching plans with Mo and the bad guys?

The door to the room opened and Mark tried not to look at the men as they filed in, not wanting them to see his weakness, but he couldn't help stealing a glance, despite his best efforts to refrain. He hoped that someone would release him now—before he began to moan. It took all his willpower to remain silent. Bill had a bag from a fast food restaurant. The scent wafted to Mark and his mouth instantly flooded. He swallowed and tried to ignore the smell. His back spasmed again and the tantalizing aroma was forgotten as he gasped and writhed.

Jim, his hands in his pockets, stood beside Mark. "Ready to talk?"

Mark panted, "Yes, sir." Whatever it took to end this. He could tell them about Mo going off alone that night. It was all he had. He prayed it was enough. Had Mo been put through this kind of interrogation? Is that how they had acquired information on Mark? If it was, he almost couldn't blame his old friend for lying.

The guard unclipped Mark's wrists from his ankles and, with the release, Mark sagged onto his back, gasping. The relief was immediate, but not complete. His muscles still quivered and jumped, and he was surprised that they allowed him a moment to compose himself. He gulped air, every breath drying out his mouth. He must have sweated a gallon.

Jim stepped back and began a slow circle around him, making him nervous. Mark was the carrion, Jim, the vulture.

Mark bit back a groan as he sat up and the guards helped him to his feet where he swayed for a moment. He felt like he had just run a marathon. The smell of French fries made his stomach rumble.

"Well, let's hear it." Jim had come around to stand in front of him.

"One night, Mo went off by himself to meet old friends." Mark paused to catch another breath and to stall, trying to make the thin bit of information sound more important than it was. He slanted a glance at Jim. "Maybe he planned something that night?" It sounded lame even to him. Mark saw a flash of anger on Jim's face. Ice rattled as Bill swished his drink, before setting it down. A drop of condensation raced down the side and pooled on the table. Mark licked his lips and tore his eyes away from the sight. No use adding to his own torture.

"That's it? That's all you're going to tell us?" Jim shook his head and turned away as if thoroughly disgusted with Mark.

Mark bowed his head. He should have gone with Mo that night. At least then he would have something to tell Jim now. Paper crinkled and Mark looked up to see Bill unwrapping a burger. Lettuce and tomato peeked out from under the bun. The scent made his mouth water.

Jim came back to Mark, his arms crossed. "I'm disappointed. Here I thought you had something useful." He sighed.

Bill opened a pack of ketchup and squirted it into a pile on the wrapping. Mark watched him dip a fry and then pop it into his mouth. Jim said something and Mark pulled his attention back to him. At least he tried to, but when Bill lifted the burger and took a bite, his eyes darted back to watch the man sink his teeth into it. Mark could almost taste the cool lettuce, the crisp tomato and the tangy mayonnaise.

"Am I boring you?" Jim's voice was low and held a note of danger.

Mark snapped his gaze back to him. "No, sir."

"We've tried to give you a break. Did you notice the extra food? The time outside? Those perks don't come for free. Now you have to pay for them. You have to give up some information. Some *real* information."

The comment was straight out of his dream. Somehow, even without the camera, his dream was going to come true. Mark locked his knees to keep from sinking to the floor. They insisted he give up something he didn't have to give.

* * *

Jessie strapped her shoulder holster on before slipping her arms into her jacket. The pictures from Mark's camera lay on her dresser, and she picked one up. She had already shown her sister the ones from the recital and just said that the group shots hadn't turned out. It was true, so she didn't feel guilty and there was no need to mention these images.

She tucked the two of Mark into her purse along with the negatives. There was a camera shop on her way to work and she planned to talk to them during lunch, if she had a chance. If nothing else, she wanted to enlarge the photos. There might be something in them that would clue her in to when they had been taken. The negative listed them as the twenty-third and twenty-fourth frames, but that couldn't be right. They had to have been on the film and she had just used up the rest photographing the recital. The frame counter had said zero, but it was an old camera. She hoped the person at the camera store could tell her something about it.

The morning dragged and Jessie kept glancing at the clock. It was a beautiful day. School had just let out for the summer and, she heard children playing at the park across the street. The clock inched towards noon, and Jessie pulled the photos out of her purse to take another look. Even though she had studied them a dozen times already, she hoped each time that something would turn up and show that the pics were only from a costume party or even some kinky sexual thing. She felt her face heat up and glanced at

Dan at the other desk, hoping he didn't notice. She shouldn't have looked because he caught her eye.

"What do you have there?" He rolled his chair across the gap between them.

Jessie turned the photos face down and bent to get her purse. "Oh, nothing, just some photos I...found."

"Yeah? So why are you hiding them?" Dan grinned and made a 'give me' gesture. "Come on, show me."

Jessie sighed and ran a hand through her hair, letting the strands settle. "Okay, but I'm warning you, they aren't easy to look at."

Dan's grin faltered and he hesitated as his hand closed over the photos. With a questioning glance at Jessie, he flipped the pictures over. The first was the one of Mark seated on the floor, his knees bent and shoulders pulled forward at a painful angle. If Dan knew who it was, he didn't let on, he just studied the photo for a minute before moving onto the second one. His eyes widened and then he shook his head, his mouth set in a hard line. "Where'd you get these?"

Jessie shrugged. "I used one of Mark's cameras to take pictures at my niece's recital Saturday. Remember I told you about how he had been evicted and everything was on the lawn? The camera was in with his stuff. When I picked the photos up yesterday, those two were in with the pictures of the little girls dancing."

"You think these were taken before he...before he was arrested?" Dan rarely spoke of Mark now. There was no reason to, since the guy wasn't always intruding in their cases, but once he had called Mark a poor bastard. It had been said with regret, like he knew something, but he had never elaborated.

Leaning over to see the photos again, she shook her head. "It makes sense. I mean, obviously, I didn't take them, but according to the negatives, these were the last two on the roll of film." Jessie sat back and pulled the envelope with the negatives out of her purse. "See?"

"That's weird." Dan skimmed through the negatives. "Maybe they cut them wrong?"

"Could be. I'm heading to a camera shop in a few minutes to see if they can tell me anything." She stood and held her hand out. "But, even if the images were on the film before I used the camera, what are they pictures of? Who is making him do that?"

Dan handed her the pictures and she traced a finger over Mark's pain-glazed eyes in the second photo. "Look at this, his hands are still shackled and it looks like he can't even raise them high enough to get proper leverage."

"It's a stress position." Dan rolled his chair back and stood, grabbing his jacket off the back. "I'd like to come with you, if you don't mind."

Jessie pushed a strand of hair behind her ear. "Sure, but what's a stress position?"

"Just what it sounds like. It's a form of persuasion used by some governments to get prisoners to give up information." Dan angled his head towards the door. "Come on. I'm curious now. Maybe someone planted those pictures in the packet somehow."

Jessie went ahead of him down the hallway. "What if they weren't planted?" So far, she had refused to consider the story Mark had told her after his initial arrest. That was crazy. She could only surmise that he'd been desperate to concoct something that outlandish. That was the only logical explanation.

* * *

"Wow, that's wild." The guy examined the negatives and pictures. "These negatives definitely came off the same roll of film. They were processed together, all the cuts on the film strips line up. They physically came from the same roll of film, and see where the film winds around the take-up spool in the camera?" He pointed to the square holes at the bottom of the negatives and continued, "Every fifth one has a tiny notch in it. The notch is on the second picture as well as the ones from the recital. I bet if I look at the camera you took the pictures with, I'll find a small defect on one of the teeth that pulls the film through the camera."

"I have the camera right here." Jessie dug into her purse and handed the young man Mark's camera. She noted his name tag. Gary.

Gary's eyes lit up. "Cool. I'm not sure of the make, but it's old. Very old." He turned the camera this way and that, skimming his fingers over the textured body. "It's in good condition too. It was probably one of the first thirty-five millimeter still cameras." Beaming, he opened the back. "Yep, there's a tiny flaw in one of the teeth on the wheel. See the sliver of metal sticking out?" The young man laid the strips of film out on the counter in order. "Right here." He tapped the edges of the strips as he kept a silent count. "The notch is on every fifth negative and this negative falls exactly in sequence. These photos definitely came off the end of this roll of film."

Jessie and Dan leaned across the counter. There was no doubt. Jessie straightened and caught Dan's eye. Now what? He shrugged.

"Where'd you get the camera anyway?" Gary asked, and then bent to get something beneath the counter.

"It's not mine. It belongs to a...friend of mine." Jessie ignored Dan, knowing that if she looked at him now, he would be grinning at her.

"Oh. Well, I can't tell you how those bizarre photos got on your film, but I have another roll of film here. You could try it out and see what happens. In all likelihood, it was just some crazy glitch."

Nodding, Jessie pulled some cash from her wallet. "I think I'll do that. Meanwhile, would it be possible to get those two photos blown up to eight by tens?"

Gary made a face. "Sure, that's no problem, but what in the world for?"

Dan leaned an elbow on the counter and smiled. "It's police business. You understand."

Gary's eyes rounded. "Oh." He rang up the film, his demeanor more subdued. "I'll get right to work on those enlargements. Should be ready by tomorrow."

Jessie smiled. "That would be great, Gary."

* * *

Jessie picked up the enlargements the next day on her lunch hour. She waited until she was back in the office to open the envelope. Bracing herself, she sat and pulled the pictures out. The larger pictures showed more detail. Mark's face was bathed in sweat, and his hands looked swollen in the cuffs. In the second picture, she saw the muscles in his arms bunched. He appeared thinner than she remembered, and his orange t-shirt was plastered to his body. Across the back, was a stenciled number? It was prison issue. That much was obvious. But which prison? Booted feet in the corner had camouflage pants tucked into the top. That meant military.

Dan entered, a bag in his hands. "Want a burger? I figured you wouldn't have time to get one, so I got an extra."

She tried to smile, but didn't quite manage one. "Sure. That sounds good. Thanks."

He handed her the burger and wordlessly took the pictures from her. After a long moment, he sighed. "It's not any easier looking at them like this, is it?" Dropping the pictures on her desk, he returned to his own and began eating his lunch.

She took a deep breath. "No. Harder in fact." As difficult as it was to look at the pictures, it was time to think logically. The pictures looked real, but where had they come from? How had they ended up in the camera? She had just happened upon Mark's stuff tossed onto the lawn of his building. Then had happened to use the camera for the recital and happened to use the photo store near her work. How could anyone have planned an elaborate scheme to plant the photos with the prior set of chance circumstances?

Jessie unwrapped the burger. The photos of Mark had been on the end of the roll. How had a man who had been gone for months wind up on the end of a roll of pictures that should have been faces of giggling little girls wearing tutus? If it was a con, it was insanely complex. Who would go to that much trouble and why?

Dan didn't know what Mark had told her about dreams and pictures predicting the attacks on nine-eleven. It had been hard enough telling anyone that Mark had been arrested as a terrorist; there had been no need to add lunatic to the list, but what if pictures like these were what Mark had experienced?

"When I went to see Mark that last time, he told me something."

His mouth full, Dan raised his eyebrows and took a gulp of his soft drink. "Yeah?"

She tucked her hair behind her ear and leaned an elbow on her desk as she turned to Dan. "He told me that he had a camera that took pictures of the future and that after developing the photos, he'd dreamed about what was in the pictures." She stopped as she tried to recall exactly what Mark had told her. "Or maybe he had dreams first and then the pictures show up. I'm not sure."

Swallowing a bite, Dan wiped his lips with a napkin, and Jessie couldn't help noticing that the corners of his mouth twitched.

"Really? That's...interesting." He tilted his head to the side with a half-shrug. "So? Taylor was always a bit odd. It sounds like something he'd say." He dipped a fry into a pile of ketchup and pointed it at her. "Does that have something to do with why he was arrested?"

"It had almost everything to do with it. He said that he had photos of the Towers and a dream. I guess he called a bunch of government agencies the morning of the attacks to try to warn someone." Jessie picked up her burger and took a bite. She wasn't hungry, but it smelled good. Her coffee was cold, but she took a drink anyway to wash down the food. "What if he was telling the truth?"

Dan balled up his wrapper and tossed it in the wastebasket. "Aw, come on, Jess. I know you liked the guy, but I think you're grasping at straws."

Jessie snatched the photos and waved them. "Then where in creation did these come from?" With a snap of her wrist, she let the pictures slide onto the desk then stood and paced to the window. Of course he didn't believe it. Why should he? It was crazy. Drawing a deep breath, she turned, arms crossed. "Look, I know it sounds...improbable. But what if it's true? I didn't believe it until these pictures showed up." She flung an arm out, gesturing at the photos. "You got a better explanation?"

Dan slouched in his chair, but he had lost the sarcastic look, and instead, bit his thumb as he contemplated the pictures covering Jessie's burger. "Well, you could test it."

"How?"

"Take some more pictures." He grinned. "See what develops."

She couldn't help smiling at his bad pun, then sat down in her chair as she thought about his suggestion. "I guess I could do that." What if another horrible scene turned up? She shivered and hoped she was wrong about this.

"Did you dream?"

Jessie pushed the awful mental pictures of what might show up out of her mind. "Did I dream?"

"Yeah. You said Taylor told you he had dreams that went along with the photos. You have pictures, but did you dream?" He pointed his chin towards the photos, "Did those scenes turn up in your dreams?"

Jessie moved the pictures off her lunch and shook her head. "No. At least, if I did, I don't recall any." With a shudder, she continued, "These would have been nightmares. I would have remembered." Without looking at the them again, she put them in the envelope. She pushed the photos back into their envelope.

"Well, I have to go interview some witnesses from that incident yesterday." He burped and pushed out of his chair with a groan. "I guess it's back to work. Are you going to finish that initial report?"

Jessie took a last bite and swept the crumbs off her desk with the side of her hand. "Yeah. And thanks for lunch."

CHAPTER TEN

A friend, when questioned, said, "Mark's a great guy. We used to go have a few beers, shoot pool, or go biking. Then, a few years ago, he got super busy. Guess his business picked up. I gave up calling him."

It was the same story with other friends, but, if Jim's memory was accurate, Taylor's business, while growing and successful, hadn't taken a huge jump that would explain the sudden inability to see old friends. Was he too busy because he had other duties?

Jim tapped a pen on the yellow legal pad at his elbow. Notes in his precise hand filled the top half of the paper. Taylor's file lay open, individual reports spread out over his desk. He re-read the transcript of Mohommad Aziz's interrogations. The guy had really done a number on Mark Taylor. The man had told his team of interrogators that Taylor had volunteered to take photos of Chicago skyscrapers and the Chicago Board of Trade as possible targets. Details were sketchier than Jim would have liked. When asked why Taylor would do something like that, as there was no documentation that Taylor had ever been a sympathizer, Aziz had said it was greed and that Taylor had demanded fifty-thousand dollars for his photos.

Jim set aside the transcript and pulled out Taylor's financial records. His debt had been moderate, a car loan and a small business loan, both in good standing with regular payments. The photographer had paid the appropriate taxes on his business, and his spending matched his reported income, with a modest amount set aside in stocks and savings.

There were no big purchases, no large deposits, and no transfers of money. In short, no red flags. If he had been paid fifty thousand dollars, he hadn't spent any of it. Jim scratched his neck. Maybe Taylor buried it all in a trunk in his backyard.

Buried beneath the financial records was the very odd file that the Chicago police had on Taylor. It contained six reports of Taylor being caught in dangerous situations, but what was strange was he had been cleared of any wrong doing in every instance. In fact, he had played a key factor in most of the situations coming out better than they could have. Better than they *should* have.

In one case, a car with two children inside had begun rolling down an embankment and ended up in a pond. Luckily for the kids, Taylor had been able to open the door and reach in and pull both kids out, tossing them onto a grassy embankment. The car had gone twenty feet into the pond and sank in deep, murky water. The kids would surely have drowned. Taylor had been mildly injured when his jacket caught on the door latch and he had been dragged. The car hit a bump, according to Taylor's statement in the report, and his jacket had ripped free.

Jim set the report down. Four others had similar outcomes, but the fifth one was different. It's the one that intrigued him. In that case, Taylor had been shot while attacking an undercover police officer. Oddly, it wasn't the officer who shot him, but instead, a member of the street gang the officer had been trying obtain evidence on. Taylor's attack had saved the officer from being hit. Taylor hadn't been so lucky and had been shot in the left thigh.

So, why was a clean-cut guy like Taylor hanging out on street corners in a drug-infested neighborhood? Jim wondered if he had been there trying to make a buy, but no reports listed him as a drug user and his drug screen upon arrest had come back negative. None of Taylor's friends or acquaintances mentioned drugs when they had been interviewed. Besides, he'd come across many addicts in his career and nothing in Taylor's behavior even hinted that the man was a user.

Tossing his pen down, Jim sat back, his hands clasped behind his head. It just didn't add up. What would make this guy join up with a terrorist group? His parents were middle America and raised their son in a loving and supportive home. They were practically a Norman Rockwell painting come to life. Neighbors remembered Taylor as the kid who was first to knock on their door to shovel after a snowstorm, or playing baseball in the corner lot with the other boys. The most trouble he had been in was when he had been caught smoking a joint behind a neighbor's garage when he was fifteen.

He skimmed the transcript from the half dozen phone calls Taylor had made to various government agencies on the day of the attacks. At the bottom of the page was a reference number for the audio recordings. They hadn't listened to the actual calls that Taylor had made as they had read the transcripts, but now Jim was curious. He called his secretary and requested that she get a copy of the tapes.

It would take awhile before the tapes would arrive, so he took a quick break to get some fresh coffee. Taking a sip, he settled at his desk once again. According to the file, Taylor had a girlfriend...a detective with the Chicago PD. That was an interesting tidbit. The notation said that they appeared to have only been together a short while. Most of his friends had drifted away in the last few years. Jim rifled through the papers to find a brief interview he recalled reading.

He sat forward and sorted through the file. Damn. There wasn't much. Just the few sketchy police reports he'd already gone over. He checked to see who had filed them. He recognized one. Where had he seen that name recently? Detective Jessica Bishop. He snapped his fingers. Wasn't that the name of the woman Taylor was dating at the time of his arrest? Interesting. He rubbed his chin, trying to remember the approximate date Taylor had begun dating her. He was sure it had been shortly before Taylor's arrest.

Jim noted the names and details on a legal pad. He intended to investigate the Bishop angle more closely. He sorted the papers and found the interview he was looking for. It had been filed under the personal contacts since Bishop had been the girlfriend. He skimmed the transcript, and scowled. The officer, Sean Daly, who'd done the interview, was either having a bad day or was lazy beyond belief. He should have pushed harder on the fact that a police detective had a relationship with someone giving tips on crimes. Daly should have pounced with follow-up questions.

The reports needed fleshing out and he decided that he needed to do it himself. He glanced out the window and pulled his shirt away from his body. It would be nice to get out of the humidity. The air barely moved outside his window, and even in the air conditioned building, his shirt stuck to him. He grinned. Chicago shouldn't be too brutal in September.

His mind still entertaining the idea of Chicago, he shuffled the documents back into the stiff expandable file and moved to the row of tall cabinets lining one wall of his office. There was a short knock on his door, and his secretary stepped in.

"Here are the tapes you requested."

"Wow, that was fast."

She held out a bundle of tapes held in a stack by rubber bands. "I have connections."

Jim took the tapes from her and smiled. "Thanks." After she left, he took the tapes back to his desk, he found his cassette player and slid in the first tape. He had read the transcripts from these tapes several times before, but that wasn't why he had requested them. He wanted to hear how Taylor sounded.

An hour later, Jim scrubbed his hands down his face and scratched his head with both hands. He was no closer to deciding what to do with his prisoner. It would have been so much easier if Taylor had sounded calm, but Jim had detected a note of restrained panic in the first calls. In later tapes, he'd been not just panicked, but frustrated and angry. The last tape was different. Recorded at 0743 Central time, Taylor sounded defeated, his voice thick. Was he crying? Either the man was a hell of an actor, or he had truly been distraught. Jim replayed that last tape. Taylor's voice filled the office.

"Please, you have to put me through to someone in charge. There's not much time left. Oh, God. Please."

"I'm sorry sir, I need to ask a few questions first."

"Goddamn it, there's no time for questions...time...oh, shit...what time is it?"

There was a short silence and then a sharp thump. Jim leaned in, his ear turned towards the machine. What had he done? Dropped the phone? There was a muffled scrape Jim closed his eyes, picturing the scene in his mind. Fear was etched on Taylor's face and tension in his movements. Jim shook his head and snapped his eyes open. He was probably just superimposing the familiar expressions he'd inspired when questioning Taylor. That's all it was.

Taylor choked out, "Never mind. It's too late."

The tape ended at 0745. One minute before the first plane had hit.

Jim stabbed a finger down on the eject button. The evidence was impossible to ignore. Even if Taylor knew the exact timetable of the plan, there was no way he'd have known exactly when the first plane would hit. There were too many variables. The terrorist pilots could have made their move sooner or later, there could have been a delay due to fighting, as happened on Flight 93 that went down in Pennsylvania. Even the wind could have been a factor. So, how had he known that by 0744, it was too late? Unless he knew that only a minute later, the first plane would hit.

How had he missed that the first ten times through the transcripts? Jim picked the phone up and called to his administrative assistant. "Jill, could you book me on a flight to Chicago?" Glancing at his calendar, he nodded. "Next Wednesday would be fine."

* * *

He sat as straight as the shackles allowed. Across the table, Jim sorted through Mark's file. At least, Mark assumed it was his file. What was the guy up to? And where were the others? As horrible as interrogations were, at least he knew what to expect. This change in procedure smacked of some kind trickery. The guards were ever present, but stood by the door instead of right beside Mark. For the first ten minutes, Jim had ignored him, looking at him briefly when he had first arrived, and then checked his watch every few minutes.

Mark shifted in the chair. What was he waiting for? Were the others late? But why were there no other chairs?

Mark jumped when there was a knock on the door, and right on cue, his heart began pounding. He knew better than to turn to see who had entered. He couldn't help himself, he prayed it wasn't a doctor.

Jim smiled and motioned for someone to enter. "Bring it in. Thanks."

Before Mark could get over his shock at seeing the other man flash a genuine smile, a woman strode past, giving Mark a wide berth and avoiding eye contact. She carried a white paper bag in one hand and a drink holder in the other. The two soft drinks sloshed as she set it down along with the bag. "There's extra ketchup, mustard and salt."

"Great. I appreciate it." Jim dug into his pocket and handed the woman some cash. "That should cover it."

Mark was torn between wanting to look at the woman—the first he had seen in months, or the bag, whose scent told him what it contained. The woman ignored him and left the room. That left him no choice, but it didn't make it any easier. He swallowed hard and studied the floor. It was the safest choice.

At the crinkle of paper, Mark raised his head. Jim dug into the bag and pulled out two large sandwiches. He pushed one in front of Mark. "I think it has the works."

Mark recoiled. What was the guy up to?

Jim frowned as he began unwrapping his own sandwich. "It's okay. You can have it."

The smell filled the air, and he hoped he wasn't drooling, but he didn't touch the food—not even when a container of fries joined the burger on the table in front of him. For all he knew, it was poisoned. More likely, it was a trick and the second he put it to his mouth, Jim would order him to drop it.

Mark remembered a dog he'd had as a kid that would sit with a treat balanced on its nose, waiting eagerly for permission to flip the morsel up and snatch it out of the air. Mark now knew how that dog had felt. It made him ashamed of teaching his pet that 'trick'. Now it seemed cruel. He studied his shackled hands clasped in his lap. Even if he dared to eat the burger, he couldn't reach it anyway. There wasn't enough slack in the chains.

"Eat the damn burger." Jim set his own lunch down, and wiped his hands on a napkin. "I'm trying to do something nice here."

Mark darted a look at him. "Why?" His voice was hoarse from disuse, and he cleared his throat. There had to be an ulterior motive. Jim's face hardened and Mark raised his chin a notch. This was the man he knew. He could handle this.

For a long moment, their eyes clashed and Mark felt a thrill of triumph when Jim looked away first and shook his head. "Fine, eat it or not. I don't care." Jim took a bite of his burger and Mark turned his head, the sight of the food making him light-headed.

The thrill of winning died in the next few minutes as he remained at the table, hearing the crunch of the lettuce, smelling the charcoal-grilled meat and the aroma of French fries. What had he won? Nothing. Mark took a deep breath. "I...uh...I'm sorry. I just...I don't know what you want from me."

Jim sighed and dropped the fry he held. "I just thought it would be something special for your birthday. We're not heartless here."

Shocked, Mark stared at Jim. "It's my birthday?" It was September eighth? He had been here only ten months?

He was thirty-six years old. Were his parents thinking of him today? Or did they think him a terrorist? Last year, he had spent the day at a Cub's game. The sun had been hot, the beer cold, and the home team even won the game. He closed his eyes, picturing the deep green ivy covered walls, the emerald diamond and the flags on the centerfield scoreboard blowing straight out. Towering above the team flags had been the American flag. He opened his eyes and blinked hard.

"You didn't know?"

Mark shook his head. How could he have known? It wasn't like he had a calendar tacked to the wall of his cell.

"Well...shit. Yes, it's your birthday." Jim waved to the food in front of Mark. " So eat up. It's not poisoned."

"I can't...sir."

"Why the hell not?" The irritation was back in his voice and he gave Mark a sharp look.

Mark bit back a sarcastic reply. This was probably just another way to torment him. He lifted his hands as far as they would go. If he stretched, he could just touch the edge of the sandwich.

Jim's face flushed. "Oh." He called a guard over and instructed him to detach the shackles from the waist chain.

The other man's embarrassment surprised him, but he didn't dwell on it. He allowed himself to breathe in the scent of the burger, letting it fill his nose and make his mouth water. Then he took a bite, closing his eyes and savoring the taste and texture. The sauce mixed with the crisp lettuce and tomato and complemented the hot and juicy burger. Pure heaven.

He washed it down with an ice cold soft drink. It made him think of all the times he had eaten this exact same meal. Usually he was with a friend for lunch or late in the evening after a long photo shoot. It was normal. Ordinary. So ordinary, it made his throat tighten and he had to take another long gulp of the soft drink to get the food down. What he missed most was normal life.

Half-way through the meal, it hit him that when he finished eating, he would go back to his cell. Back to his surreal life in a nine-by-six room with white cinder block walls. This meal— this taste of his usual life—it was just a brief interlude. Nothing more. His hands shook and his stomach churned. No longer hungry, Mark set the half-eaten sandwich down.

"What's wrong? Don't you like it?" Jim balled up his wrapper and stuffed it in the bag. He tried to quell his anger. Jim probably hadn't meant to be cruel, but that only made it harder. Mark took a deep breath. "I liked it fine, sir." For the first time, he lied to the other man. "Thank you. I appreciate the meal." He touched his stomach. "I'm full, that's all." A wave of nausea ripped through him and he prayed he would make it back to his cell before the food came back up.

CHAPTER ELEVEN

Jim drummed his fingers on the armrest of the cab as it inched through Chicago's morning rush hour. His superiors had denied his official travel request, stating that they felt Officer Daly's report was sufficient and that nothing more could be gained from that line of inquiry. Undeterred, he'd put in for some personal time and paid for the trip himself. So, he was here unofficially. That might be better anyway. If he didn't find anything useful, he wouldn't have to admit it to Bill.

Almost an hour later, Jim tossed his bag on the bed in his room. He thought about following it down and taking a quick nap, but it was already after ten. He had a lot of ground to cover before his return flight tomorrow evening. First on his agenda was finding Detective Jessica Bishop. According to his notes, she worked out of the fifth precinct. Jim changed from his rumpled traveling clothes and put on a crisp white shirt, blue tie and black pants. Just because it was technically vacation didn't mean he couldn't look official.

Jim paused outside the police station, double checking the precinct number. Satisfied he was at the right one, he pushed through the doors and strode up to the desk sergeant. "I'm looking for Detective Jessica Bishop. Can you direct me to her office please?"

"Who are you?" The man squinted up from his paperwork.

This was the tricky part. Bishop didn't know him. This wasn't official business so Jim couldn't declare that he was with the CIA. He didn't want to lie, either. He settled for a half-truth. "I'm Jim Sheridan. Detective Bishop and I have a mutual friend, so I thought while I was in town on business, I'd come by and introduce myself." He pulled out his wallet and showed his driver's license.

The sergeant raised an eyebrow, but then shrugged. "Whatever." He waved a hand towards the right. "Her office is third door on the left. But she ain't there now." With that, he went back to whatever he was doing with the papers.

Jim braced his hands on the desk and leaned towards the sergeant's face. "Any idea when she might return, or where she might be? I promised I'd meet her when I was in town."

The man sighed and rolled his eyes. "Look, I ain't her secretary. You might find her in the file room. It's back that-away." He jabbed a thumb over his shoulder.

"Thanks. You've been so much help." Jim headed in the direction the man had indicated and peered in three offices, inquiring in each if anyone had seen Jessica Bishop. No one had any idea and he was beginning to wish he had called first. He'd thought about it, but didn't want to give up the advantage of surprise. He had found that it was easier to read a person that way. A door marked FILE ROOM was ajar, and he pushed it open and stepped in.

"You the one looking for me?"

Jim turned towards the voice behind him. She was taller than he expected, only a few inches shorter than his five-foot ten. He had seen a standard file photo of her, but in person, even with her hair in a tight bun, she was striking. She watched him warily.

"Detective Jessica Bishop?"

She nodded, her eyes never leaving his face. "And you are?"

Jim stuck his hand out. "Jim Sheridan."

For a long moment, she studied him before she shook his hand. Her grip was strong and her eyes hard. "What can I do for you?"

Jim looked over her shoulder to the busy station. "I know this is unexpected. I flew out on the chance I could talk to you when I should have made an appointment, but do you have some time? I'd like to talk to you. Somewhere quiet, if possible. It's about a mutual acquaintance."

"Who is it?" Jessica glanced away, and he saw her reluctance and irritation. She held a stack of files and her eyes went from the clock then down to the files in her hand as though weighing in her mind if she had time to waste talking to him

"I see I've caught you at a bad time, but I promise you'll be interested in who this acquaintance is." He paused a beat letting her realize the importance of his next words. "I'd rather wait to disclose who it is until we can go somewhere else to discuss it."

She raised her head, her expression wavering between annoyance and curiosity. "Look, I don't know you from Adam, so why should I go anywhere with you?"

He stepped closer and said in a low voice, "I saw Mark Taylor the other day. I'd like to ask you some questions."

She lost her grip on the folders, but juggled them quickly and looked like she was going to ask him something, but changed her mind. Hope had sparked in her eyes for an instant before she masked it with a shrug. "Okay. Let me get my purse out of my office."

As she entered an office, she glanced over her shoulder. "Are you hungry? We can get some lunch."

"That sounds great." Jim realized that he was starving, his stomach reminding him that the granola bar he'd eaten on the way to the airport this morning was a distant memory. He waited outside the detective's office. Purse in hand, the woman started for the door, stopped, turned back, and pulled a large white envelope from a desk drawer. Tucking it firmly under an arm, she breezed past him.

She drove, not saying much beyond asking him what kind of food he wanted. He shrugged and told her to pick the place. His hopes of putting her at ease turned to regret when she pulled up in front of a grungy hot dog stand. Jim hid a grimace. Maybe she was trying to give him food poisoning. He ordered a hot dog with the works along with fries, and Jessica ordered the same. He followed her to one of the picnic tables sitting on the hot pavement. Jim bit into the hot dog, and then grinned. "This is good."

Jessica nodded, her mouth full. After taking a sip of her drink, she said, "Yeah, it's one of my favorite spots." She glanced around. "It doesn't look like much, but what it lacks in ambiance, it makes up for in flavor." A few wisps of her hair had escaped confinement and the gold strands fluttered as she tilted her face to the sun, eyes closed. "Besides, sometimes I just need to get outside for a bit."

They ate, occasionally making awkward small talk. It was odd having lunch with a complete stranger, and he knew she felt more than a little uncomfortable. At least the food was good even if it was greasy as hell. He chuckled. That was why it was so good. If he ate like this too often, he'd get soft, and what kind of image would that project? He vowed to run an extra five miles to make up for the greasy meal.

The last time he had indulged in fast food had been with Taylor. Jim picked up the last bite of his hot dog, scooping up some errant pickle relish and replacing it on the end of the dog before polishing it off. That meal hadn't ended as well. The guy had puked upon returning to his cell. The hot dog churned in Jim's stomach at the thought. Taylor had been nearly catatonic for three days.

Jim took a sip of his soda, then used the straw to loosen the ice. There was always the worry about crossing the fine line between breaking the man's defenses or just breaking the man. If he pushed too hard, he risked pushing Mark Taylor into insanity. Not hard enough, and they wouldn't get any information. He glanced at Jessica and held up his cup. "I'm thinking of getting a refill, you want one?"

She swirled the cup, as though weighing it. "No thanks. I'm good." Her eyes rose to his face, studying him. "For someone who flew out...from where ever the hell you came from, you sure don't have much to say."

He hoped the heat disguised the flush he felt creeping up his face. It wasn't that he didn't have news, but it wasn't good news. "Sorry."

Jim swiped his finger through the ring of condensation his drink had left on the picnic table. Jessica finished her hot dog, but picked at her fries. The silence of the meal was awkward, but small talk would have made it worse.

He tapped his fingers on the table and tilted his head to work a kink out of his neck. The sun beat down on the pavement creating shimmering waves of heat. His prediction that it wouldn't be hot in Chicago in September had been a faulty one, but that was par for the course lately. He sighed. It hadn't occurred to him that Taylor would have no idea it was his birthday. He hadn't meant to cause pain, but he'd seen it flash across the other man's face when he'd learned the date.

Jim ate his last fry and gathered his wrappers, tossing them on the tray. Jessica finished eating, and now sat staring across the parking lot, her drink straw in her mouth as she sipped.

"You done with that?" Jim indicated her meal and she nodded. He took the tray and tossed all the garbage in the trash can next to the building. When he turned back to the table, he found Jessica watching him, her expression intense. He had been right. She had questions and the grace period was over.

"So, where is he? Where are you guys torturing him?"

Jim paused and tried to hide his surprise before resuming his seat at the table. He had to admire her directness. Maybe he'd been too quick to criticize Officer Daly's interview. "Excuse me? Who said anything about torture?"

She shook her head. "I'm sure you'll deny it, but I know who you are. I've been around long enough to know a Fed of some sort. If you were FBI, you'd identify yourself as such. That leaves CIA or DOD."

The lady was smart, he had to grant her that. Jim shrugged, but didn't admit to who he worked for. "He's in a brig in South Carolina." He narrowed his eyes. "But nobody is torturing anyone."

She snorted and shook her head, her face twisted into a smirk. "He's innocent, you know." Jessica's chin went up, challenging him to contradict her.

Anger burned in her eyes and he let her statement hang there for a long moment before crossing his arms on the table and leaning towards her. "What makes you say that?"

He'd found that the best way to get answers was just allow the other person to talk. If pointed in the right direction, they often spilled more information than they intended.

"Because I have evidence that what he said about the pictures is true."

That was the last thing Jim expected her to claim, and he cocked his head. "You're serious?"

Jessica slid the envelope in front of him. "Look for yourself."

Jim glanced at her before pulling two pictures out of the envelope. He tried to control his expression, but shock pulsed through him as Taylor's image stared back at him. He recalled that interrogation. They had only done that particular position one time. "Where'd you get these?" Damn it. There must be a leak on his team. It had to be a still from the video because there were no other cameras in the room. This was highly classified material. If these stills ever found their way to the press, heads would roll. Whoever had sent them either had top clearance or knew someone who did. Jim clenched his jaw to keep from spewing his anger at Jessica.

"I got it from one of Mark's cameras. His belongings were tossed out of his loft when he was evicted." She emphasize the last word, her tone accusing. "I just happened to be passing by and grabbed what I could. The rest is all gone." Jessica took the picture of Taylor seated in the rowing position and looked at it for several seconds, her face awash in disgust. "Is this how you get people to confess? If I did something like that, I'd be brought up on charges." She slapped the picture on the table in front of him.

"I follow the guidelines set for me." He shook his head and tried to repress the urge to walk away. The last thing he needed was condemnation. "You know, we get blamed when something happens, for not knowing, yet when we try to do our best to gather important information, we're labeled barbarians." Jim stabbed his finger down on the picture. "This isn't some goddamn game we're playing, Bishop." He waved a hand towards the tall buildings a few blocks over. "This city could be next for all we know. And maybe your boyfriend has information that could prevent innocent people from being killed."

"So the ends justify the means?" Her voice was incredulous.

"Damn straight. It's justified when it decreases the harmful impact on citizens."

She flushed and he bit back a smirk. She wasn't dealing with some Neanderthal government flunky. If she wanted to throw that threadbare expression at him, he could quote Machiavelli right back at her.

Jessica put both hands flat on the table and leaned towards him. "That's...bull—" She broke off as a couple of customers passed on their way to the order window. When she tried again, her voice was quieter, but just as angry. "That's bullshit and you know it. What kind of information are you going to get from someone who's in so much pain he'd name his own mother as a terrorist if it meant that the torture would end?"

Jim had no answer to that and conceded she had a point. He had harbored his own doubts about the authenticity of some of the information gathered, but there had been some proven successes with some prisoners using the same methods used on Taylor. One success might mean that there would be more, and nobody would know who would give up that important bit of information. He leaned his elbows on the table and rubbed his temples, then dropped his hands and let his anger drain away. "I understand your concern.

Believe it or not, I do have Taylor's health in mind and try to make sure that there's no permanent damage."

Jessica recoiled. "Oh my God. You mean you're the one who actually does these things to him?" She paled.

This was not going as planned. "I'm sorry. I shouldn't tell you this, but I guess I need to explain what my role is and why I'm here." He took a deep breath. "I am the head of a team that questions Taylor. We're not the only ones though. There are a few agencies dealing with him. Frankly, the reason I'm here is because I harbor some doubts about his guilt. I shouldn't tell you that either, but I hoped to get more information from you or anyone else you can think of." Jim opened his arms, palms out. "I just want to find out the truth. That's all."

Color crept back into her face and her throat jumped as she swallowed. "First, I'm not sure that anyone would call what Mark and I had a relationship. It was too new. Just so we're straight on that."

Jim believed her but could also see that even though she denied any relationship with Taylor, she still cared about him. Curious, he asked, "How were things going before Taylor was taken into custody?" He allowed a note of humor to inflect his voice, "For what it's worth, he seems like a nice enough guy."

Her cheeks turned pink at that and she actually chuckled. The smile transformed her face. No wonder Taylor had asked her out. "Yeah, he is, but he has some odd quirks." Jessica's gaze became distant. "For instance, on our first date, we were having a pleasant dinner...until he had to leave suddenly. Said he didn't feel good or something. Only, I saw him at a mini-mart on my way home that night. Long story short, the place was about to get robbed and he inter-fered, and if he hadn't, I would have shot and probably

126

killed a fourteen year old robbing the store. The kid had a very real looking water pistol. Mark never explained how he knew except that he got a good look at the gun. I know guns, but that one fooled me."

She went quiet for a few moments. Jim fought the urge to ask questions and was rewarded when she then shook her head and continued, "Anyway, I felt like he ditched me on our date. He apologized and asked me out for the next weekend— literally begged for another chance. I agreed, but the day before our date, he shows up in the middle of our narcotics bust."

Eyes wide in exasperation, she waved a hand to emphasize the story. "So, he tackles the undercover guy about to make a buy, and right then, a rival gang-banger decides to pepper the street corner with an AR-fifteen." Jessica looked down at her hands and rubbed them together and took a deep breath. "The officer came out without a scratch, the drug pusher took a couple of rounds to the chest, and Mark was wounded in the leg. After he recovered, we tried again. Things were going well, but then..." She bit her lip and shrugged. "Well, you know what happened then."

"So, you're telling me that the marks on his record with the Chicago P.D. came about when he was trying to help?" The official reports barely made mention of Taylor's role, but now Jim understood. What police officer wanted to admit to being saved by a civilian? Instead of awarding a medal, they arrested him for interfering in a case. They couldn't make any of the charges stick, but just the fact that he was charged in the first place remained on his record. "I noticed that the charges were dropped."

She shrugged. "It was an embarrassment to the department. I can't claim to be innocent. I felt the same way when he began showing up."

"But you don't anymore?"

"I didn't understand it then, but I think I do now." She swept the loose strands of hair out of her face. "I used his camera to take pictures of my little niece's dance recital. When I picked the film up, most of the pictures came out great. Little Maggie did a wonderful job." Jessica's face softened and a smile curved her lips. "The last two pictures I took were of Maggie with her dance class. The girls were so wound up, I had a hard time getting them to sit still long enough to snap the picture, so when I finally got them to cooperate, I took two pictures, just to be sure." She separated the photos of Taylor, looking from one to the other, then up to Jim. "Only instead of laughing little girls, I got these. I had the negatives checked, along with the camera. I thought maybe the pictures had been staged before he left or something, but according to the negatives, that would have been impossible. These were the last two on the roll." Jessica slid the pictures together and put them back in the envelope. "Now, I believe his story."

While interesting, Jim wasn't sure that it was related in any way to Taylor's innocence or guilt. There was still the time in Afghanistan. "You are aware that Taylor spent several weeks in Afghanistan back a few years ago?"

"Yes, he mentioned it to me. I didn't know him at the time he went, but he showed me some pictures he brought back. I was touched at how he captured the fear and strength in the women's faces. He wanted to help tell their story. It's too bad that book wasn't published. Mark's photos were stunning."

"I'm sure he's an accomplished photographer, but our source claims Taylor agreed to take photos of possible Chicago targets. The Sears Tower, the Hancock building and others."

128

Jessica crossed her arms and shook her head. "I don't believe it. No way."

"Your belief in Taylor is admirable, however, you don't have the same information nor responsibility that I have."

She stared at him, eyes narrowed, then without a word, swung her legs to the outside of the bench and stood. "I have to return to work." She strode towards the car.

Jim slid to the end of the bench and hurried after her. He caught up and put his hand over hers, stopping her from opening the car door. "I'm sorry. I know this must be hard on you. Nobody ever wants to believe that someone they care about could do horrible things."

"Take your hand off me." She didn't raise her voice. With the look she gave him, she didn't have to.

"Sorry." Jim snatched his hand away and took a step back.

Her shoulders sagged a fraction. "You have no idea what I do or do not feel for Mark. I'm not even sure, but I do know one thing—that man is not capable of the things you claim. I'm saying that as someone who has been a police officer for ten years and a detective for three." She opened the door and nodded towards the passenger door. "Get in."

It took a moment for Jim to register that she didn't intend to leave him here, and then he jogged to the other side and got in before she changed her mind. "Thanks. I thought I'd have to find a cab."

Jessica shrugged and started the car. "Well, it's not like I'm doing it out of the goodness of my heart. I would like nothing more than to leave you here to bake on the pavement, but I want to show you something."

* * *

Jessica gripped the wheel and forced her hands to relax before her fingernails dug into her palms. The thought of the things this man had done to Mark and God knew how many others, made her skin crawl. She glanced at him. There he sat, looking like an accountant, all neat and crisp. Like he never got his hands dirty. "Can I ask you something?" She faced forward and eased the car into traffic.

"Sure. That doesn't mean I'll answer." He sounded weary, but not in the least intimidated. "I hope you don't mind if I roll the window down. It's a gorgeous day."

"Doesn't it bother you to do these things to other human beings?" She knew it was a bold question and that he would probably deny that what he did was wrong.

Sheridan remained silent for so long, she thought he was going to ignore the question, but then she saw his jaw tighten, and knew that she hit a nerve. Good.

"Believe it or not, I don't like that part of my job at all. It's like asking a surgeon if he enjoys amputating a patient's diseased leg. It's not pleasant, but sometimes you have to cut away the diseased portion to get healthy again." He rested his elbow on the windowsill, his hand disappearing above the car. She could hear him drumming his fingers on the roof.

There was another long pause then he said, "There's nothing I want more than a healthy country. One that isn't afraid to carry on with business as usual. If I do my job right, the rest of you will be able to live, work and travel without having to worry that the next terrorist plot will tear your world apart."

She shot back, "I have the same goal for the city of Chicago, and maybe it's small-scale, but I don't torture my crime suspects until they confess and point fingers"

Her building was just around the corner and she turned right.

"That's very admirable, but then I doubt your suspects were trained to withhold or to give false information."

"Withhold information? Are you serious? One look at Mark's face would tell you if he's telling the truth or not. The guy can't tell a lie if his life depended upon it." She rolled to a stop in front of her building. "I'll be right back."

She wasn't sure why she needed to show him the camera. For all she knew, the two images of Mark had been a one-time thing. Since buying the new roll of film, she had been too afraid to take more pictures. Who knew what might show up? She even wondered why Mark had ever continued using the camera. The fear of what might develop made her mouth go dry every time she thought about trying it again. Some things were better left unknown. Had Mark known he would be shot that time?

"Well, here it is." She moved the driver's seat back. "I haven't used it since that time, but I planned on testing it again."

"Go ahead if you want, but just to let you know, I have a feeling that those pictures of Taylor are the product of a leak on my team. That's all it is. I'll get to the bottom of it and I promise, you'll see no more of those kinds of photos."

Jessica ignored him, and instead, loaded the film. It was a bit trickier than she was used to, but after shutting the compartment, she advanced the film to the first frame. She turned to Jim. "Say cheese!"

CHAPTER TWELVE

"What the hell are you doing?" Jim glared at Jessie as she snapped off three photos. Who knew what she would do with the photographs? He wasn't even supposed to be here.

"Just testing the camera to see if it works like it did before. You saw me load it, now I'm going to run through all the frames." She advanced the film and thrust the camera at him. "Here. You do the honors. Take pictures of whatever you want. We can go down to the park at the end of the block."

Jim held the camera with his thumbs and first fingers. "It looks old. I don't know much about cameras. What if I break it?"

"The thing looks like it's made it through some rough times, I doubt a few pictures in the park will be the end of it." Jessie slid her seat forward and started the car, pulling out when it was clear.

"Fine." He turned the camera over. "Do I just push the button here?" Jim held his finger over one of the gadgets on top of the device.

"Yep." She eased against the curb, stopping the car. "Here we are. Have at it."

He sighed and exited the car; he had better things to do than take pictures. Hopefully there weren't many exposures on the film. Might as well get started. The sooner he used it up, the sooner he could get do some more investigating. He had a few of Taylor's friends he wanted to chat with before flying back to Charleston in the morning. Lifting the camera, he snapped a picture of Jessie as she came around to his side of the car.

He shot photos of trees, the slide, a swing, and even a butterfly that landed on a bench. Jim didn't want to admit it, but it was kind of fun to try and find something to photograph. The goal was to simply take random pictures just to use up all the frames, but he couldn't help trying to find interesting subjects. It seemed like such a waste to just point the lens anywhere and click the shutter button.

Jessie followed him, making suggestions, and when she mentioned taking a picture of a wildflower poking through the slats of a boardwalk surrounding the play area, he tried to suppress a grin. If the guys on his team could see him now, lying on his belly trying to get a good picture of a flower.

In fifteen minutes, he had used all the frames and handed the camera back to Jessie. "Well, that was fun," he said, his voice dry.

She raised an eyebrow, the corner of her mouth quirking. "I think you need to get out more. It seems like you have a natural eye."

Jim felt his face heat up. "I think you'll discover differently when the pictures come back. They probably aren't even in focus." He sat on a bench, leaning forward with his hands loosely clasped, absently watching a couple of little boys have a sword fight with sticks.

Jessie sat beside him and rewound the film, taking it out when it was complete. She made a show of holding it up for him to see and putting it in the canister. Jim shook his head and hid a smile. Maybe he would buy a decent camera and learn how to use it. It had been fun.

He stood and twisted, getting a kink out of his back. "Now what?"

Jessie handed him the canister. "There. You keep it. I wouldn't want you thinking I switched rolls somewhere. Maintain the chain of evidence and all."

Jim rolled his eyes, but took the film. "Fine."

"Now, we get it developed. I know a place that should be able to do it in a few hours."

After dropping off the film, Jessie took him back to his hotel and agreed to pick him up after she got off work. They'd go together to get the prints. In his room, he dug out the numbers of Taylor's friends and tried calling them. None were home, and he left a short message, saying he would get back to them later that day. Then, with nothing to do, he stretched out for a nap. It had been a long day already.

* * *

Jessie tapped on the glass counter. Jim felt a surge of apprehension and shook it off. Her nervousness was rubbing off on him. The same guy who had promised to develop the prints earlier came from the back room, a film envelope in his hand.

"Here you go." He set the envelope down and looked from Jessie to Jim, his face twisted in disgust. "I know it's police business, but there's some seriously disturbing pictures in here." He rang up the purchase. "Don't you guys normally have your own lab people develop film for you?"

Jessie snatched up the envelope. "Yeah, but like before, this is a special case. We need to keep this quiet. Will that be a problem for you? I suppose we could go elsewhere if we need to..."

"Oh, no ma'am. I can handle it."

Jim had to hand it to her, she had the young guy puffing up his chest, no doubt feeling important to be part of an 'investigation'. Amused, he turned to Jessie, about to crack a joke about how awful his photography skills were if the photos scared the poor guy, but he bit the comment back when her face drained. "What?" He circled behind her to see the photo in her hand. "Damn it!"

Jessie swung around, her face twisted in fury. "Doing *this* to a person is how you keep our country safe?"

Jim snatched the print out of her hand to take a closer look. There was no mistaking what was going on. Taylor lay stretched on his back, cellophane pulled tight around his face except for his nose. A hand, just visible at the top of the picture, held a pitcher of water, the stream shone silvery as it poured onto the cellophane. The man's eyes were wide with fear and the tendons on his neck stood out as he strained to get away. Sickened, Jim closed his eyes and swallowed.

Jessie glared at him and the guy behind the counter stood mouth agape at her comment. Jim sent him a hard look, then gripped Jessie's elbow. "Can we take this conversation out to the car?"

She jerked her elbow free and marched ahead of him, slamming the door.

Jim took a deep breath and turned to the guy. "Look, I'm sorry you got involved in this." Pulling his ID out, he flashed it in the young man's face. "It's imperative that you don't tell anyone about what you've seen and heard. Understand?"

He nodded, his Adam's apple bobbing as he swallowed. "Sure. Not a word."

"Good." Jim grabbed the envelope of photos, exited the shop, and climbed in the car beside Jessie. The implication of what the photo meant sank in. At first, he had thought it was an old photo of the time they had waterboarded Taylor, but then he recalled that they hadn't used cellophane. He hated that method, feeling like it was going too far. Bill was a fan of it though. Insisted it was a more compelling technique, very effective on the more reticent prisoners and had produced some actionable intelligence when he had used it on another detainee.

Jessie sat arms crossed, her face a mask of loathing as she watched him. Jim tried to form an explanation but couldn't come up with one. "I just want you to know that I didn't order this. I gave explicit instructions that Taylor was to be left alone until I returned." He wasn't sure why he wanted the woman to believe him. Even if he had ordered it, he had the authority to do so and didn't need to explain his decisions to a civilian.

"So, you're saying that you believe the photos weren't planted?" Her voice rose, and for the first time, she looked at him like he was human.

Jim shrugged. "I don't know what the hell is going on with this picture." He hesitated, not wanting to admit to any of this. "The one time we did that, we used another... method. Maybe it wasn't us."

She narrowed her eyes, her tone skeptical. "Not you? What does that mean?"

"Taylor has a couple of agencies questioning him." He was fairly certain that FBI didn't waterboard, but sometimes guidelines were...bent. Maybe this was one of those times.

"Do all the others use this method as well?"

He'd hoped she wouldn't think to ask that question. It was time to end the discussion before it went any farther. "Listen, I can't discuss this with you." It was bad enough that he was even here talking to her. He was in line for an official reprimand if his superiors found out he was talking to a civilian about any of this.

She raked him with a scathing glare and then stared out her side window. They sat in tense silence for about five minutes, and he had his hand on the door handle ready to step out, when she turned to lean against the door, tucking one leg up under her. "I'm not exactly sure how it works, but I think the picture comes first, then Mark has the dreams. Maybe it fills in the details."

Jim suppressed a sigh. If she wanted to focus on the unlikely, no, make that the impossible, then he'd go along with it for now. At least it got her off the subject of methods of interrogation. He pulled out the photo, steeling himself. He wouldn't cringe—not in front of her. He was used to seeing this kind of thing, but usually he was prepared and was able to detach from what happened to the subject. With Jessie sitting there, it was impossible to remain distant. For her, Taylor wasn't a subject. He was a man, and not just any man, but someone she had feelings for. The fear and panic on Taylor's face was palpable. "You think he's going to dream this?" He held the picture up.

Shuddering, she looked away. "Maybe." Jessie sighed. "I'm just not sure. I didn't listen to him when he tried telling me."

Jim sat back and stared out the windshield. Traffic whizzed by and horns blasted in the late afternoon rush hour. He rubbed his eyes. This whole thing was crazy. Magic wasn't real. Everyone knew that. Magicians used sleight of hand and tricks. Religion wasn't one of his things either and he had no idea what people would say about this. Most likely, no one would believe him if he tried to argue that Taylor did have a way to see the future. A rock formed in the pit of his stomach. No one would believe him, just like no one had believed Taylor. "I'll see if I can change my flight home to an earlier one."

"Does this mean you believe that he had nothing to do with 9/11? That Mark will be set free?" Jessie's eyes opened wide, hope shining out of them.

He averted his gaze. There was too much hope in them. "I don't know what I believe, but it's beyond my control anyway. If I come to the conclusion that there's not enough evidence to continue holding him, I can make that recommendation. I could try to convince the rest of the team. But that is the limit of my authority. I have to go through channels." Jim took a deep breath. " You should know how this kind of thing works. It's not so different. People higher than me have the final determination." There. He hadn't promised anything.

The light in Jessie's eyes fizzled. "I see."

* * *

Mark tried to control his fear as he stood in the inter-rogation room, but his heart knocked against his ribs and sweat ran down his back. He locked his knees to keep the chains attached to the bolt in the floor from rattling. Jim wasn't here, so maybe his dream had been wrong. Maybe it was a just flashback nightmare to when they had done the water thing to him before. He closed his eyes and as he re-called the details, bile burned his throat. Jim had been absent in his dream too.

Bill approached and Mark saw the same shaving nick on his chin that had been there in the dream. "I'm sorry Jim couldn't be here with us today, but he had some business to attend to. I hope you don't mind if I ask all the questions this time." He smiled and paced in front of Mark, his expression amused.

"No, sir." He hated all this small talk shit. His fear mixed with anger. What would they do if he said he did mind? Take him back to his cell? It was a sick game they played with him. "Just get it over with."

Bill did a double take, his mouth dropping open. "Excuse me?"

Mark straightened as much as he could and looked him in the eye. "I know what you're going to do. I dreamed it. So, let's just get it over with."

Eyes narrowed, Bill stepped right up to Mark and jabbed him in the chest with his finger. "Oh, you do, do you? Tell me about it."

Mark opened his mouth to recount his dream, but snapped it shut. If he told them, he might change things. Sure, maybe he wouldn't have the water poured in his face, but then what? This was his chance to prove what he said was true. "I can't. Not yet. I...I could write it down for you, and put it in an envelope. You could seal it, and when we're...done, you could read it." He swallowed and tried to control his trembling. If he survived, he would have his proof.

Bill looked at the other men on the team. One guy shrugged, tore a sheet of paper off his pad, and slid it across the table with a pen. Bill grabbed them. "Fine. Let's do that." Pointing towards the eye bolt on the floor, he barked an order to the guards, " Release that, but stand by."

Relief at the chance and dread at what was to come, warred within him as he was shoved onto a chair. Closing his eyes again, he pictured everything. When it was clear, he wrote it as a quickly as he could, trying not to leave anything out. He told of the plastic wrap, and how the water had been ice cold. He recounted all the questions asked of him, and even a snide comment made by one of the guards when he'd called Mark a drowned cat. Bill would say how Jim would be sorry he'd missed all the fun. His hand shook as he wrote that part.

Mark wrote of how the water had run out by the time the guard had counted to forty-four and Bill had sent someone for more. He came back with a full pitcher, and Mark recalled the next nineteen seconds. How Jim had burst through the door. He didn't remember any more of the dream, but hoped that would be sufficient. When he'd finished writing, he had filled the front and back of the yellow paper. An envelope was pushed across the table and Mark folded the sheet and tucked it in. His mouth was so dry, he had trouble forming enough saliva to wet the flap, but managed to seal it.

Bill made a show of taking a piece of duct tape and sticking the envelope to the wall where Mark would be able to see it as he underwent the interrogation.

The guards pulled him to his feet, and dragged him to the spot, stretching him out and strapping him to the board. The scene played out just as he saw it in his dream. Mark heard the rustle of the plastic, but before he could react, a guard ran the clear wrap over his eyes, tightened it around his head, brought it down over his mouth and continued winding until only his nose was uncovered. He gasped for air and the plastic tightened across his open mouth, forcing his lips against his teeth. Already feeling like he was suffocating, Mark tried to turn his head. The cuffs ground into the bones of his wrists and ankles. He struggled, unable to stop himself.

Mark gagged and gasped as the torment progressed. The counting by the guard filtered through his panic, the only thing he had to hold on to. When the count reached nineteen in the second round, the torment would end. One way or another.

His hearing faded and darkness crept into the edges of his vision. Jim leaned over him, his mouth moving, but Mark's world faded.

CHAPTER THIRTEEN

Mark's eyes rolled back. Jim tore at the plastic, his fingers slipping against the wet film. "Goddamn it. Someone help me before he dies." He hoped he wasn't too late. Damn traffic.

The guards stooped, one working on the wrap, while the other released the shackles. When they rolled Taylor onto his side, water poured from his nose. Jim pounded on the unconscious man's back and was rewarded with a weak cough, then a stronger one as more water drained.

Relief swept through Jim as he knelt on one knee. Taylor gagged and choked, then his eyes fluttered open. *Thank God.* Jim stood, fury rising in him, replacing the relief. Turning towards Bill, he ground out, "What the *hell* were you doing?"

Bill glared back. "I was interrogating the subject. What does it look like?"

Ignoring him for the moment, Jim addressed the guards and pointed to Taylor still lying dazed and gasping on the floor. "Take him to the infirmary and have him checked out."

Jim faced the interested expressions of the others in the room and strode to the table. How the hell could these guys just sit here and watch? None had bothered to help make sure Taylor didn't die. It took every shred of his self-control to speak in a calm voice, "If you would all excuse us.

I need to confer with Bill. I'll let each of you know what is going on as soon as possible."

Dr. Weiss, the medical expert on the team, looked like he was going to argue, but Jim gave him a hard look. "You have an objection, Doctor?" He, of all people, had the duty to make sure no lasting harm would be done. And yet, here he sat, looking befuddled.

The other man stood and shook his head as he gathered up his papers. "No, but I wanted to let you know about the unusual circumstances before the interrogation began."

Jim leaned on the table with both hands. "What kind of circumstances?"

"The subject insisted that he knew what was going to happen, and he asked to write it down and put it in a sealed envelope."

Dr. Weiss pointed to the corner where Mark was now standing on trembling legs. The guards shackled him, and Jim had to bite his tongue to keep from telling them not to do so. Protocol had to be followed. Mark had recovered enough to send a hate-filled glare in Jim's direction.

"The envelope hasn't been touched since Bill taped it there. I'm curious and I'm sure the team is as well." The other two members hesitated at the doorway.

At a tearing sound, Jim looked over his shoulder to see Bill yank an envelope off the wall. Jim straightened and held his hand out. "I'll take that."

Bill's mouth set in thin line, but he gave Jim the envelope. As the senior member, Jim had the authority. He knew it rankled Bill at times, but this was the first time he had seen outright anger. He decided to spare Bill any further embarrassment and nodded to Dr. Weiss. "Thank you for telling me about this. I'll let you know if it's pertinent to the investigation." He waved a dismissal to the others.

Jim would have liked to open it with Taylor present, but that would mean the guards would be privy to the contents as well only he had a feeling that this information should be kept secret. He nodded towards Mark. "I hope you'll feel better soon."

It was the closest he could come to an apology. The anger in Mark's eyes wavered, and then his shoulders slumped. The guards led him away.

"Well, aren't you going to open it?" Bill sprawled into a chair, pointing with his chin at the envelope in Jim's hands. "The guy was a real pistol tonight. Told me to just get it over with."

"Get what over with?"

"What we were going to do. Claimed he dreamed it last night." Bill clasped his hands behind his head and grinned.

The hairs on the back of Jim's neck rose and he paused as he tore the seal. "He said that?"

"Yeah, but he wanted to write it down instead of telling us. I decided to go along with it. Thought maybe he would write something useful while he was at it."

"Huh. Well, let's see." Jim unfolded the paper and smoothed it on top of the table. The handwriting scrawled across the page, but it was still clear enough to read without any problem. Taylor had outlined in stark detail exactly what was going to happen.

Jim read it and slid it over to Bill. "I wasn't here for most of this, so, I don't know if he's right or not. What do you think?"

Bill lowered his hands with a sigh and slouched forward to read the paper. Seconds later, his back straightened and his eyebrows rose. He flipped the paper, his eyes racing across the lines of print. When he finished, he looked up at

Jim. "Well, holy hell. What do you know? He has it verbatim, right down to a...remark I made."

Jim pulled out a chair and flopped onto it. "So, what do we do about it?"

"What do you mean?" Bill sounded puzzled. "It's interesting, but doesn't change anything."

Jim narrowed his eyes and leaned forward. "How can you say that? Either what he's been telling us all along is true, or someone on the team set this up."

Bill shrugged. "Who the hell would set this up?" He stood and pointed a finger at Jim. "Are you accusing me of arranging this...this scam?" Leaning one arm on the table, he swept the other in a vague motion towards Taylor's cell block. "Maybe the guy got lucky. He's had enough sessions in here that he could have guessed. But if this is his attempt to get released, it's not going to work."

Jim felt his jaw tighten and exerted every measure of his self-control to keep his anger in check. His instinct was to jump up and stand toe-to-toe with the guy. Instead, he tilted the chair back on two legs, put his feet on the table, and crossed his arms, giving Bill a hard stare until the other man sat down.

As if the outburst hadn't occurred, he said in a calm voice, "Of course I don't think you set it up, but there were others in the room. We'll need to keep alert for troublemakers." He let his feet drop to the floor and stood. "However, this fiasco notwithstanding, I do have doubts about Taylor's guilt. Unless you uncovered anything with this session today?"

Bill shook his head. "Nope, just more of the same denials."

"Either Taylor is the world's toughest guy or he's not connected to any terrorists." The implication that Taylor was innocent, and had been caught up in a post 9/11 witch hunt wasn't something that he wanted to think about. There were too many people involved. Something like that wouldn't happen. The designation of enemy combatant needed approval from the highest authorities. It wasn't Jim's job to question it.

"It doesn't matter anyway, we can't just let him go. Who knows, maybe the guy is tough. Maybe he's just stupid or a martyr." Bill stood and waved his hand. "Besides, there's still the confession by his friend and his trip to Afghanistan to consider."

"That's all bullshit, and you know it. His 'friend' named half of his address book. From what I read, that guy was a bit player. A wannabe terrorist. His confessions have yielded a big fat zero as far as actionable intelligence. In fact, the last memo stated that he's already been released back to his home country."

Bill shot a Jim a look of surprise. "Oh. I missed that one, I guess." He sank back onto his chair and drummed his fingers on the table.

Jim nodded. "I'll find it and forward it to you."

"But Taylor was still in Afghanistan..."

"So? Lots of journalists and photographers were in that country in the last several years. Should we go round them all up?" Why was he defending the guy? Jim shook off the thought. He wasn't defending, he was simply playing the devil's advocate.

Bill sighed, and rubbed circles on his temples. "What other evidence do we have? The calls? Is that it?"

"Exactly. The evidence we do have, the calls warning of the attacks." Jim began ticking off the list on his fingers. "His association with someone who has contacts within al-

Qaeda, and his trip to Afghanistan, hasn't been built upon since his detainment began. We're still at square one."

"You think he's innocent." It was a statement.

Jim flipped the envelope against one hand, tapping it as he paced in front of the table. Innocent? It was hard to contemplate. Difficult to accept. "I don't know, but I'm not comfortable with what we have so far. If we don't get more soon, we're going to have to make some serious decisions."

Shaking his head, Bill said, "Even if the guy is innocent, how can we let him go? You know he'd go running off and telling the press."

"That's a possibility, but not a reason to keep him prisoner. It shouldn't even be a factor in our decision. We're not some communist country who locks up dissidents. If he wants to speak, it's his right."

"Well...shit." Bill propped his elbows on the table, his hands on either side of his head. After a moment, he dropped his hands. "What about a non-disclosure contract?"

"You mean an agreement to keep quiet?" The idea put a sour taste in Jim's mouth.

"You have a better idea?" Bill spread his hands. "Look, Jim, I'm not so sure the guy is innocent, however, like you said, we haven't been able to get any hard evidence. I concede that. None of the teams have, so we're not alone."

Jim halted his pacing, tucked the envelope in his inside breast pocket, tugged on the lapels. "I think we dig in deeper. Try some new techniques. If those don't work, then, I don't think we have any choice but to recommend release."

* * *

Mark paced his cell. It had been weeks since the last interrogation and he hadn't heard anything about what he

147

had written. This whole time, from the beginning of this nightmare, despite the accusations and the interrogations, hope had burned in him. He'd tried to quash it—had tried to go numb, but it flickered anyway. Then the dreams came again, and as terrifying as they'd been, they gave him a reason to hope, a way to prove his innocence.

Now, even after his predictions came true, nothing had changed. He'd seen the envelope in Jim's hand before they took him to the infirmary, he was sure he remembered that. Had they thrown it away? Had he gone through hell for nothing?

Hope. He hated hope. It was insane to cling to it. He was insane. This whole goddamn *place* was insane.

He balled his fists, his body tensing as rage raced through every cell of his being. *The bastards!* The confines of the cell, with no way to vent the anger, served as a pressure cooker. He yanked the thin pad off his bed, slamming it against the wall. Why didn't they let him go?

The dark bubble over the camera up in the corner caught his eye. There they were. Watching him. They were *always* watching him. The lights shone all the damn time. Everything he did was caught on tape. He couldn't even take a piss without an audience. Shame combined with the anger, and Mark's gaze dropped to the half-eaten bowl of grits on his tray. Grabbing it, he whipped handfuls of the congealed substance at the bubble. Let them just try to see through that mess.

When the grits were gone, he gave a hard flick of his wrist, sending the bowl bouncing against the wall. His chest heaved while he watched it spin and wobble in a circle before coming to rest in the corner. The sticky grits plopped from the bubble onto the floor. Damn it. Even the grits wouldn't cooperate. Mark stared at the splotches of food on the floor and burst out laughing. What an idiot he was for thinking anything would make a difference. A stupid, naive idiot. They had probably snickered over the note in the envelope.

He staggered back, bumping into the wall, and slid down to a sitting position. Hysterical, mirthless laughter bubbled up in his throat, choking him before it dissolved into a sob. Pain squeezed his chest. Why had he allowed himself to feel anything? Hope hurt.

"*Shit!*" He crossed his arms over his knees and buried his face, wrapping his hands over the back of his head.

* * *

The mattress was gone, taken as punishment. Even his blanket was confiscated. The temperature in the cell dropped precipitously. It had to be deliberate.

To keep warm, he did jumping jacks, push-ups, and any other exercise that he could do in a nine by six cell. That worked, until he tired. His muscles quivered as he paced to and fro. Less than four steps from end to end, and he'd about face and repeat the march. For hours, he continued, his pace slowing until he was stumbling and lurching across the cell. They would turn the heat on soon. They wouldn't let him freeze to death.

He hadn't seen anyone in days. Maybe they had gone off and left him. But someone delivered the meals. They still came at regular intervals. Not the usual fare. Instead, he received cold meals ready-to-eat. He ate them, if only to keep from getting a feeding tube, but the cold sapped his energy, and he got up only to use the toilet or push the meals out. After awhile, he didn't need to get up as often. His fingers were clumsy and stiff, and the meals too hard to open. He gave up, and sent them back out untouched. Nobody seemed to care.

Mark curled on the metal shelf and shivered. His teeth chattered until he was sure a few had chipped. He clenched his jaw to stop the chattering. How many meals had come since the cold hit? Six? Eight? He lost count. He slept in short spurts, getting up to move around, but finally, he sank onto the floor, with a sigh. He had to rest.

Arms pulled into his shirt, he hunched over his drawn up knees. At least one more meal arrived, but he was so stiff, he couldn't get up to retrieve it. He moved onto his side, the cement no colder than the metal shelf. Why bother trying to move? His eyes grew heavy. How cold did someone have to get before they died? Would they let him get to that point?

After a bit, the cold didn't bother him so much. He must be getting used to it. Growing up in Wisconsin, and then living in Chicago, he was accustomed to cold weather.

Once, he'd gone hunting with his dad when he was a kid, and had broken through some ice, falling into a shallow pond. He recalled pushing against the ice, breaking it with his hands as he waded out, but remembered his father's warnings to keep moving until they got back to the campsite. There, he'd been stripped of his wet clothes, and wrapped in warm blankets. His dad wouldn't let him sleep until he had warmed up. The next day, he'd asked why, and was told if he'd fallen asleep when he was that cold, he might not have woken up.

Mark pushed an arm out of his sleeve and bent it under his head for a pillow. He closed his eyes. Falling asleep now might be the answer to his problems. Just shut his eyes and never open them again. He'd be done with interrogations, done with the shame and fear. He'd be free.

* * *

Jim sighed as he read through the memos from the head of security. Taylor had gone crazy with some food and as punishment, they had removed his mattress. It was also noted that he was no longer getting grits. One side of his mouth quirked in a smile. He couldn't blame Taylor. Even after living in the South for a number of years, he had never acquired a taste for the dish.

He glanced up as the subject of his thoughts was led into the room. Taylor kept his head down as he shuffled to stand beside the chair. There he waited, never raising his eyes.

Jim motioned to the guards. "He can sit." With that, the guard secured Taylor's shackles to the bolt in the floor.

Bill took the first turn. He circled to the front of the table. "Hello, Mark. How are you feeling today?"

"Good, sir." His head rose, but he simply stared at a spot ahead of him on the floor.

"Glad to hear it. You had a rough time of it lately." Bill paused and sent Jim a glance. They'd discussed their strategy. Bill would sympathize with Mark's plight and show concern about all the guy had been through, the water-boarding, extreme isolation, and temperature control. They hoped sympathy would cause him to break down.

Taylor didn't respond.

Bill leaned into Taylor's line of sight, forcing the man to see him. "You're not going to answer me?" His tone was light, as though joking.

"You didn't ask a question, sir." Taylor sounded as flat as his expression. There was nothing there.

Bill chuckled. "You're right. I didn't." He half sat on the table, his pose relaxed. Jim marveled at the tone of concern Bill managed with his next question. "How are you holding up, Mark?"

Taylor remained silent for so long that Jim was sure he wouldn't reply, but finally, he shrugged. "Okay. I guess. Sir."

"That's good. Anything I can do for you? Do you need anything? Cards? Books?" Taylor's request for books had been sent through the channels several times, but still hadn't been cleared.

"No, sir."

Bill spread his hands, and shrugged at Jim with a 'what do I do now' look.

Jim decided to take his turn early. He stood, letting his chair scrape the floor with a harsh screech. Taylor didn't flinch. It was time to get tough. Obviously, being nice was getting them nowhere. He reached into a folder and removed a pile of photos. Moving around the front of the table, he shoved a picture under Taylor's nose.

"Recognize these?"

Taylor's head moved a fraction as Jim flipped through the photos, allowing Taylor to see all of them. "Yes, sir."

So that's how it was going to be. Every response would have to be pulled out of the guy. "Care to enlighten us?" Jim was well aware of what the photos were, but wanted to hear Taylor confirm it.

Taylor replied in a monotone, "They're photos I developed from my camera on September 10th, 2001."

Jim paced across Taylor's line of vision, but if the man noticed, he gave no indication. His gaze still appeared to be fixed at a spot on the floor.

"Do you know where we found these?" Not letting him reply, knowing it would be either a yes or a no, Jim moved to the point. "These were in a box in your home." Jim circled around the table to retrieve a stack of photos out of a file. Returning to the front of the table, he thumbed through the stack. "They were mixed in with these other pictures."

He leaned against the table and crossed his ankles. With a shake of his head, he studied the photos. "You know, Taylor, for a guy who's supposed to be a professional photographer, these photos are crap."

He held one up, biting back his annoyance when Taylor only flicked a glance at them. "Look at this. Why did you take a picture of a car parked on the side of the street? Or one of man eating a hamburger?" Jim sorted through the pictures. "Or how about this one. It's my favorite. It's the front door of an apartment."

He remained silent, so Jim stepped closer and kicked the leg of the guy's chair.

Taylor started, his eyes widening briefly. Jim bent, bringing his face within inches of the other man's. "Look at me when I'm speaking to you."

After the initial surprise, Taylor sighed and lifted his gaze. It rested in the vicinity of Jim's face, but didn't quite meet his eyes. "Yes, sir."

There was no spark. Just weariness and resignation.

"Well, now that you're awake, shall we get on with this?"

"Yes, sir."

"Explain why you kept all these photos. They weren't in your studio, they were in a box under your bed." Jim found the one of a baby wrapped in a towel. "Except for this one. This one was found on your person at the time of your arrest. Care to explain it? Is this a relative?"

"No, sir. Not a relative. Just a baby."

"Why does a single guy keep pictures of an unrelated baby in his pocket?"

The insinuation hadn't been lost on Taylor and for one brief second, his eyes flashed anger. "That's the last picture I changed." He drew in a deep breath, as though the effort to speak taxed him. "That's the end result." His brow furrowed in confusion and he seemed to lose his train of thought. After a pause, he clarified, "She drowned in the first picture."

The statement caught Jim by surprise. Taylor sounded matter of fact.

"So, after you...saved her, you took her picture as a memento?" It was hard to maintain the insinuation in his voice.

"No. I puked. Then I was...arrested." His head lolled back for a moment, as if he didn't have the energy to hold it up. After a pause, he straightened, but it seemed to require incredible effort. "The photos change. If I succeed."

"Okay. I think I get it. You go on your little missions and keep the happy pictures as mementos. So, why did you keep the pictures of the attacks?"

He focused on Jim, his eyes dull and filled with defeat. "As a reminder that I can't fix everything." Taylor swallowed, his throat bobbing as his gaze slid away.

CHAPTER FOURTEEN

Jim watched as the guards led Taylor away. The man shuffled out in the same manner he'd arrived, his shoulders hunched and head bowed.

Bill remained at the table with him while the rest of the team left. "That was a bust."

"Yes, I guess so...or if we look at it another way, it could be seen as the subject simply has no information." Jim gathered up the photos and returned them to the files.

"It could be seen that way." Bill folded his hands on the table and turned his head, his expression serious. "Is that how you're seeing the situation?"

Jim lifted the folders and tapped them against the tabletop to align the contents. "I think I do." The moment he said it aloud, a weight seemed to lift from his shoulders.

"So, at the next meeting with the council, you'll state that you think Taylor is innocent?"

"I'll state the truth, that after close to a year of intense questioning, no team has gathered any actionable intelligence. In light of that, and my opinion that Taylor is no threat to this country, that I recommend his release as soon as it can be arranged."

Bill sighed. "I can't argue with that. I guess I'll go along with you." He ran a hand over his head and rubbed the back of his neck. "You realize that the next meeting isn't scheduled until after the holidays, don't you?"

"Yes. I'll send some memos urging an emergency meeting." It felt wrong that Taylor would remain in custody

155

due to something as simple as the schedule of a meeting. "I'm not sure it'll make a difference though. They might not even take our recommendations." He stood and pushed in his chair.

"Then why did they have us do the questioning? It wouldn't look good to ignore us. You think the other agencies will go along with it? What about law enforcement?" Bill rose and walked alongside Jim as they exited the room.

"I believe they will. If they have info that they're withholding, they'll have to show it, or give a damn good reason to keep Taylor in custody." Jim strode down the hall, hoping like hell he wouldn't ever have to return to that room.

They reached Bill's office first, and Jim leaned against the door frame after Bill entered. "We have to make this happen ASAP, Bill." Jim tapped the files against his thigh. "I don't know how long Taylor will hang on. He's spiraling down."

Bill plopped onto his chair. "Yeah, I noticed." He leaned back. "In the meantime, we can try and lighten things up a little."

"Will the protocol allow that? We're supposed to follow the same guidelines as the other place."

"Screw the protocol." Bill grimaced.

Jim smiled. "See what you can do in that regard. I'll get on the horn and start making calls, see if I can expedite the matter."

* * *

In the weeks since he and Bill had made their suggestion for an emergency meeting, nothing had happened. Someone always had a reason they couldn't attend. The fact that a man languished behind bars didn't seem to add any urgency in the other council members' minds.

Bill's attempts to lighten things had only gone as far as halting further interrogations. The security at the prison had enforced their own measures after Taylor's outburst of throwing food around his cell. Now, he was confined to his cell at all times, except for showers.

Jim opened Taylor's file to add another email to the list he'd begun after the decision to make their recommendation to free Taylor. He hadn't realized what a tricky and protracted task it would be to convince the people with authority that Taylor was not a security threat to the United States. If nothing else, Taylor should get an official hearing. The fact that one hadn't taken place yet rankled Jim. It wasn't the American way.

Two hours later, he printed out his advisement that in light of no new information, and the questionable sources for the Afghanistan claim, it was his opinion there was no merit for keeping Taylor in detention. Bill had completed his own recommendations that he held doubt about the man's guilt.

He stretched, grimacing at a twinge of stiffness in his back. He'd been sitting so long, his back creaked when he stood and crossed to the window. Would the powers that be follow their recommendations? If they did, how long would it take? The wheels of government spun at a snail's pace, but maybe since there had never been formal charges, it wouldn't take much longer to straighten the mess out and free Taylor.

* * *

Mark stopped mid push-up when the slot on his door opened. It was too soon for the next meal. The command to present his hands and feet for shackles came over the speaker.

Since his outburst a few months ago, his outdoor excursions had been curtailed. Since he had showered yesterday, that could mean only one thing. Interrogation.

He pushed back to a kneeling position, unable to force himself to stand right away. Since the last interrogation, his thoughts had touched on finding a way to end it all. In his whole life, he had never felt that way, but there was no end in sight here. He didn't want to die, but he didn't want to live like this.

So far, whenever the despair hit and his mind flashed to suicide, he had been able to shove the thought out of his head. If he underwent another brutal questioning, he wasn't sure he would be strong enough to quell those demons.

The command came over the speaker a second time and Mark stood, swiping his head on his shoulder as sweat dripped. His feet felt encased in cement as he approached the door.

He tried not to react when in addition to the usual shackles, they used the blackout goggles and the earphones. Did that mean he was going somewhere besides the interrogation room? Swallowing hard, he couldn't help balking at the application of the goggles.

Interrogation was bad, but at least he knew what to expect. What if they had something worse in store? Mark couldn't imagine anything worse, but he was sure that they could.

Lost in a vacuum of sensory deprivation, Mark stumbled along, sitting when pushed down, standing when pulled up and walking when tugged forward. He felt vibrations under his feet, and knew he was in a vehicle, but time blurred and he had no way to judge the distance he'd been driven.

After leaving the car, he was walked another distance before they stopped him and hands worked at the goggles and earphones, removing them. Mark blinked in the bright lights and squinted at his surroundings. A locker room? What the hell was he doing here? The guards removed his shackles and instructed him to strip. Mark hesitated as fear boiled within him. An image of the Nazi death camps and the gas chambers shot through his mind and he shook it off. That was crazy. He removed his clothes, hoping that his shaking wasn't apparent. One guard pointed behind Mark. "Okay, let's go. There's a shower back there. Supposed to be everything you need to get cleaned up."

A shower? They did all this for him to take a shower? Confused, Mark followed the guard, alert for any tricks. Not that he could do anything to protect himself even if there were.

To his amazement, there was a shower stall. Several in fact, but the one they directed him to had a bottle of shampoo and a bar of soap—brand new—sitting on a metal shelf. He needed no further prodding.

The soap smelled clean and fresh, not the antiseptic smelling stuff he normally had to use. He raised the bar to his nose, closing his eyes as he breathed deeply. Images of sand and surf and lazy summer days lying on the beach swirled through his mind. The scent filled the stall as the hot water beat on his back. He wanted to stay in that stall and never come out. In here, he could push aside the worry of what was coming next. He could stay in the present. Forever.

When he finished, he was given a razor and shaving cream, and the guards didn't seem to be in a hurry to get the blade back. They led him to a locker that held a clean set of clothes, and told him to get dressed. Mark clasped the white button-down shirt, looking from it to a pair of dark dress pants. Where was the orange prison suit? He squashed his fears and decided to just enjoy each little luxury instead of ruining it with worry. If they were getting ready to take him to the gas chamber, at least he would be wearing real clothes and he'd be clean.

Sitting on the bench, he pulled on black socks and shoes. The shoes were the biggest surprise. He hadn't worn any for so long, and he wiggled his toes as he admired the shiny leather. They felt good. Real good. Standing, he looked down at himself and took a deep shaky breath. He felt human for the first time in over a year.

* * *

The guards put the shackles back on, and Mark tried not to let that bother him, especially since they didn't reapply the goggles. They led him down a long hallway that looked like it could be a courthouse. He squared his shoulders. Maybe he would finally get to plead his case before a judge.

He was led to a small room, over to a table and instructed to sit. Beside him was an empty chair. The guards remained standing behind him. Across from the table where Mark sat, was a longer table. An American flag and a state flag in tall stands, flanked it. Four chairs faced him.

Across a narrow aisle was a table identical to his own, complete with two chairs. Mark glanced at the chair next to him, wondering who it was for.

160

The only sound in the room was an occasional creak of Mark's chains and one of the guards coughed a few times. After waiting for several minutes, four military officers entered the room and strode past Mark without a glance in his direction. While watching the officers, Mark almost missed the two men in suits who walked down the aisle and sat at the other small table. Mark tried to get a closer look at them, but the one nearest to him had his back turned, blocking the other man from view.

A rustle at his elbow distracted him. An older man with gray hair slicked over a bald spot slid into the chair next to him. The man leaned over and whispered, "I'm David Cox, your attorney." and offered his hand.

Seeing the manacles when Mark made no move to return the handshake, Cox fumbled with the catches on his briefcase. "My attorney?" Mark wasn't aware he'd had one. The guy was sweating bullets and looked as if he had run a marathon before arriving.

"I've been working on your behalf for months. I even took your case before the U.S. District court." He pulled a handkerchief out of his pocket and mopped his brow. "The government is getting pressured about all this enemy combatant status. Technically, we won our case, but—" Cox broke off and glanced at the guards behind Mark, his expression wary. "I'm sure you have a lot of questions, but I feel we should continue this conversation after the hearing."

Mark nodded but couldn't help doubting that he would actually get the chance to discuss it.

Cox withdrew a stack of papers from his briefcase and began sorting through them. "I wasn't notified of this hearing until about an hour ago and I'm not even sure what it's about. I'll try for a continuance if I don't feel prepared to answer on your behalf."

He swallowed hard. So, he hadn't been forgotten. "Thanks." A voice cut through the room. A voice he recognized and one that raised the hairs on the back of his neck. It came from one of the men at the other table. Jim and Bill...shit. Mark must have made a sound because Jim broke off his conversation, his eyes meeting Mark's. He nodded, his face impassive.

Mark faced forward with his hands in a white-knuckled clasp on the table. The men in the room busied themselves with settling in. Papers rustled, briefcases clicked, and muted conversations drifted in the heavy silence. A woman entered with a pitcher of water, Mark froze, until she began pouring it into glasses in front of each officer. Everyone had their glass filled. Mark received one too, but he could only look at it. At least he hadn't been left out. That was something.

His knee began to jerk, the rattling clink of the leg chains loud in the small room. Cox gave him a warning look as the court was called to order.

At the long table—a man who looked vaguely familiar to Mark—addressed Jim. "Officer Sheridan, I received your report and we have discussed it at length. Thank you for clarifying some issues we had. We have come to a decision." He shifted his focus to Mark. "Mr. Taylor, would you please rise?"

He stole a look at Jim, but the man faced the front. Was he being sentenced now? How could he be sentenced when he hadn't been tried? Hell, he wasn't even sure of the charges. His legs felt like jelly. Cox prodded him with an elbow, followed by a grim, "Stand." Mark wanted to shout at him that he was trying, but instead, he shoved out of the chair and stood. He took a deep breath and raised his chin.

"Mark Taylor, this council has found insufficient evidence that you had any involvement in the events of September 11, 2001. You are to be released from custody immediately." The man gathered his papers and he and the rest of the tribunal rose, and without so much as a nod in Mark's direction, left the room.

His legs wobbled, and he sat hard. That was it? He was free? Mark rested his elbows on the table, propping his head in his hands as the realization sunk in. The nightmare was over. He was going home. Emotion welled up and he lowered his head onto his arms, his body shaking as he tried to suppress a sob. His head felt stuffed with cotton, and it took a moment before he heard his lawyer speaking to him. Mark swiped his eyes on his shoulder before he turned his head. "Huh?"

"I said, 'congratulations. You're a free man." He clapped Mark on the back.

Mark shook his head. "It's...it's kind of surreal. Is it true? I'm free? They won't take me back there?" Please, God, let it be real.

David Cox smiled, his eyes crinkling in the corners. "Yes, it's true."

Blinking, he tried to return the smile, but he noticed Jim stuff a large white envelope in his briefcase. What if it was a trick? After over a year in custody, now he was just free to walk out? Just like that? It didn't make sense, and he didn't trust them.

One of the guards stepped forward. "Stand please."

Mark did as ordered, and when the guard removed the shackles, his whole body felt light, as though he might float to the ceiling. He rubbed his wrists and waited, hardly daring to breathe. It could be a trick, give him a taste of freedom in hopes that he'd spill his guts to stay free.

Jim approached the table and handed a stack of papers to Cox. "These need to be signed by your client."

He made no attempt to acknowledge his former prisoner. The entire proceeding, with two exceptions, had been handled as if Mark hadn't even been in the room.

"Okay. Give me a couple of minutes to go over these, please." Cox accepted the packet and turned his attention to Mark. "Well, this was an unexpected turn of events. I have to tell you, I had my doubts that you would be released. The government has been hell-bent on keeping enemy combatants locked up without even a trial."

He flipped through the papers. "These look like standard documents. There's one about your personal and business bank accounts. It looks like it might take awhile to unfreeze them." Cox frowned. "Wait a minute..." He glared up at Jim. "What's this? You want him to sign a statement waiving his right to pursue a lawsuit against the government?"

A muscle near Jim's jaw tightened for a second, his mouth set in a hard line as he glanced over to Bill, who nodded in response to some unspoken question. "Apparently so." His voice was calm.

Cox shook his head in disgust. "Could you give me a moment to confer with my client?" It was not a request.

"Certainly." Jim moved over near Bill, but continued to observe.

"Think it over, Mark. They've taken away more than a year of your life, and I don't even know what else might have happened in there."

Jim's face remained impassive as he waited, but his hand tighten on the handle of his briefcase. If Mark signed, it meant never getting a chance to get justice for what they did to him. Would they send him back to prison if he refused?

Could they do that? He glanced over his shoulder. The guards were gone, but they could be lurking out in the hall. It wasn't much of a choice. In fact, it was no choice at all. His heart hammered and he looked from Jim back to Cox. He couldn't take a chance when freedom was so close.

"Give me a pen."

When he finished, he set the pen down and ran a hand through his hair. It was official. Mark let out a shaky breath.

Jim set his briefcase on the table and pulled out a lumpy envelope and extended it towards Mark. "Here."

Mark flinched, but didn't take the package. He wanted to ask what was in it, but his throat spasmed as the possibility that he might truly be free began to sink in.

"Go ahead. It's just your wallet and personal effects you had when you were taken into custody."

Mark's hands shook as he tore the envelope open and flipped it over. His wallet, keys and even some loose change tumbled onto the table, along with a white letter-sized envelope. Thumbing through his wallet, he was surprised to see that there was about eighty dollars in it. He pocketed the billfold, keys and change. He stared at the envelope for a moment before pushing it back towards Jim. "I don't think this is mine...sir." What if they had planted some evidence in there? As soon as he touched it, they would say that he claimed it, and must be guilty.

Shoving it back, Jim snapped, "Take it. You're going to need it."

"Yes, sir." Swallowing hard, Mark picked it up.

"I'll see what it is." Cox reached over and took it from him and opened it. "There's a plane ticket to Chicago." He squinted at the ticket. "The flight leaves in just a few hours." He pulled out a stack of bills. "And some cash. Eight hundred dollars."

Mark shot a look at Cox. "That's not mine." He rose, backing away with his hands raised, palms outward.

"Listen, it's just money for food and lodging for a few days until you get settled." Jim clicked his briefcase closed.

Cox snorted. "Oh, I'm sure that'll cover all his expenses. You know he's going to need more than that."

Jim shrugged. "It's better than nothing."

Stepping forward, Mark took the envelope. Despite the limited amount, he realized he would need it. "Thank you." The words lodged in his throat.

Nodding, Jim drummed his fingers on top of his briefcase and looked at Mark as if he had something he wanted to say, but instead, he swung the briefcase off the table and put his hand out. "You're welcome."

Confused, Mark looked at the hand, then up at Jim. He couldn't do it. Even if they put him back in prison. "I...ah—"

"Never mind." Jim dropped his hand and strode to the back of the room, disappearing out the door.

In the sudden silence, Mark tried to focus, but his mind was whirling, and he remembered Cox had said something about his assets. "My bank accounts?"

"Yes, they were immediately frozen when you were designated an enemy combatant. I wish I could tell you when it'll be all cleared up, but I can't say for sure."

The eight hundred dollars didn't seem so generous now. What would he do until his accounts were available? Mark pushed it from his mind. He could deal with that back in Chicago. Right now, he just needed to get out of here.

CHAPTER FIFTEEN

At the airport an hour later, Mark approached the security checkpoint. People were taking off their shoes, and some were pulled out of line for no reason that Mark could tell. His hands began to sweat, and he swiped them on his thighs. He didn't want to take his shoes off. Glancing at the man behind him, he started to ask what was going on, but that man had a cell phone to his ear, and just glared at him.

Mark's mouth went dry as his turn approached, then a security guard tapped him on the shoulder. "Step to the side please."

He hesitated. Freedom was so close. "Is...is something wrong?"

"No, sir. I just need to ask you a few questions."

The phrase sent a chill through him. Jim and Bill said they were just going to ask a few questions. It was stupid to be worried. He had nothing to hide and others had been questioned. "Okay."

It took only a few moments even though it felt like much longer, but in the end, they let him pass through. He tugged his shirt away from his body, feeling like he had just run a few sprints. With no bags, check in went quickly. Mark sank onto a chair and ran a hand through his hair. He tried to relax as he waited for the flight to be called, but he couldn't keep still. His leg bounced and when he noticed, he stopped, but then began drumming his fingers on the arm-rests.

A harried looking woman approached. With one hand, she dragged a small suitcase on wheels, and a huge purse hung off her shoulder. Her other hand clutched the hand of a little girl.. The child poked a finger in her mouth and stared at him with wide brown eyes. "Sit in the chair, Olivia." The child didn't budge, just kept her gaze on him. Mark squirmed.

"It's okay, honey." She lifted the girl and set her in the chair. Mark gave her an encouraging smile. He'd always been good with the children that came to have their portraits taken. The girl scooted as far from Mark as she could. The woman stood beside the chair and looked at her watch before tugging on the straps of her purse. It looked heavy.

He saw that all the other chairs were taken. The woman should sit beside her child. He stood, waving towards the chair. "Here, you can have my seat, ma'am." Mark shoved his hands in his pockets as he stepped away. His heart raced, and he tried to shake off his nerves. It was just a mom and her kid. Nothing scary about that. Except that he had only spoken to a handful of people in the last year, and most of them had been interrogating him.

"Oh no, that's all right. I don't mind standing." She plunged her hand into the depths of her purse, but one strap came off her arm, upending the bag. The contents tumbled out onto the floor. "Shoot!" Mark gaped at the pile of miscellaneous items. He was sure that MacGyver could build a whole car with the contents of that purse. Bending to pick up the items, the flustered woman knocked the handle of her suitcase, and it tipped, resulting in more angry words from the mother. The little girl began to cry. "Olivia, hon, it's fine. Don't cry." Her voice shook.

Mark bent, retrieving a lipstick, a medication bottle, and some change that had rolled under the chair. He then righted the suitcase. "Here." He handed over the items. "Please. Take my seat. It's okay."

"Oh, bless you." The woman gave in and dropped onto the chair. "You have no idea what a bad day this has been." She fanned her face and chuckled. "No, make that a bad week. Our flights have been canceled and delayed due to bad weather."

Mark nodded. "I'm sorry to hear that. I've had some rough days recently. It's no fun. I hope things go better for you." His stomach rumbled and he wished he would have thought to buy some food before checking in. There was no time now. Oh, well. He would live.

The woman grinned at him. "You hungry?"

He cleared his throat, embarrassed that she'd heard. "Uh, just a little."

Reaching into another pocket of the purse, she pulled out a chocolate bar. "Here. I know it's not much, but take it."

Mark hesitated, and she leaned forward, pressing it into his hand. "I'm not supposed to eat the stuff and I have another for Olivia."

"Thank you. I appreciate this." He brought the bar up to his nose, even through the wrapper, he could smell the aroma. Heaven.

The woman raised an eyebrow and Mark couldn't help letting a small smile quirk his mouth. "It's the first one I've had in a really long time."

She waved to him, then sighed when the flight was called. "Have a good day."

The plane circled O'Hare for thirty minutes in a holding pattern due to rain and sleet. Traffic on the highways below crawled along, the headlights snaking around the airport and branching in towards the city. Looking south, he saw the Sears Tower, its lights hazy, but reaching high

169

into the twilight sky. His throat tightened. It wasn't the most beautiful skyscraper in the city, the Hancock was more elegant, but the Sears Tower represented Chicago. It jutted up out of the prairie, bold and broad, soaring head and shoulders above the surrounding buildings. Mark craned his head as the plane banked and he lost sight of the building. How could anyone think to destroy something like that? He sat back with a sigh. How could anyone think that he'd wanted to destroy it?

Mark stood on the moving sidewalk inside the terminal. Normally, he disdained them, preferring to walk, but he was drained. As the belt carried him through the terminal, it suddenly occurred to him that nobody knew he was coming home. In Charleston, he hadn't had time to call his parents, and they lived four hours north of Chicago, just outside of Madison. In this weather, no way would they be able to come down to see him.

He stepped out of the airport, the blast of cold damp air cutting right through the thin shirt he wore. Nobody had thought to provide a coat for him. In the south, it was still warm, but in Chicago, winter was just beginning to flex her muscles.

The cab should be warm enough and when he got home, he could dig out his winter gear. After asking for an address, the cabbie glanced at him in the rear-view mirror. "Dude? You crazy? Where's your coat?"

Mark shrugged. "I wasn't thinking when I got on the plane. Forgot it." He tried to suppress a shiver, but the chill swept his body.

The man shook his head, but he reached down and turned the heat on high.

"Thanks." Mark hunched into the seat, and soon, the warmth of the cab soaked into him. They got caught in the same traffic that had been visible from the plane, and it wasn't long before he began blinking, each time, his eyes staying shut longer. He hoped the cabbie was honest, because he was beat. He'd tried to doze on the flight, but was so keyed up, he couldn't relax.

"Here you go."

Mark started and sat forward so fast, he bumped his head on the roof of the car. "What?" He rubbed his head and looked out the window. They were in front of his building. He was home.

The cab pulled away, and Mark hurried up the steps to the front door, keys in hand. It was so familiar. Huddled against the cold, he fumbled for the key on his chain, and tried to slip it into the lock, but it wouldn't fit. That was strange. Was it the wrong key? The one for the storage closet in the basement looked a lot like the door key. He tried the other one. Neither opened the door.

He sat on the brick ledge bordering the entryway. Once a unit had been burglarized and the front lock had been changed. Mark ran his finger down the list of names beside the buzzers. His neighbor would buzz him in if he was home. There were some new names on the list and it took him a moment to realize that one of them was in his apartment. He wiped a drop of water off the name plate. It had to be wrong. That was his apartment. He scanned the other names, found one he recognized, and buzzed it. Nothing. He tried again. And again.

Shaking from cold and rage, he slammed the heel of his hand against the panel, hitting several buttons at one time. A voice came over the speaker. "Hello?"

Mark leaned in. "Hey! I'm trying to get into my apartment, but my key's not working."

"What apartment?"

"303. My name's Mark Taylor."

The speaker hissed with static, and he pushed the button again.

"Get lost before I call the cops!"

Mark staggered backwards, the hatred in the voice hitting him like a blow. He managed the first couple of steps, but missed the next. Flailing, he tumbled onto the sidewalk into a pile of dirty slush. The sudden stop jolted up his spine, but he hardly felt it. The slush soaked into his pants, and his hands stung from the pavement and the cold. He winced as he stood and looked down at his knee. The material was torn and his shirt was dotted with black greasy stains. He tried to swipe some of the dirt off, but it just smeared so he gave up. Wrapping his arms around him, he shivered.

Right upstairs, someone was sitting in his loft. His shoulders sagged, and he swore as a shudder swept him. Bitter disappointment rose in his throat. He'd come home, only it wasn't his home anymore. Why hadn't he thought ahead?

Who could be living in his loft? What about his furniture and clothes? Were they in storage? Craning his head, he found his window and sure enough, light shone in it. Damn it! Mark turned, hoping he'd see his Jeep where he usually parked it on the street. It was gone. What had he expected? That everything would be just as it had been when he'd left?

The rain turned to sleet as he trudged along the street, flinching as cars whizzed past, splashing slush on him. Both hands were firmly tucked under the opposite arm, and he shivered non-stop. What should he do? He could get another cab and go to a hotel for the night, but then what? His money wouldn't last a week if he did that. Even a cheap hotel would put a serious dent in his finances. There was a diner down on the corner. He used to eat at least three meals a week there. Seeking warmth, food, and a place to gather his thoughts, he entered and took a seat at a booth. His teeth chattered so hard that when the waitress came, he couldn't speak.

The young woman looked him up and down as she narrowed her eyes. "Hey, buddy, this isn't a shelter. If you need one, you gotta go down to St. Paul's around the corner." She pointed with her pen over her shoulder.

Mark blinked. She looked vaguely familiar. "No. I, uh, I came for dinner...but, I fell." He took the napkin and tried to blot the front of his shirt. He couldn't look at her.

"You got money to pay for your food? I need to see it before I can take your order."

If he hadn't been so cold, he was sure that his face would have been burning. Pulling out his wallet, he withdrew a twenty and held it up.

Her face broke into a smile. "Oh, okay. My name's Brittany, and I'll be your waitress. Sorry, about, you know..." She flicked her wrist. "It's just we get so many that come in here, especially on days like this." Launching into the special for the evening, she stopped and cocked her head. "I've seen you before."

Mark nodded, not returning the smile. "It's been awhile since I've been here." His body shuddered, and he rubbed water off his face as it ran from his hair into his eyes. "I used to live down the street."

"Ah, so you're back to visit the old neighborhood." Brittany smiled. "Did you move close by?" She jabbed her pen at him and said, "I sure hope so, because you're going to freeze your tush off on the way home."

Like a Mack truck, it hit Mark. He was homeless. His stomach twisted and the ache swelled, filling him. For a long moment, he couldn't answer but finally managed to mumble, "No. It's not that close. I'm looking for a new place."

Brittany sighed. "You don't have anywhere to go, do you?" She slipped her order pad into her apron pocket. "Look, St. Paul's has a soup kitchen tonight. It's not far, and you can sleep there."

Mark sat straight. "I have money." He lifted his chin.

"I know, but, I hope you don't mind me being nosy, but I bet you don't have much, do ya?"

He tried to hold her gaze but then turned away, shrugging. "I have enough for a meal."

"Yes, but St. Paul's has a good one, and you could save your money. I know they call it a soup kitchen, but it's really more than soup. It's a regular meal." Her voice had become soft and encouraging. "I mean, if you want, you can eat here. God knows, my boss would shoot me if he knew I was sending a paying customer away, but I'd feel guilty taking your money. Do me a favor, and go to the shelter tonight."

Exhausted in body and spirit, he gave in. He just didn't have the energy to fight. Mark slid out of the booth, stood and nodded at Brittany. Without a word, he exited.

He knew where St. Paul's was and Brittany's 'just around the corner' was in reality, a good half-mile away. The few minutes of respite in the diner made it feel even colder outside, and it took him almost twenty minutes to walk to the church.

* * *

"Good lord! You're half frozen." The woman, stout and with tight gray curls, shook her head then motioned for Mark to follow as she headed across the lobby of the church to a door labeled 'Basement'. "I just don't think I'll ever understand what you people are thinking, running around in this weather improperly dressed." She opened the door, then looked back to see that he was still behind her.

He should have just bought his dinner at the diner. Saving a few bucks wasn't worth this. If he hadn't been so cold and miserable, he would have marched right back out, but his shivering had grown fierce and constant. His jaw ached from clenching his teeth.

"John, grab a blanket for this guy, would you?" the woman asked a young man sweeping the floor as they entered.

"Sure." The kid leaned the broom against a table and jogged to the far side of the room where Mark saw stacks of sheets and blankets on a table. Between Mark's spot and that table were approximately three dozen cots. "Here you go, Mister."

He took it. "Thanks." At least the kid didn't have that tone in his voice. Mark tossed the blanket over his shoulders and pulled it tight, clutching both ends in his hands.

While he ate some kind of baked pasta casserole and bread, his shivering gradually subsided. Soon, he became so drowsy that even as he swallowed the last bite, he nodded off for a second. Blinking rapidly, he shook his head to clear it, unable to stifle a yawn. His feet felt like they weighed a hundred pounds each as he crossed to throw his paper plate and cup in the garbage. All he wanted was sleep, and at the moment, he wasn't picky about where that sleep would take place.

Some other men had lined up for linens, so Mark joined them. Someone complained when he saw that Mark received another blanket, but the stout lady shut him down with a look. "The rules are out by sun-up, which at this time of year, is around seven. Bathrooms are that way." She pointed down the hall, then took in Mark's ragged appearance, her mouth pursed. "Do you need some personal items? Like a toothbrush, deodorant, that kind of thing? We have some personal care packages stashed away. Would you like one?"

"Yes, ma'am." He hadn't thought about those things. "I'd appreciate that."

"Well, at least you're polite. I'll be back in just a minute. You can make up your cot while you're waiting."

Mark pulled off his shoes and socks. His feet were pale and wrinkled from being wet, and he hoped his socks and shoes would dry during the night. He stretched out on the cot, intending to only lie down until the lady returned with the care package, but the next thing he knew, it was morning. It was time to rise and shine.

He found the care package stashed behind his shoes and cleaned up in the bathroom. After a cold breakfast, Mark headed out. The shelter gave each person a bag lunch to take with them, but he munched on the apple as soon as he reached the street. He couldn't recall the last time he had eaten one and savored the tart sweetness as it burst over his tongue.

He walked his old neighborhood, recalling names of people who lived in adjacent buildings. Did Mrs. Scott still live in the old house on the corner? The older woman walked everywhere with her cute pug, Sparky, at her side. The sleet stopped and the sun shone in a deep blue sky despite the frigid temperatures. A blast of cold air tore at him and he huddled into the old navy pea coat he had found under his cot. The stout little lady must have put it there for him while he was sleeping. The wool had a dank musty odor, but kept him warm.

First thing he needed to do was call his parents. He headed for a mini-mart that he remembered had a phone. After buying some water, gum and a bag of peanuts, Mark asked for change. Outside, he lifted the receiver, but hesitated—what if they thought he was guilty of the things he was accused of? He didn't think they would believe it, but he had to see their faces. He had to know for sure. Reluctantly, he set the receiver back on the hook.

He rode the EL out to the Greyhound station and bought a ticket to Madison. Getting from the bus station in Madison to the little town where his parents lived ten miles outside of the Wisconsin state capital would be a challenge, but if it came down to it, he could always walk.

Mark boarded the bus and opened the bag lunch. The fast food restaurants he'd seen outside the bus terminal tempted him with the tantalizing aroma of French fries and hamburgers, but he stiffened his resolve and bypassed them. Every penny counted and he had the bag lunch. As it was, the bus ticket had set him back almost forty dollars.

The turkey sandwich was dry, but not bad, and he washed it down with a gulp of water. A granola bar rounded out the meager meal. Taking another sip of the water, he reasoned that he'd survive the three hours to Madison easily.

The bus made a few stops on the way towards the Wisconsin border. At one, a young guy took the seat beside Mark. The buzz cut and his politeness as he asked Mark if the seat was taken, had Mark guessing he was a new basic training grad even before the guy mentioned it. He told Mark he was on his way home on his first leave before starting A school at Great Lakes Naval Base.

Mark smiled and nodded, hoping the kid wouldn't talk the whole way, but he didn't have to worry; the second the bus began moving, the sailor fell asleep.

In a way, Mark envied the guy. Fatigue burned his eyes, but, there was too much on his mind, too many things had happened in too short a time, for him to relax. The feeling haunted him that if he closed his eyes, he'd wake up back in the cell.

Resting his head against the window, he watched the flat Illinois farmland slide by. Ragged rows of corn stretched on either side of the highway, the shriveled tan leaves flapping in the wind.

Dairy farms, dotted with cows huddled in the corner of the pastures, grass worn down to bare patches from last summer's grazing, alternated with the jarring rawness of new housing developments. It was as if a stray wind had dumped the seeds for subdivisions, leaving them to sprout up randomly across the landscape.

Mark yawned. His childhood had been spent in a tiny town in the middle of nowhere too, but at least there had been a whole village with a town hall, a main street and even a movie theater. Summers had flown by, the memories melding together into a warm golden haze of playing baseball on an empty lot, and then heading to the Dairy Maid to get ice cream afterwards. As soon as dinner was over, they all met up again for one more game of ball before it was too dark to see. Then they would catch lightening bugs or play kick the can. Mark smiled. Sometimes they'd put the poor bugs in the can before playing, and when it was kicked, the bugs had shot out like a shower of living sparks. It had been a great place to grow up.

When was the last time he had been home? He shifted in the seat, his cheek resting on the ice cold pane of glass.

It felt good in the overheated bus. His dad's sixtieth birthday was the last time he could remember. That was the June before the terrorist attacks. Mark recalled sitting on his parents' front porch and watching the neighborhood flicker at dusk as the bugs flashed yellow up and down the street. Childish laughter had echoed from the backyard of some house as a new crop of children carried on the summertime traditions.

He should have gone home more often. It wasn't like his parents didn't invite him. His mother understood though. She knew that he didn't like to be away from Chicago. She didn't know about the dreams or camera, but he had a feeling that she knew there was something important in Chicago. Mark wondered if a previous owner of the camera had been from a city. He had lost count of the number of times he had studied the camera, searching for a clue to its power. Was there a previous owner? The camera was old, so it likely had a series of owners.

Was it just chance that brought it into a person's hands or did the camera decide who would get it? Where was it now? Had someone else discovered the unusual properties it possessed and did they get the premonitions? The bus hit a pothole and his head bumped against the window. If they got premonitions, would they recognize them as such and know that they could change things? Well, *some* things anyway. Mark grimaced. Some things weren't meant to be changed. His stomach tightened and he took a deep breath.

The sailor stirred and stretched, narrowly missing Mark's head with a clenched fist. He opened his eyes, his mouth rounding in surprise when he saw where his hand was. "Oh, wow. Sorry, man."

Mark shrugged. "No harm done." He fished in his pocket for the pack of gum and offered a piece to the sailor.

"Sure. Thanks." He slid a piece out and popped it into his mouth.

Taking one for himself, Mark put the pack away and wondered what time it was. He noticed the watch on the other guy's wrist. "Hey, you got the time?"

"It's about a quarter to four." The sailor smiled. "I can't wait to see my girlfriend. She was going to come down for my graduation, but she had finals. She goes to UW-Madison. My parents wanted to come too, but couldn't get off work." He made a face and shrugged. "It wasn't a big deal though. At least I'll be staying at Great Lakes awhile so I can come up to see them pretty often."

He chewed the gum and pulled his wallet out, flipping it open to a picture of a smiling young woman with short red hair. She had a delicate nose and a heart-shaped face. He beamed as he showed it to Mark.

"Cute girl. You're a lucky guy."

"She didn't want me to enlist, but after nine-eleven, I just had to, ya know?"

"That's great of you. I'm sure your parents must be very proud." Apparently the stick of gum acted as an ice breaker.

"How about you?"

The gum lodged in Mark's throat for a second. "Ah, no, I didn't enlist."

The sailor laughed. "No, that's not what I meant. I figured you're too old to enlist. I meant are you going to see someone special?"

Mark didn't know whether to be offended about the age comment or relieved that the conversation had shifted off nine-eleven. He chuckled and shook his head. "Nope. No girlfriend. I'm going home to see my parents."

"No girlfriend? Are you married?" His eyes darted to Mark's left hand. "Guess not. Divorced?" His face scrunched in sympathy, and before Mark could set him straight, he went on, "That's gotta be rough. I'm sure you'll find someone else soon."

Mark began to correct him, but then thought better of it. It didn't matter. He just nodded. "Yeah. Maybe."

"Aw, now don't get all down. You're decent looking. I'm sure you'll hook up with someone eventually. I've heard some people use those Internet dating sites. You could even use your own picture. Even though you're kind of old, the chicks might go for you. They like tall guys with dark hair. This one guy in my unit looked a little like you, except, well, you have more hair." He laughed at his joke, then continued, "He got letters all the time from different girls. One time..."

Mark tuned him out, just nodding and occasionally saying 'uh-huh.' Two days ago, he had thought that he would give anything to have another person to speak with, but now that he was out, he found it difficult to make small talk.

It wasn't the kid's fault and Mark tried to pay attention, but his mind wandered. His future was shot to hell and he faced an uphill battle to get his life back together. Just trying to figure out where to start left him drained. Then, at odd moments, he would flash back to his cell or an interrogation. It didn't take much to trigger it. A word, a smell, and sometimes, nothing at all. It just happened. When it did, his muscles tensed up and he would break out in a cold sweat.

Mark rubbed his palms on his thighs and craned his neck to see past the sailor and on out the other window. Along the highway, a sign said that Madison was only fourteen miles away. At least they were close to their destination.

"So, they coming to pick you up from the bus station?"

"Huh?" Mark had completely lost track of the sailor's monologue.

"Your folks. You said you were going home to see them."

"Oh, yeah, I am, but no, they're not expecting me." Mark crossed his arms and turned towards his window. "I'll probably catch a local bus in Madison, take it to the edge of town and walk from there." He could use the time to think. Already, he second guessed his impulse to come home unannounced. His leg bounced. What if they didn't want him there? Mark shook that off. His mom, at least, would be happy to see him. He was sure of that.

Had his detention been mentioned in the paper? Leaning an elbow on the window ledge, he rested his chin in his palm and hoped his dad hadn't died of embarrassment. He sighed.

"Hey, man...you okay?" The sailor touched his shoulder and Mark flinched. The sailor reeled back, his hands up as though to ward off an attack. "Whoa! Take it easy."

Heat crept up Mark's face, and he shook his head. "Sorry, I'm just a little jumpy." He wasn't sure why he felt a need to explain his actions, but he added, "I haven't seen my parents for over a year, and, well, I'm just a little nervous about seeing them again."

The sailor nodded, his expression sober. "I understand." He was quiet for five minutes or so. Mark felt bad for reacting the way he had.

It figured that he would scare off the very first person to talk to him normally in over a year.

"It's going to be dark out soon. I'm sure my parents wouldn't mind giving you a lift."

The sailor was like young puppy, and even though Mark kept nudging him aside, the kid came back for more. Mark saw the earnestness in his eyes. "My parents live about ten miles north of the city. That's way out of your way, I'm sure."

His face lit up. "No, it's not. We live in the north end, just inside the city. They won't mind."

The kid looked so eager, Mark didn't have the heart to say no, so he shrugged. "Well, ask your parents when you see them. If it's okay with them, I'd appreciate a ride."

"Great!" The sailor grinned. "Wow, I don't even know your name." He stuck a hand out. "I'm Tommy Wilson."

Mark looked at the hand, then shook it and smiled. "Mark Taylor."

* * *

A few minutes later, the bus pulled into the station. The driver exited and began unloading the luggage from the compartment underneath the bus. Mark stood and stretched. Tommy zipped up his coat and peered out the windows. His face broke into a grin and he pointed. "There they are!" His enthusiasm made Mark smile. The kid was practically dancing down the aisle of the bus.

Mark followed and stood back as Tommy hugged his parents. They were all talking at once, smiling and laughing. The reunion went on so long that Mark began to sidle away, figuring Tommy had forgotten about him. With a last look at the happy family, he turned and shoved his hands into his pockets. There was only about an hour of light left and he quickened his step.

"Mark! Where ya going?"

He turned to see Tommy jogging towards him. "I...ah, well, I don't want to bother anyone."

"Naw, no bother. My parents are okay with it. Come on." Tommy made a follow motion with his hand and turned back towards the parking lot.

Mark saw no graceful way out of the situation and as a cold wind whipped his hair around, he decided that a nice warm car was preferable to walking in the frigid dark. He just hoped there wouldn't be too many questions.

Tommy made introductions, and his parents greeted Mark with in a friendly tone, although his dad, who wasn't much older than Mark, did study him for a long moment before saying, "Well, I'm freezing, so let's get going."

Mark trailed behind the group and got in the backseat beside Tommy. He gave the father the address then settled back, listening to the parents quiz Tommy on what had gone on in basic. Had it been hard? Were the drill instructors mean? Was the food good? He was glad for all the chatter because it allowed him to remain silent.

Tommy borrowed his mother's cell-phone and called someone, and judging from the grin on the kid's face and the way he turned away from the rest of the car, Mark guessed it was the girlfriend.

Tommy's dad glanced at Mark in the rear-view mirror. "So, Tommy said you're going home to see your folks."

"Yes, sir."

"Sir? That's awfully formal. My name's Jeff." Every few seconds, he would take his eyes off the road and look at Mark. "I bet they'll be glad to see you." Was there a hint of a question in that statement?

Mark nodded, meeting Jeff's gaze for an instant before averting his eyes. The other man knew something. He could tell by the tone of his voice and how he regarded Mark. Feeling a need to fill the silence and to answer an unspoken question, Mark said, "They're not expecting me. I want to surprise them."

"You live in Chicago?" He was digging.

"Yes, sir." Mark didn't offer more. He squirmed and glanced at Tommy, who was oblivious to everything except the voice on the other end of the phone.

"Are you military? You sound like it."

"No, sir..., uh, Jeff. I've just been around military people a lot lately. Guess it wore off on me." He tried to chuckle and make a joke, but it fell flat.

The car stopped at a light and Mark saw Jeff exchange a glance with his wife. The light turned green and Jeff focused his attention on driving and didn't ask Mark any more questions. The rest of the drive continued with only Tommy's voice breaking the silence.

* * *

"Thank you for the ride. I appreciate it." Mark wanted to jump out of the car before it came to a complete stop in front of his parents' house, but instead, he tried to smile at the Wilsons. "It was a pleasure meeting all of you." Mark opened the door and shook Tommy's hand again. "You take care, and good luck with the Navy." With a last wave, he shut the door and began walking up the drive.

The house looked the same as he remembered. The porch, with its white spindle railing, hugged the sunny yellow home. The flower beds lay fallow, but he pictured them bursting with flowers as they usually were in the summer.

The memory was so vivid, he could almost hear the lazy buzz of the bees that had been a melody from his boyhood. How many times had he sat on those steps and guzzled lemonade underneath a blazing summer sun?

The second floor was dark, but warm light shone from the front windows, and he knew that the kitchen in the back would be bright. Mark sniffed. Wood smoke. His dad always loved a good fire in the fireplace. He squared his shoulders, took a deep breath, and mounted the steps.

Should he knock? Normally, he just walked in because his parents never locked the door. There was never a need. He didn't want to scare them though. He compromised and knocked, then opened the door a tiny bit. "Hello?" The scent of wood burning mingled with another tantalizing aroma. Beef stew?

Mark winced as something in the kitchen hit the floor with a loud crash. Then his mom's face peeked around the corner from the kitchen into the long hallway to the front door. "Hi, Mom."

"Mark?" She looked like she didn't believe her eyes, then she gave a shriek and flew towards him and into his arms. "Oh my God! It really *is* you." She alternated between hugging him and pulling back to see his face. Tears streamed down her cheeks.

"Norma? What the hell is going on?" The basement door opened and his dad, his protective goggles pushed up on top of his head, froze as he saw Mark. "Jesus Christ!"

His mom broke away, but kept an arm around Mark's waist. "Mark's home, Gene. He came home!"

Not seeming to comprehend, his dad looked from Mark to his wife for a few seconds before he finally moved, his steps hesitant as he approached.

Mark swallowed hard. "How have you been, Dad?"

His father's steps quickened. "Mark." It was all he said, but it was enough. In a heartbeat, his dad's arms were around him, his hand going up to the back of Mark's neck and pulling him close. "We've missed you, son." His voice was thick.

Wood shavings clung to his dad's flannel shirt and he smelled of pine and varnish. Mark could only nod and his throat swelled. He sighed when his mom reached up and feathered his hair.

His dad broke off the hug and took a step back, eyeing him from head to toe. "Are you okay? Did they treat you well?"

Mark saw the worry on his mom's face, and said the only thing he could, "Yes, sir. I'm fine." He tried to smile, but then had to duck his head and bite his lip to keep his emotions in check. "I don't really want to talk about it now, if that's okay."

She ran her hand up his arm, stroking it gently, and tilted her head. "Oh, hon, we don't have to. Are you hungry? Dinner is almost ready."

"I'm starved." Mark did smile then, and rubbed his hands together. "I can't wait to taste your cooking again."

His dad clapped him on the back. "It's good to have you home." Nodding, his lips tight, he turned and abruptly went back to the basement.

CHAPTER SIXTEEN

Steam rose from his plate. Mark closed his eyes and inhaled. Damn. It smelled great. The carrots and celery added color to the stew. Big pieces of beef swam in thick gravy, bumping up against chunks of potatoes. Two corn muffins perched on the edge of the plate where they dripped melted butter to mix with the gravy.

Mark took a bite and knew he was home. His mother poured him a tall glass of milk and he gulped it. "Ah. This is great, Mom." He swiped his hand across his mouth and dug into the mound of food on his plate.

His mother beamed and hardly touched her meal. Every time Mark looked up, he found her watching him like he might disappear any second.

"Your son is right. This is a wonderful meal, Norma." Using his muffin to sop up some gravy, his dad made quick work of eating. "I bet you didn't get food like this in prison."

Cornbread lodged in Mark's throat, and he thought he might gag. Grabbing his milk, he took a swallow. "No, sir. Nothing like this." He still had a half a plate of food, but his stomach churned and his appetite had deserted him. He poked at the carrots with his fork.

Prison. Did that make him an ex-con? He had never been convicted of anything. Hell, he had never even been charged with anything. He felt his mother looking at him and kept his head down.

"I didn't think so. You look kind of skinny, but no worries, your ma will put some meat back on your bones." His dad chuckled and laid his fork and knife across his plate.

"*Gene.*" She gave him a stern look.

"What? It's true." He patted his stomach. "Got any dessert?"

"There's apple pie."

Mark bit the end of a piece of carrot, but couldn't manage any more. He sat back and gave his mom an apologetic smile. "Dinner was delicious, but I guess my eyes are bigger than my stomach." After the talk of his weight loss, he wanted more than anything to polish off his dinner, but he just couldn't.

She frowned at his plate and then held his gaze for a long moment. Nodding, she stood and held her hand out for his dish. "I'm sure it's probably just all the excitement getting to you."

"It's okay. I can get it, Mom. You sit and eat." Mark rose and crossed to the sink. "Apple pie sounds great, but I think I'm going to have to take a rain check."

"Well, maybe later on tonight you'll be hungry again."

"Maybe." Mark rinsed his dish and stuck it in the dishwasher, then grabbed a cup and poured coffee from the fresh pot. "Anyone want some?"

"You can pour me a cup," his dad said, then he cleared his throat, and continued, "If you don't mind watching me eat my pie, I'd like for you to sit and talk with us."

He'd known the questions would come, but he'd hoped to delay the inevitable as long as possible. "Yeah. Sure." Grabbing two more cups, he poured coffee for his parents. His hand shook and he spilled a few drops on the counter.

In the window above the sink, he saw the table behind him. His mom shook her head at his dad, but his father only nodded. Mark was surprised at the expression of sadness that stole across his father's face. His mother sighed, stood and moved to the other counter where she began cutting the pie.

After all he had been through in the last year, this should have been easy, but as he carried the cups to the table, his heart thumped so loudly he could hear it inside his ears. He told himself it was just his parents, it wasn't like he was going to be interrogated.

He blew on his coffee as his father stirred some cream into his own. Done stirring, his father set the spoon on the saucer with a clink. "Tell us what happened. We don't know much."

Mark rolled the mug between his palms, watching the coffee swirl inside. "Honestly, I don't know much either. One minute, I was elated because I helped save a baby, the next, the police were slapping cuffs on me. The FBI showed up, whisked me to their office and asked me about some phone calls I made on September 11th. I had dreamed about the attack, and thought I could stop it." Mark couldn't keep the bitterness out of his voice.

His mother shot a confused glance at Mark's father before turning back to Mark. "A baby? We didn't hear anything about a baby. And what phone calls?"

Of course the baby part hadn't made the reports. It might have ruined the image they tried to paint of a heartless terrorist.

His dad pinned Mark with a hard look. "There has to be more to it than that."

Mark rubbed circles on his temples. " It's complicated. You guys remember my trip to Afghanistan about four years ago?"

His dad shrugged and his mother nodded.

"Well, the guy I went with, Mo—Mohommad Aziz—was also arrested. It seems he had some connections to al-Qaeda. He told officials that I was involved too." It still hurt to think of his friend's betrayal and he took a sip of coffee to hide the pain. The only explanation was desperation on Mo's part. If he received the kind of questioning Mark had, well, he could hardly blame the guy.

"*Were* you involved?"

The accusatory tone hit Mark physically with a sharp stab to the chest and his cup rattled when he set it down. "What do you *think*, Dad? Tell me. I want to know." He couldn't keep the anger out of his voice.

"I don't know what to think." His father drummed his fingers on the table, his mouth stiff. He glanced off to the side, as if composing his thoughts. He spit out the words as if he was tasting something nasty. "I'll tell you what I *know* instead. I *know* that my son—my only child—who I raised to respect people and to love this country, was taken away and accused of one of the most horrific crimes imaginable against his own countrymen."

Mark shook his head, cradling it his hands. "No. I didn't—"

His dad froze him with a look as he cut him off. "My son is gone with no word, and I have to get my information from the news media—when they call to get interviews with the parents who raised the 'monster'."

"Gene, he's not a monster. He'd never do something like that."

"I'm just repeating what was written." He glared at Mark's mother before pinning it on Mark. "Do you know what this did to your mother? I'll tell you. She was kicked out of half the clubs she belonged to, and the other half hardly speak to her. Everywhere we go, people whisper and point. We're pariahs in our own community."

Mark turned to her but she evaded his eyes. "I'm sorry, Mom."

She shrugged, her eyes bright with tears. "It wasn't a big deal. Not compared to not knowing where you were or how you were doing."

His dad didn't let up. "I lost about half of my patients, other doctors shun me, and it's become so bad, your mother and I were thinking of leaving town." He stabbed a finger in Mark's direction. "So don't go thinking this has just affected you." He circled his finger to encompass the three of them. "It's affected all of us, and your mother and I deserve to know the truth. We deserve to know why you've shamed us."

"I never meant to shame anyone." His voice broke and he cleared his throat, taking a moment to gather his composure. "I...I went to Afghanistan, but I only took photos for Mo's book. I never did the things they said I did. I never went to any training camps. I never said a bad word about the U.S."

He rubbed his eyes with his first two fingers and thumb. "While I was there, I bought an old camera. An antique." He cursed that day. "I never told you guys because it sounds crazy, but when I'd use that camera, I'd get photos of things that were going to happen."

His dad scoffed and crossed his arms. "I thought you could do better than that."

His mother remained silent, which was almost worse.

"Let me finish, dammit!" Mark glared at his father. "It's true, and not only that, but after seeing the photographs, I dreamed about them. Dreams like you never imagined, Dad. Three dimensional dreams, movies almost. Only, it's never good stuff. It's always someone dying or getting hurt."

He used to hope for good pictures and dreams. He took plenty of happy photos with the camera, catching images of blissful couples strolling in the park, but the dream pictures never had happy endings. "When I wake up, I know exactly what's going to happen to the person in the dream. If I'm lucky, I can stop it. I can turn the photo into a good one."

He could see they weren't buying it. His father shook his head, and his mother had tears welling in her eyes. They thought he'd lost his mind. "It's true! I swear it." He wracked his brain for a way to prove it, but had nothing. "Remember when I was shot?"

"Of course, hon." She reached across and took his hand, giving it a squeeze. "How is your leg now?"

Mark pulled his hand away in frustration. "It's fine, but I didn't get shot because I was taking photos in a bad neighborhood. A cop was going to be killed. I had the photos and dream the night before so I took my camera to the neighborhood as a cover. I had to wait until the right moment, then I tackled the officer just as the drive-by shooting began. That's a fact." He pointed at his father. "You can check it out. I never told them the cop was going to get killed, but nobody can dispute that I tackled him just as the passing car sprayed the corner with bullets."

"Son, I know a doctor, he's a good guy. You could talk—"

"I don't need a shrink, Dad. I'm not crazy. I was able to stop it because I knew. It's not the only time. I stopped dozens of things since I got the camera." He scrubbed his fingers through his hair and plowed ahead, "That's what happened to me on September 10th. I took some photos. Nothing special, just some shots of the Chicago River, only that's not what developed. What I got were pictures of the planes hitting the Twin Towers."

His mother wiped her hand across her cheek, leaving a wet smudge. "And?"

"Don't play along with him, Norma."

Mark ignored his father and focused on his mom. "As soon as the pictures developed, I started calling around. I didn't know what to do. It was so much bigger than the other things. I looked up numbers of different agencies, but I didn't have anything concrete to tell them. The details don't come until I dream."

He took a sip of his lukewarm coffee. It was the best he'd had in ages, but he couldn't enjoy it. Not with his dad looking at him with a mixture of revulsion and pity. "I woke up around five o'clock, and began trying to warn somebody. I called the FBI, the U.S. Marshals, the airports, police. Any place I could think of. Hell, I even called the National Guard."

"Well, you didn't do any good."

"No shit, Dad." He never swore at his father and hated to now. The anger, withheld for so long, burst out despite his attempt to stifle it.

"I know I didn't do any good. If only people would have listened." His anger drained out of him along with his energy. There was no point in it. It wouldn't change anything for the better. He sat back and massaged his brow. "Anyway, I don't have proof. Not anymore. I did before I was locked up, but I never showed anyone. I don't blame you for not believing me. Nobody else did either."

"Didn't it occur to you that you could get in trouble for making those calls? They're practically bomb threats."

Mark nodded. "Yeah. I realized that afterwards, but at the time, I thought I could do something, ya know?" The frustration he had felt that day came back and he shoved a hand through his hair. "What was I supposed to do? Wouldn't you have tried to do something if you had known?"

His dad's eyes narrowed. "Where's this 'mysterious' camera? If it's so special, why didn't you just show it to them?"

It was difficult to ignore the sarcasm, but he did his best. "I never got a chance. I suppose they took all my equipment, and your guess is as good as mine as to where it is now."

"You didn't get anything back?" For the first time, there was a shred of sympathy in his father's voice.

"No. I went back to the loft and someone else is in my apartment." Mentioning it to his parents dredged up the pain of his loss again, so he swallowed the lump in his throat and hurried to change the subject. "I told the Feds everything. I told them about the dreams and the camera. I told them about other things I had stopped, but they just thought I was crazy."

"Oh, Mark." The sorrow in his mother's voice tore at his defenses. At least she wasn't crying any more.

"So, why did they let you go if they didn't believe you? Couldn't they make the charges stick?"

"I wasn't charged with anything."

"What? That doesn't make sense. So, it never went to trial?" His dad sounded surprised.

Mark picked at his finger with his thumbnail, worrying a ragged cuticle. "I never had a hearing let alone a trial."

His father leaned forward. "I don't understand. What happened? Start at the beginning, without all that camera crap."

Mark sighed. "First, they locked me in a cell in Chicago for a few weeks, I guess. I spoke to a lawyer once, but then I was moved to another place. A naval brig. I only found out yesterday that it was in Charleston." He shivered at the memory of the first terrifying transport spent in near total sensory deprivation, when he hadn't known where he was going.

"What's wrong? Did something happen?"

Surprised at his dad's perception, Mark shook his head.

"You're not telling us something." His mom's brow furrowed.

He glanced between his parents. They didn't need to hear anymore; didn't need to know the ugly details. Especially his mother. "Listen, I'm kind of tired. Can we talk about this tomorrow?"

Mark couldn't maintain eye contact and pushed the coffee aside, gripping one hand in the other. He raised his head. His mother's eyes brimmed and as he watched, a tear escaped and slipped down her cheek. His dad sat with his arms crossed, and when he spoke, his voice was low and hard, "And you've been there all this time? Couldn't you even call us?"

Hunching over the table, Mark worked at the cuticle again. "No, sir. I never got to use the phone." Guilt filled him and he wasn't even sure why. It wasn't like he had a chance to call and passed it up. Is that what his dad thought? "I wanted to call. And a couple of times, I was allowed to write letters." He leaned both elbows on the table and ran his hands through his hair, then rested his head on his palms. The bastards. They had promised that they would mail the letters. "I guess they never sent them."

Mark pushed up from the table, his hands curling into fists at his sides. "I'm sorry. I...I thought they told you guys." He turned and stepped to the sink, bracing himself against it. He had caused his parents so much pain.

A warm, heavy weight settled on Mark's shoulder and he felt his father behind him. His dad tightened his grip near Mark's neck, giving him a squeeze. "You're home now. That's all that matters."

Mark clenched his jaw and didn't dare look at his dad's reflection, so he just nodded and tried to breathe through the pain twisting inside his chest.

There was a rattle and clink of dishes behind him and a few seconds later, his mom set the stack beside the sink. Mark stole a glance at her. She caught his look and despite the tears still streaming, she smiled. "I prayed every night that you were safe and that you would come home. My prayers came true."

* * *

The wooden stairs creaked, the third one loudest of all, and Mark remembered that particular step giving him away once when he was seventeen and trying to sneak out of the house to go to a party. Amusement lifted the corners of his mouth as he turned to the right, his hand spinning around the wooden knob at top of the banister. The action came naturally, from a childhood spent racing up the steps, and careening down the hall. The knob had been the only thing that had prevented him from catapulting out the window at the top of the steps.

His old room still looked like he had left for college the week before. On the wall was a poster of Walter Payton, and opposite that, one of the Dallas Cowboy Cheerleaders. The double-bed looked huge and the blue down comforter puffed when he sank down into its softness. It was all he could do to keep from falling back and sleeping right then, but he wanted to shower first.

He rubbed his eyes and wandered over to the oak dresser. Some of his clothes were still here. He tended to leave his dirty clothes unless he needed them. It had made traveling from Chicago easier if he didn't need to pack every time.

In the top drawer, he found some boxers and a tee shirt. Perfect. He shut the drawer and the jolt knocked over a couple of photographs on top of the dresser. Mark lifted one. His senior prom. He was decked out in a white tux with a pastel pink cummerbund that matched Becky Harris's chiffon dress. They both grinned into the camera. His arms circled Becky, resting on top of her hands at her waist. Her blond hair, so curled and sprayed that it looked like it would crack if touched, came to just below his chin. She had been tiny, even in heels, and Mark remembered feeling so big and invincible holding her. He ran a hand through his short hair. In the photo, it had been longer and feathered. Mark chuckled at how much time he had wasted every morning making sure it looked good.

A soft knock sounded and Mark turned to the door. "Come in."

His mom entered carrying a couple of bath towels and held up a new toothbrush. "I found this in the downstairs medicine cabinet. It was a free sample. There's toothpaste, shampoo, and some disposable razors in this bathroom. If you need—"

"Thanks, Mom. I got it." Mark smiled and cut her off. There was an awkwardness between them that had never been there before. He cleared his throat and set the towels on the bed. "I was just looking at my prom picture. What a goof I was." The comment was meant to be funny, but his voice cracked. Mark averted his eyes from hers.

She crossed to the dresser and held the picture. "I remember taking this picture. You looked so handsome all dressed up." A smile softened her features as one finger traced Mark's outline in the photo. "I was a nervous wreck all that night. I was sure you were going to get drunk and crash the car on the way home."

This was news to him. Vaguely, he recalled that a boy had been killed in a car crash after a prom night party a few years before his own prom, but like most kids, Mark had never considered it happening to him. "Why did you let me go?"

"It was your prom. What else could I do?" She shrugged. "Besides, I worried every time you walked out that door. But, you always came home okay." Setting the picture down, she faced him. "Until today."

Mark swallowed down the lump that threatened to choke him and picked at a snag on the towel, working the thread until it stuck out another inch. He tore his gaze from the towel and tried smile. "I'm fine."

She shook her head and stepped close, wrapping her arms around him. "No, Mark. You're not." Her hands ran up and down his back. "But you will be."

He nodded into her neck, not trusting his voice. After a moment, he stepped back. "Well, I probably should get that shower before I stink up the room."

She didn't smile at his attempt at humor, but nodded. "Good night, hon."

* * *

Mark grabbed the soap and lathered up the washcloth, scrubbing his skin in an attempt to wash the stench of prison right out of his pores. The mint and vanilla scent of the shampoo filled the shower stall. It smelled so good, he was half-tempted to taste it. The hot water poured over his head and eased the tension from his muscles as the suds swirled down the drain. He watched them disappear and wished his memories from prison could disappear so easily.

Later, he lay in bed, his hands clasped behind his head. He had to figure what to do with his life beginning tomorrow. He couldn't stay with his parents indefinitely. His thoughts drifted to Jessie. Would she have waited for him? For her, life had marched on, while his life had been captive in a cell. Mark turned and tugged his pillow, pounding a fist into it. Why should she wait?

She had feared and doubted him. Not that he blamed her. His story sounded impossible even to himself. Jessie dealt with cold hard facts, not mystical dreams and magical cameras. He punched the pillow into a ball and pulled it back under his head. As hard as it was, he had to accept that their relationship was over and had been for a year now. Just because his life had been on hold didn't mean hers had been.

It was just as well. He had nothing to offer. At least before, he'd had a successful career. Now he had nothing. Thanks to the damn camera, he had been too busy to keep in touch with most of his friends, and the few he had were sure to have heard what happened to him. He doubted any would want to associate with him now.

Mark tried to push the negative thoughts aside. It would do no good. Better to think of the positive things. He was free. The bedside clock ticked and the tree outside scratched at the window as the wind blew the branches. Try as he might, he couldn't think of another positive thing. Hell, he hardly had more than the clothes on his back and less than a thousand dollars in his pocket.

Maybe he could start a little photography business in Madison. He would have to get another job to save some money to get more equipment. His throat clenched at that thought. It was like losing part of himself. Being a photographer wasn't just what he did, it was who he was.

The FBI had taken some of his equipment he knew, and probably all of his files. They had certainly gone through them all, but where they were now was anyone's guess. The other equipment though, like his backdrops and lights, probably hadn't been part of the investigation. Would they give any of it back to him? He hadn't been guilty of anything. He didn't have the first clue who to call to find out where his things had gone.

Mark wondered if his parents had any idea where it all might be. He rolled over, closing his eyes as he settled into the lavender scented comforter. Inhaling deeply, he smiled. As a teen, he had hated the smell. It was too girly and even his dad had backed him on that, but his mom always insisted the aroma would help him sleep. As he drifted off, he concluded she was right.

* * *

His shoulders ached and Mark gritted his teeth, trying to rise up in his toes enough to ease the pressure. How long would

*they leave him here this time? Bill circled him, a mocking grin
stretched across his face.*

*"You know what we want. Come on, Mark. Who are you
protecting? Is it worth it?"*

*He tried to gasp out an answer, but it was so hard to talk
and concentrate with his shoulders aching so badly. "I'm not protecting anyone. I don't have anything to tell you. I swear it."*

*Bill reached up and yanked on something, tightening the
rope. Mark groaned. "Stop!" Head hanging down, he panted.
"Please...just...stop!"*

* * *

"Mark? Are you okay, son?"

A hand shook his shoulder and Mark bolted up.
"What?" His heart raced as he took in the golden sunlight
that filled the room. He sagged back against the pillow. It
had been a dream. It was too real; like he was back in the
interrogation room. Mark ran a shaky hand through his hair,
then scrubbed his eyes. His shoulder still ached and he rotated it. He must have been lying on it wrong.

His dad stood beside the bed, his eyes lit with worry.
"What's going on? You were yelling."

Mark shook his head. "Nothing. Just a bad dream."
He didn't meet his eyes. "I'm fine."

"You don't sound fine."

"It's nothing, Dad." He winced at the hard tone in
his voice as he swung his legs over the side of the bed. Taking a moment, he rested his elbows on his thighs, hands
dangling, as he tried to get his body to stop shaking. "What
time is it?" He dared to look up, hoping that he didn't appear as rattled as he felt.

His dad gave him a long look before answering, "About seven-thirty. Your mom is making some breakfast. It should be ready in about fifteen minutes."

Mark wasn't sure he could eat with his stomach twisted up like a pretzel, but he pasted on a smile. "Sounds good. I'll be down soon." Standing, he stretched, wincing as pain lanced through his shoulder.

"You okay?" His dad nodded towards Mark's shoulder. "What's wrong?"

"I must have slept on it funny, that's all." That was true enough even though he didn't think his shoulders would ever be the same as they had been. The joints just weren't designed to hold all of a man's weight, especially when pulled at unnatural angles.

His dad gave him a doubtful look, but finally left.

Mark sighed and gathered his clothes. He didn't need another shower, but took one anyway just because he could. This time, he shaved afterwards.

For a year, he had avoided looking at his face in the mirror. The blank look in his eyes had scared the hell out of him, and so he had stopped looking. When he shaved in prison, he had focused only on the patch of skin he was shaving. Nothing more.

Seeing his face now was like looking at the face of an acquaintance. His skin was dead white from months without sunlight, the dark bristles of his beard a marked contrast. As he scraped the razor over his jaw, he held his skin taut with his free hand. He noted how sharp his cheekbones appeared. They were more defined with hollows beneath them. The changes in his face shocked him. He scarcely recognized it. Ducking his head, he rinsed the razor.

* * *

A plate stacked high with steaming pancakes greeted him when he entered the kitchen. A bowl of sausage sat beside a pitcher of warmed syrup. Mark didn't know which was watering more, his mouth or his eyes. He was home.

"Wow, Mom. This looks great. After I couldn't eat for a few days, they tried to tempt me with pancakes, but—" He was going to say that they were tough and dry, but the look of horror on his mother's face stopped him cold.

"Why couldn't you eat?"

Mark opened his mouth but then realized that he couldn't tell her about the things they had done to him. He shrugged and grabbed the syrup, pouring it on the pile. "I...uh...I got a stomach bug. You know how those things are."

His dad entered the kitchen, the newspaper folded under his arm and interjected, "How what things are?" He pulled his chair out and set the paper beside his plate, giving Mark a questioning look.

"Mark said he was sick and couldn't eat for awhile when he was...when he was gone."

"When I was in prison, Mom. You can say it." He cut into the pancakes and shoved a forkful in his mouth, catching a drop of syrup with his tongue before it dripped onto his shirt. They were cooked just the way he liked them, crispy around the edges and tender in the middle.

"What kind of illness?"

Mark wanted to smack himself for bringing up the subject. Now his dad would grill him about symptoms and try to diagnose him. "Nothing I want to talk about over breakfast."

Hopefully they would think of the worst symptoms associated with stomach problems and drop the subject.

"Vomiting? Diarrhea?"

Stifling a groan, Mark shook his head. "It was nothing. Forget it." He should have known his dad wouldn't care that they were eating. How many times had he discussed some nasty symptom a patient had while they were eating dinner when he was a kid? His mom had become so used to medical talk that she never protested. He stood and poured a glass of milk. He lifted the gallon in invitation. "Anyone want some?"

Neither answered so he took his glass back to his seat. His mom looked at him with concern and his dad with speculation. "You never caught stomach bugs growing up." There was a note of challenge in his dad's voice.

Mark set his fork down and watched the syrup drip down the side of his remaining stack. Not only would telling them force him to remember the worst time in his life, but subjecting them to the details would force them to picture him being...questioned. Once that image was out there, it couldn't be erased. Ever. It was better for them to remain ignorant. "It was a prison, Dad. Weren't you always telling me that disease and illness run rampant in places where people are crowded together?"

"Son, what are you afraid to tell us? We realize you were in a prison, not on a luxury cruise. You don't have to spare us the details." His dad's eyes locked on his, full of more sorrow and anguish than Mark had ever seen him show. "Our imaginations have probably conjured up the very worst."

Overwhelmed, Mark broke the visual connection. "They never beat me." He couldn't bring himself to lie, but he didn't want them to imagine things that never happened. " Most of the time, I was treated okay." The pancakes were soaking up the syrup. Soon they would be soggy and cold. He took another bite.

"Hon, we won't think less of you no matter what happened in there, okay?" His mother smiled, her bottom lip trembling.

"I know. But you don't have to worry. Mostly, I was just bored." He shoved in the last forkful of pancakes.

CHAPTER SEVENTEEN

"So, what are your plans?"

Mark looked over the top of the newspaper at his dad. "What do you mean? Today? I was gonna—"

His dad shook his head and cut him off. "No. I mean, for work. For getting on with your life." He took the seat across the kitchen table. "It's been a week. You have to start thinking about your future."

Mark folded the paper and set it down beside his coffee cup. His father's tone took him back to when he was twenty and had rebelled against returning to college. He had gone two years and done okay. School had been easy for him, but he found it boring. How many times had he tried to make his father see that it just wasn't the path that he wanted ed to take? Especially not pre-med.

It had been drilled into him his whole life that he would be a doctor like his father. "I've been looking through the help wanted ads every day, Dad. I made a resume and sent that to a few employers."

Mark put both elbows on the table and raked his hands through his hair and flashed a brief humorless smile. There hadn't been a single ad seeking a newly-freed terrorist suspect. He took a deep breath and folded his arms on top of the paper. "I have an unexplainable gap in my employment history, and all my references are shot to hell. I'm not expecting much response."

His dad rose and poured himself a cup of coffee. "If you would've finished college, you wouldn't have this problem now." He leaned against the counter, feet crossed as he sipped from his mug.

The muscles in the back of Mark's neck tensed. "Yeah, well hindsight's a bitch, isn't it?" He tried to quell his anger and took a gulp of his coffee. What had he expected from his father? Support and warm fuzzies? The glimmer of warmth the first few days after Mark had returned had faded and now his dad was back to his classic ways.

"Are you still having your special dreams?"

The coffee sprayed across the paper as Mark choked at the question. When he could talk, he stammered, "N-None since I was in prison." He evaded his father's gaze and blotted the paper with a napkin.

Those two dreams still puzzled him. Why had he had them when he no longer had the camera? The other question he had was why had the dreams been about him? That had never happened before. Mark closed his eyes and recalled the details. The interrogations blended with reality until he couldn't tell which had been dreams and which had been real. The memories of the interrogations and the dreams wove together in his mind and now he couldn't, with certainty, separate them.

"So you're done with that non...stuff?"

"Nonsense?" Mark jerked his head up. "Isn't that what you were going to say?" He jumped up from the table, ignoring the coffee that sloshed and made a puddle. "I know you always hated that I chose photography instead of medicine, but goddamn it, even though I don't have a bunch of letters after my name, I made a difference in people's lives, Dad." Mark clenched his jaw and fought to speak through the spasm in his throat. "I *did*."

His voice broke as anger burned through him at his own emotions. He shoved the chair under the table and picked up his cup, dumping the contents into the sink. It took every fiber of self-control to keep from hurling the mug across the room. Instead, he rinsed it and put it in the dishwasher. He thought he had learned to shrug off his father's comments. After all these years, it shouldn't hurt so much.

He heard his dad come up behind him, but the steps stopped a few feet away. "Listen, son. I didn't mean it like that."

Mark bit his lip and stared out the kitchen window. It had snowed the night before and icicles shimmered and glinted in the sun as they hung from the eaves. Out of habit, his mind framed them in a shot, then with a snort, he pushed the image out his mind and dried his hands with a kitchen towel. "Well, whatever. The camera is gone and so are the dreams."

* * *

"Mark, you know your dad. He just wants the best for you."

His mom stood in the doorway of Mark's bedroom, but he couldn't look at her. The tears on her cheeks tore at his resolve to leave.

"Yeah, that's what you always told me, but he has a strange way of showing it." Mark stuffed his meager wardrobe into an old duffel bag. He owned just a few pairs of jeans and sweat-shirts. When he used to come visit, he'd left his good clothes at his loft. At his parents' house, he tended to do odd jobs, helped in yard and other chores. If they went out to eat, it was to a local diner, so there was no need to dress up. Now, he wished he had left a few decent things here. A few days before, he had picked up some socks, underwear and shaving gear at the discount store. After shoving those in, he grabbed the old pea coat. It would do for the rest of the winter. It would have to if he was going to make his money last for any length of time.

"Don't do this, hon. Don't leave angry. Please." She clutched at his arm as he brushed past her.

Mark clattered down the steps, trying to ignore the tendril of pain that began in his gut and wound its way up to squeeze his heart. He stopped at the front door and set the duffel down. "I'm sorry, Mom. I have to go. I'm not angry...I just...I just can't stay here." Earlier, he'd dug a pair of gloves out of the hall closet and now he held them up. "I hope it's okay if I take these."

His mother looked at them blankly, then nodded. "Yes, of course. I think there's an extra knit cap in the closet too. I'll get it." Her voice shook and he swallowed hard. He was the worst son ever.

Her eyes brimmed a few minutes later as she handed him the cap along with a lumpy paper bag. "I tossed some things in there in case you get hungry on the bus. Do you have any money? I think I have some cash in my purse and I can send you some more when you get settled."

Mark shook his head. "I'm okay. They gave me a little money when I left." Even if he had been penniless, he wouldn't have taken any help. His mother wouldn't care, but his dad would attach so many strings, the loan would look like a vast spider-web and money would be the fly in the middle. He swept her into a hug and kissed her cheek. "I love you, Mom." He tightened the hug. "I'll keep in touch." He broke away and scooped up the strap of the bag. "Bye."

"Good-bye, and I'll tell your dad you said good-bye too."

Mark just nodded as he pushed the door open. He flinched at the sound of it closing behind him. Was he doing the right thing? There was no alternative. When he was younger, his dad had seemed like the most powerful man on Earth. Nobody stood up to his dad. He wasn't a bad guy. In fact, Mark had felt pride in the way other kids had seemed a little afraid of his father. He hadn't blamed them. His dad could be scary sometimes. Now, Mark knew better. There were scarier men out there. He knew because he had met them.

His feet crunched across the frozen gravel as he made his way to the main road. The air bit his nose while his breath steamed around his head. He was glad for the gloves and cap and turned the collar up on the coat. It was going to be a long hike.

His mother thought he was going to catch a bus to Chicago, but he had decided to try and hitch-hike instead. Every penny counted now.

Three hours later, his feet almost frozen, he finally got a ride from an old trucker. Mark's lips felt stiff as he tried to smile and thank the man.

"No problem. It's awfully cold out there to be trekking very far. I'm going to Gary, Indiana. If you're going farther, you'll have to find another ride." The man sounded the horn as he merged into traffic, his eyes darting to the passenger side mirrors. "Damn cars can see I'm trying to get going. I don't know why they can't switch to the middle lane."

Mark cringed as a little red sports car whizzed past. "I'm going to Chicago, so if it's not too much trouble, you could drop me off somewhere as you pass by. It doesn't matter where."

"You got it." The other man reached out and turned the heat up when Mark couldn't suppress a shiver. "You look half-frozen."

"I am. And the other half is cold as hell." Mark took his gloves off and blew into his hands then held them out to the vent.

The trucker laughed and nudged an open package of cookies across the seat. "Help yourself. I eat too many of the damn things." He patted his impressive belly.

Mark ate a few cookies and then settled into the seat. The heat seeped into him, relaxing him until he dozed.

The cell felt like an inferno and Mark stripped down to his boxers, but the sweat poured off him. Had the air conditioner broken or was there a fire somewhere? The water in his sink had been shut off and he didn't think it was close to a meal time yet. He'd give anything for a drink of ice cold water. He sank onto the steel shelf, at first it felt cool, but as his body warmed it, his skin stuck to the metal. His head ached and his throat felt raw.

The cell morphed into the interrogation room and Mark stood in front of the team, acutely aware of his almost naked state of dress. The chain around his waist scraped against his back.

A man Mark had never seen stuck his face close to Mark's. "We're turning up the heat .You brought this upon yourself by not telling us the truth." Even in a dark suit and tie, the man wasn't sweating.

How was that possible? As Mark wondered about that, the man snapped his fingers and pointed towards a long board in the corner of the room. "We got some water for you. Ice cold. You said you'd do anything for it."

"I didn't say that! I only thought it!" He knew what that board was for. He tried to swallow the fear, but his throat was too dry. "You don't need to do that."

The guards grabbed him and wrestled him to the board and strapped him down. One gripped Mark's head and the man in the suit held a pitcher of water just above Mark's face. A shudder shook him. "No!"

"Whoa there, buddy. Time to wake up."

Mark started awake, and brought his hands up to wipe his face. It was dry. The lights of Chicago lit the interior of the cab.

"You okay?" The trucker raised an eyebrow.

"Just a dream." He scrubbed his eyes. The cab had grown hot and Mark unbuttoned his coat. His mouth felt parched, but the thought of water sent a wave of revulsion through him. He tried to cover the shudder by stretching.

The cookies were gone and a smattering of crumbs covered the trucker's belly. The man noticed Mark's gaze and looked down, swiping the bits away with a grin. "Told you I'd eat too many. Any place in particular you wannabe dropped off?"

Home would be good, but that wasn't an option. Ducking his head, he caught sight of a green road sign that announced the Addison Street exit one mile away. He shrugged. "I guess since it's not too far away, Division or Ohio would be fine." He recalled a little hotel right off Ohio that shouldn't cost too much. At least it didn't look expensive. In the morning, he could look for work. There were plenty of warehouses just west of the highway. They weren't too picky about who they hired as long as the person had a strong back.

"You got it. I'll exit on Ohio and loop back around."

Ten minutes later, Mark stepped into the parking lot of a McDonald's. He grabbed a quick meal then headed for the hotel. The price wasn't outrageous, but he would have to find something cheaper as soon as he could. He lay on the bed, his hands behind his head. The only light in the room was the dim green cast by the bedside clock.

The hotel was in the heart of the city and he was literally surrounded by millions of people. The mattress shook

213

whenever a heavy vehicle passed the motel. Cars beeped their horns, and down the hall, a door slammed. The city pulsed with life. It surrounded him, pushing and prodding him to dive back in, but as much as he wanted to, he didn't know how. He glanced at the door. He held the key and he could leave anytime he wanted, but where could he go? It wasn't places that he had missed, but people. Someone to laugh with, have a beer, see a movie. He ran through a mental list of some of his old friends. Even before he'd been locked up, he hadn't called them often. It was his own fault for ignoring the friendships in favor of using the camera.

The only one he'd been close to was Jessie. He rolled his head to look at the phone. He could call. In twenty seconds, he could be talking to her. What would he say? She hadn't believed him before he left. For all he knew, she had a boyfriend now. It had been a year. Hell, she could be married. Mark shifted on the bed and swung his legs over the side. It was only a little after seven p.m.

He rubbed his hands on his thighs, then reached for the phone. It took him a minute to recall her number and another minute to work up the nerve to dial it. After four rings, a machine picked up. Mark slumped as he listened to Jessie's voice asking him to leave a message. He couldn't do it. Not without knowing what her life was like now. The phone made a gentle click as he set it onto the cradle.

Well, that was that. There was nobody else to call. He flopped back on the bed and sighed. It was just as well. Better to start over fresh with no reminders of his previous life.

* * * *

He awoke to bright sunlight streaming into the room. His melancholy mood from the night before had passed and

214

he felt a spark of energy. After dressing, he grabbed his duffel bag and left the hotel. Hopefully, he'd find a cheaper place today. First on his agenda was breakfast and a newspaper. He obtained both at a diner a few blocks away. Over a plate of pancakes smothered in syrup and a side of sausage, he perused the help wanted section. The waitress lent him a pen, and he circled some possible opportunities. There were a couple of warehouse jobs, just like he had expected, but the job listing that piqued his interest was one for a photo lab. The pay wasn't great, but it would be a step in the right direction.

After noting the location of the lab, he looked for rooms to rent. He saw a couple that sounded decent, but decided he should find a job before he committed to an apartment or room. Location had to be a consideration and walking distance to the job was first priority. After that was price. As he circled the phone numbers, it occurred to him that he had no way for any prospective employers to contact him. He couldn't get a room until he had a job, but he couldn't get a job until he had an address and phone number. Shit. Mark slapped the pen down on the paper and blew out a breath.

"Something wrong, hon?"

Mark turned to the waitress, who stood beside the table holding a pot of coffee. She frowned and looked genuinely concerned. He shook his head and tried to muster a smile. "No. I just...I have a small problem I was thinking about." He reached for his wallet. "I guess I'm ready for the check."

"Sure. You want a refill on the coffee?"

He thought for a second. It was foolish to waste time, but then again, he'd wasted over a year in prison; what was a few more minutes lingering over a cup of coffee? Just the luxury of being able to sit and watch people come and go while sipping the hot brew was something he wanted to savor. "Yeah, another cup would be great."

She poured, then before moving off to the next table, paused. "I'm being nosy, but if you want to share your problem, I'm a good listener."

Surprised, Mark glanced from the sugar packet he held in his hand up to her. He hadn't had anyone to share a problem with in a long time. She was probably just being polite, but he shrugged and answered anyway, "I just got into town last night. I don't have a job yet, and haven't found a place to stay tonight—I have money, that's not the problem," he added hastily, not wanting her to think he might stiff her on the bill. "I was looking in the paper for both a job and a room, and realized I need one to get the other." He shook his head and poured the sugar into the cup. "It's a catch-22."

"Hmmm...it is." She put a hand on her hip and cocked her head. "What kind of job are ya looking for?"

"Anything, really."

"Well, what have you done before?"

"I was a photographer, but it's been awhile. Someday, I'll get back into it, but for now, I'm not picky."

"We get lots of folks from the neighborhood, and one of the regulars was just moaning about having to work all the time because he couldn't find good help. You might try him. He runs a camera shop around the corner." She pulled out her pad of paper and jotted something down and tore it off, handing it to him. "You just give this to Gary and tell him Lois sent you."

"I—I will. Thanks." He glanced at the note. She had written that Gary better hire Mark because she was tired of listening to Gary's complaints. Mark grinned. "He'd hire me on your say so?"

Lois shrugged. "Sure. Why not? I know a good guy when I see one. Serving people all day, you get an instinct." She tapped the eraser on the pencil against her temple. "Besides, I got a son about your age. You remind me of him."

Touched, Mark smiled and tried to cover his emotion with a joke. "So he's a handsome son-of-a gun too?"

The waitress threw her head back and laughed. "You bet."

He tucked the paper into his wallet, took out a twenty and handed it to her. "Here's for my meal. Keep the change."

"But breakfast only cost about seven bucks. This is an awfully big tip."

"Nope, for what you're doing for me, it's not big enough." Feeling better than he could remember in a long time, he left the diner and headed around the corner.

CHAPTER EIGHTEEN

"You look familiar."

Mark shook his head, at a loss. "I'm sorry, I don't recall ever meeting you. I did have a photography business a few years ago, but I used a different place to process my photos."

The manager of the camera and film store shrugged. "Maybe it'll come to me. So, your application looks impressive, but..." He paused and cleared his throat. "I gotta admit; I'm a little leery of the big break in your work history."

Mark scratched the back of his neck. He'd known this could be a problem, but didn't know how to answer. He'd never been convicted of anything, let alone a felony, so he truthfully answered no to that question, but the whole truth was complicated, and he didn't think he should reveal it. Not if he wanted to be hired. He sighed and met the younger man's eyes. "I know. I totally understand your reluctance. All I can say is it was a personal issue. It won't happen again."

His leg bounced as he waited for the man to make a decision. "Mr. Parker, I'd appreciate if you gave me a chance to prove myself to you. Please." He didn't want to sound like he was begging, but when it came down to it, that's what he was doing. His future rested on the shoulders of a guy ten years younger and with half the experience.

"Gary."

"Excuse me?" Mark leaned in, his hands resting on the store counter.

"Call me Gary. It feels kinda weird being called Mr. Parker. Makes me feel like I'm your ninth grade English teacher or something. And if you're gonna be working here…"

Mark's fingers pressed against the glass, and his leg froze mid-bounce. "You mean I got the job?"

"Yep. You're hired. You know it doesn't pay much? Just ten bucks an hour, but if you take up photography again, you can use the equipment to develop your prints." Gary smiled and stuck out his hand. "Free processing is one of the perks. Not much of one anymore though."

Mark shook the offered hand. "Why? Sounds good to me." Right now, everything sounded good. He had a job. It wasn't much, but it was a start.

Gary shot a look around the store. "I shouldn't say this 'cause it's probably gonna put us out of business one day, but if I were you, I wouldn't even bother with film anymore."

"You think digital is going to be that big? The quality of the prints isn't nearly as good." He'd looked into digital a few years ago, but hadn't liked the fuzziness of the photos. It was fine for family snapshots, but not professional photos.

"I know you've been out of photography for a year or so, but haven't you kept up at all?"

Mark tensed. What if the kid withdrew the job offer? "I'm afraid I haven't. Tell me what I missed." He hoped his appeal to Gary's knowledge would flatter the guy.

Gary grinned and came around the counter. Apparently he liked the role of teacher. He pointed to a row of cameras on display. "My pleasure. These babies are going to be the future of photography." He picked one up and showed Mark. "All digital. You're right, it used to be that pictures printed from digital looked bad, but that's changed." He tapped a framed photo beside the display. "See how crisp that looks?"

Mark picked up the photo. The colors were bright, the image sharp. "You're right. This is gorgeous." He glanced at the camera in Gary's hands. "One reason I didn't switch was because I had lots of different lenses. I couldn't see investing in all new ones just for the digital cameras."

Gary held up a finger. "Ah, but now they fit. They wised up."

"No kidding? That's great." He set the photo down and picked up another camera on display. It felt good in his hands. Automatically, he raised it and looked through the viewfinder. His finger twitched on the shutter button, and he accidentally snapped a photo. "Aw, shit. I'm sorry." He set the camera down and stepped back.

Laughing, Gary set the one he held down and grabbed the one Mark had used. "It's not a big deal. We can just erase it. That's the beauty of digital. No more expense of paying to process bad shots."

Mark wiped his hands on his thighs then shoved his hands in his back pockets to keep from touching anything else. "Yeah, I guess that could be a good thing." It had only been a little over a year, but he felt like so much had changed. Would he ever get caught up with all that he'd missed? "So, when should I start?"

* * *

"I'll take it."

"I need first and last months' rent up front." The landlord held out his hand.

Mark reached for his wallet. That would take almost all of his money. "Can I give you the first month and then give you the rest when I get my first paycheck?"

The landlord folded his arms across his ample chest and scowled. "I don't run no charity house here, buddy."

Mark forced a smile. "I realize that, sir. It's just that I'll need to eat in the meantime."

"Try the soup kitchen around the corner." The man rubbed his fingers together in the universal sign that meant money.

Mark, hands on his hips, surveyed the dingy walls and cracked floor tiles. Roach motels decorated the corners of the studio apartment. A layer of dust covered the windowsill and the glass was so smudged with dirt that the bright sunshine only supplied a dim murkiness to the room. A battered sofa matched with a scratched end table were on one end of the room, an old chest of drawers on the other. The dining area consisted of a rickety table and chairs pushed up against the wall by the kitchen.

The apartment was a shit hole. It galled him that the greasy little guy had the nerve to act like an ass. Mark's jaw tensed as he tried to check his anger.

"You know what? I just changed my mind. I think I'd be better off sleeping on the streets." He shoved his wallet back in his pocket and turned for the door.

"You ain't gonna find nothin' better if ya can't afford this."

Mark lifted his hand and waved it dismissively. Whatever. He was down the steps and had his hand on the door to leave when the landlord came puffing down the stairs.

"Wait. I'll let ya have it for the first month and only half the second month."

Mark released the doorknob. "First month's rent, and I'll paint the place, clean it up."

The guy cocked his head, considering. "You buying the paint and supplies?"

"We split the cost, but I get a hundred bucks off the second month's rent for my labor." Mark calculated that even with the price of the paint, he'd still be ahead. He didn't think he could live in the place looking like it did. The ugly, drab little room wasn't much better than his cell had been and in some ways, worse. At least the cell had been relatively bug-free.

"Fine."

Mark paid the agreed amount. "I can get started cleaning this afternoon. Is there a broom around?"

The landlord handed him a receipt. "I might have one in the basement. I'll check." He reached in his pocket and took out the key. "Here ya go."

The key warmed Mark's palm. He took a deep breath, easing it out as he squeezed the piece of metal. He had a home. Not much of one, but he had the key and he could come and go as he pleased. "Thank-you, sir."

* * *

The landlord had surprised him by dropping off not just the broom, but sponges, a bucket and a mop. The rest of the day, and into the night, he scrubbed walls, windows, and floors. Finally exhaustion and hunger brought him to a halt. Scrounging into his meager stocks he came up with a couple of peanut-butter and jelly sandwiches and a glass of milk, which he ate sitting on the floor so he could survey his progress. The window sparkled, the floor was clean, and the walls weren't quite so dingy, although they still needed paint. That would have to wait until the next night.

There were a number of things that would have to wait their turn and the list grew. He had taken so many things for granted his whole life. Now, he was happy for the sliver of soap he'd found stuck to the shower caddy. He should have thought to take the soap from the motel, but at least he had snagged the shampoo.

The mattress in the sofa bed looked suspicious so he slid the mechanism back and replaced the cushions. The couch would do just fine. It would feel as luxurious as a bed at a five-star hotel. Before settling in for the night, he went to the refrigerator and poured milk in his lone glass. Tilting his head back, he downed it in four satisfying gulps. Gasping, he swiped his arm over his upper lip, and grinned despite the brain freeze.

Easing down on the couch, he kicked his feet up, wrapped his coat around him and tucked his head into the crook of his arm. For the first time since his release, he slept through until morning.

Sun glinted through the windows, filling the apartment with a warm glow. He blinked at the brightness and rubbed his eyes. A surge of adrenaline shot through him. Today was his first day at work. The thought propelled him off the sofa, and he rummaged through the clothes in the dresser, pulling out his least faded jeans and a plain black sweater. He made a mental note to ask the super about the closest laundry facilities. It would be too much to hope there was one in the building, not that he was complaining. As an afterthought, he grabbed a clean pair of sweatpants to use as a towel. It was one more thing to add to the growing list of necessities.

After showering and shaving, he stood in the kitchen, a glass of milk in one hand, a granola bar in the other. As he crunched the bar, he gazed out the window onto the street below. Mornings in his loft, he'd often awakened early, catching the first rays of the sun as they gilded the waves on Lake Michigan. He'd loved that loft. By some stroke of luck, the view of the lake from his windows had been unimpeded. He missed sipping a cup of strong black coffee as the city stirred awake. It was his time to think, to let his creativity take flight as he planned the day's photo shoots. Taking the last bite of the bar, he washed it down with the milk.

Between getting the job and finding the apartment yesterday, he'd gone to his old apartment building. The super was a different guy, someone Mark had never met. The man had checked the records, and confirmed the eviction.

"It says here that since nobody came to claim the belongings, they were put on the curb."

"What about my car?"

The guy had simply shrugged.

"So, that's it? There's nothing left?"

"Sorry, buddy. It was all legal."

It was all gone. His apartment, his equipment, his photos, his business, his old life.

A taxi blasted its horn, and Mark started. He blinked, dragging in one long breath and then another. Life marched on. There was nothing to do but stumble along and deal with it. His earlier eagerness faltered with the memories. Trying to regain it, he glanced around the kitchen. Sure, it wasn't his old loft, but it was his new home and things could be a lot worse. He set about making sandwiches for lunch. Peanut butter and jelly was quick and cheap, and he rounded his meal with an apple, tossing it all in a bag.

His spirits perked up as he stepped into the crisp morning air and took a deep breath. Above the smell of exhaust and stagnant puddles scattered on the pavement from melting snow, came the scent of spring. Bicyclists sped past, seemingly unfazed by the early morning chill in the air.

A bike would be great. He wondered what had happened to the one that he'd kept in his loft storage area. He hoped it had gone to a kid. He mentally added a bike to his wish list. Food, shelter and clothing were the priority. He had those three now even if the clothing and food weren't in abundance.

After work, he'd stop at the store and get some more basics for meals. He planned to hit the thrift shop again, see if he could afford some sheets and towels. So much to do, so little time. It hit him how much he'd missed having plans. To having a purpose to each day. It was what life was all about.

The walk to the camera shop only took about twenty minutes. At an intersection, he stopped for traffic and took a moment to turn his face to the sun. It didn't have much heat, but the light against his eyelids warmed him. Opening his eyes, he smiled at an old lady waiting beside him. She scowled and tottered off the curb, muttering something about young people on drugs. His smile stretched to a grin. Life was good.

* * *

The next week passed quickly. During the day, he fed film into the processing machine, tended to customers and sold a few cameras. After work, he put a fresh coat of paint on the walls of the apartment. He painted one wall a deep blue, and the other three cream-colored. He'd found an area rug at the thrift store. It wasn't a necessity, but as he laid it on the floor in front of the sofa, he knew he'd been right to purchase it. Even with a couple of tattered corners, it added a homey air to the room. It was a cheap replica of an Afghan rug, which he thought somehow fitting. Or ironic. He wasn't sure which.

A week after moving in, he'd fallen asleep on the sofa while reading when he startled awake, disoriented and unsure of what had awakened him. The book he'd been reading slid from his chest to the floor. Nothing looked out of place, so he reached for the book, the movement freezing when someone pounded on the door. Heart thumping, he crossed the room but didn't touch the doorknob. "Yeah?"

Why wasn't there a damn peephole? He put an ear to the wood. It was silly to think that there'd be men in dark suits lurking in the hall.

"It's Bud. I came for the receipts."

Mark ran a hand through his hair as his heart settled to a normal rhythm. He opened the door. "Sure. Come on in while I get them." He strode to the dresser, opened the top drawer and withdrew an envelope.

"Jeezus, this looks damn good, Taylor." Bud touched the blue wall. "Not sure if I like the blue-it's gonna be hell to paint over someday-but, it looks good."

"Thanks. Here's the receipts. I deducted some of the stuff that I bought for myself." Mark pointed to where he'd subtracted the cost of a can opener and a few other things.

Bud shrugged. "I trust ya. Just tell me what I owe you."

Mark swallowed, feeling stupid for the gratitude that washed through him. "I circled it there at the bottom. It came to forty-three dollars."

"What'd you do? Steal the paint?" Bud chuckled as he flipped open his wallet.

"Uh...no, I got it cheap because it was a return. Not the right color for someone." Mark shuffled his feet and jammed his hands in his pockets. "It's all there on the receipt."

Bud paused as he counted out some bills. "I was just jokin'." He gave Mark a questioning look, then handed him the money. "All I have is two twenties and a five-"

"Sorry, I don't have change right now. I'll just run down to the mini-mart and get some." Mark knew without looking that he didn't have change. He'd spent his last two dollars on milk.

"Nah, don't worry about it." Bud waved him off. "Hey, I was thinking. You got any more of that paint?" He jabbed a thumb at the blue wall.

"Sure. It didn't take much to cover the one wall. Just a couple of coats. Why?" Mark put the bills in his wallet. Grocery money. He'd worked for himself for so long, it hadn't occurred to him that first paychecks were delayed a week or two. Now he could eat.

"I got another empty apartment below this one. You think you might be interested in painting it like this one?"

Surprised at the request, Mark shrugged. "I guess. I could probably paint it this weekend."

"Great! Same rate? A hundred bucks?"

The job was worth more, but it was money and he was desperate. Working around cameras every day was torture. His fingers itched to try them, and every moment he wasn't processing film, he played with the digital models. Gary had let him test one at a park and then uploaded the pictures to be printed. A few of the prints now decorated the shop. He wanted to save enough to buy his own, but at ten bucks an hour, it would take forever. "How about one twenty-five?"

Bud narrowed his eyes, but then grinned. "Deal."

After that, Bud called on him with other jobs. Mostly painting, but when he found out Mark knew a thing or two about photography, he asked him to take some pictures of the newly painted apartments to put in a brochure for the building. He even admitted that he'd been able to raise the rent on the units.

Some jobs, Bud paid him cash, others, he knocked a few bucks off the rent. Either way, Mark felt like he came out ahead. The weather eased from brutal cold to spring dampness, and when he wasn't working at the camera shop or fixing up apartments, he jogged. The freedom of running wherever he wanted never got old.

CHAPTER NINETEEN

Jim leaned back in his chair, gazing out at the Chicago skyline. Relief at getting through the first week as head of the new FBI Counter-terrorism task squad swept through him. The two months of preparation that had gone into accepting the position had been worth it. Standing, he plucked his suit coat off the back of his chair and draped it over his arm. It was too nice of a day to wear it home. The office was mostly empty, but he nodded to the few agents still putting in time at their desks.

A couple of guys nodded back, and one told him to have a nice weekend. Jim smiled in response. Maybe there was hope that they would eventually accept him. His reception by the agents had been guarded, and he'd sensed a bit of resentment that their task force was headed by a CIA officer. It made no difference to them that some CIA offices were headed by FBI agents. The cooperation between agencies wasn't new, but that didn't make it easier for the agents under his authority. He'd already discovered that FBI and CIA had different ways of looking at things, and he'd made a point of emphasizing that as strength in his first staff meeting.

The weekend loomed and he had absolutely nothing to do. Maybe he'd go out and have a big juicy burger at that pub he'd seen a few blocks from his apartment. The game was on and he'd be able to catch a few innings.

The pub wasn't busy and he took a seat at the bar. Sitting alone at a bar watching a game and eating a burger felt acceptable. Sitting at a table alone in a restaurant just made him look lonely. While he waited for his burger, he sipped a beer and ate peanuts from the bowl in front of him. Pool balls clacked from the back of the room. A game would be fun. Too bad he didn't have anyone to play against. He set his beer down and mopped up the condensation that had dripped onto the wood near his elbow. If the table became free, he could shoot a bit.

His dinner arrived and he bit into the burger. It was just as juicy as he'd hoped. A couple of guys near the end of the bar laughed about something. A group pushed through the front door and worked their way across the room. Law enforcement. Jim could peg them from a mile away from the way they carried themselves.

He observed them for a few seconds but then the sound of the crowd on the television caught his eye. The Cubs had a rally going and he forgot about the others in the room, so when he felt a tap on his shoulder, it took him a second to respond, and when he did, he jumped, rattling the silverware on his plate.

"Jim?" Jessica Bishop stood on his left, her arms crossed and eyebrow raised. "What are you doing here...again?"

"Detective Bishop." He wiped his mouth and hands with the napkin, and then put his hand out, noting her hesitation.

After a second, she shook his hand, but had to move in closer to allow the rest of her group to squeeze past them.

She stepped back and called over her shoulder to the retreating group. "I'll be there in a sec, order me a beer, okay?" She turned back to Jim. "You didn't answer me."

He sighed. "I don't think it's any of your business, but as it happens, I work in Chicago now."

She glanced around, then leaned forward and said in a quiet voice, "There's not a CIA office in Chicago."

Jim shook his head and took a swig of his beer. "I'm heading a task force in cooperation with the FBI here." He gestured to the empty stool beside him. "Would you care to sit and allow me to buy you a beer?"

Her lips thinned. "Why the hell would I want to do that?"

Wincing, Jim jerked his head down in a nod of acknowledgment. "I understand. My apologies." He pulled his wallet out and removed some bills, setting them on the bar near his empty plate. He'd intended to stay and watch the whole game, but the atmosphere no longer felt welcoming. "I'm sorry for keeping you from your friends."

Behind her, the group settled at a table. "They're co-workers; I wouldn't exactly call them friends." She looked like she was going to say something, but bit her lip instead and looked at the floor.

He waited for her to step back so he could go past her, but it was if she'd put down roots. "Excuse me, ma'am. I'd better be going."

"I thought you were going to help him."

Jim leaned against the bar, puzzled. "What do mean?"

"Helping Mark. When you were here last summer, you promised to see what you could do."

"I did." Jim shifted his weight. Taylor's written prediction had shaken him at the time, but the more he thought about it, the more he wondered how much had been a guess. Or a set-up. He didn't think Bill would do anything like that, but what of the others in the room? The photos could have been prearranged also. It made a hell of a lot more sense than the crap about a magical camera.

Her shoulders sagged. "I'm sorry. I shouldn't have expected that he would be released based on the images you saw. Not sure what else it would take." She gave him a hard look and turned to leave.

"He is free. What more do you want?"

"I don't understand." Her fingers tightened on her purse strap, the knuckles whitening.

He shrugged. "It's not a trick question. He got out a few months ago."

* * *

"Thank you, Mrs. Taylor. I'll be sure to let you know if I find out anything." Jessie set the phone back on the cradle and tapped the end of her pen against the ink blotter on her desk. Why did she even bother looking for the guy? Obviously, he didn't want to see her. If he had, he knew where she'd be.

Dan entered the office, a stack of files in his hands. She sighed and held out her hand for her share. So much for lunch hour. "Thanks."

He grinned. "Next time, say it with feeling."

Reluctantly, Jessie smiled. "Oh, shut-up."

With a wink in her direction, he sat and began sorting through the files. "So, what did you find out?"

She opened a folder, perused the contents and set it on the left side of the desk. "Mark came home, spent one night in Chicago, and then took a bus to his parents' house near Madison." Another folder joined the one on the left. "Apparently, he'd had no idea about his apartment, so when he got back, he had nowhere to go."

"Ouch. That's rough." Dan grimaced, his finger holding his place on a paper as he jotted a note down.

"Yeah. I'm sure it was. He spent about a week with his parents, but left after some kind of disagreement with his father. She's only had one phone call since. He said he had a job at a camera store and was doing fine."

"That's it?"

"Yep." Pausing in taking a note about one of her files, she added, "His mom didn't think he had much money; everything was frozen by the government, and there was no telling how long that red tape would take to clear. He refused to take any cash from her."

They fell silent as they each concentrated on cross-checking files for a case, but Jessie found it difficult. Where was Mark? Why hadn't he called her? She thought they'd begun something special. Was he okay?

"What are you going to do?"

Jessie glanced at Dan. "Pardon?"

"About Taylor. Are you going to find him?" For once, the man didn't have a teasing glint in his eye.

Trying to act unconcerned, she shrugged. "I shouldn't, but I promised his mother I'd find out what I could." She waited for him to get in a smart remark, but he didn't; he only nodded.

Thirty minutes later, Dan spoke again. "You know, he might not want to see you."

Jessie stacked her completed files, stood and crossed to the file cabinet, tossing over her shoulder, "Why wouldn't he?" Setting the stack on top of the cabinet, she turned towards Dan.

Dan wore a somber expression. "I had an older brother who was a prisoner of war in Vietnam." He held up his hand when Jessie began to tell him she was sorry about that. "Let me finish. When he came back, he didn't want to see any of his old friends, especially the female ones."

Jessie crossed her arms and shook her head. "That doesn't make sense. I'd think he'd want to re-connect."

He sighed and stacked his files. "You'd think, but he said once that he couldn't stand the pity in their eyes. I think there was more to it, but he never said much." Dan held out the stack and she stepped forward and took them, adding them to her own on top of the cabinet. "Eventually, he did marry and have a family, but it was rough at first."

She leaned against the cabinet, digesting his words. "Yeah, but Mark wasn't a prisoner of the North Vietnamese. I mean, he was held by his own country. It couldn't have been that bad...right?"

Dan turned his head and shrugged, his expression grim. "You saw the pictures."

* * *

Jessie debated for a week what to do, but finally decided to find Mark to give his mother some peace of mind. There were a couple of dozen camera shops in Chicago, but she only had to call four before she found him. Or rather, she spoke to the manager who confirmed that Mark worked there, but he was on his break. She thanked him and said she'd try again later. After hanging up, she noticed the address of the shop and felt the hairs on her arms rise. It was the same shop that she had used to develop the pictures from Mark's camera last summer.

An hour later, she stood in front of the shop, working up the nerve to enter. Should she force her presence on him? What if he'd changed? What if he was like Dan's brother? There was only one way to find out. She removed her sunglasses in the dim interior of the shop. Mark had his back to her, his attention focused on a customer examining a camera. He looked leaner than she recalled. His hair was longer too, but it looked good.

"Can I help you?"

To her right, she found the young man who had helped her the last time she had been in, when Jim had been with her. His eyes widened in recognition.

"Hey, I remember you." He stepped closer, his head bent as he said in a low voice, "I never told anyone about those photos, but if you have more like them, I'm afraid I'll have to refuse to develop them. I don't want to get mixed up in anything like that."

Jessie held up her hand in a stop gesture. "No, I didn't come for that reason. I'm actually here to see if I could get a moment to speak to Mark Taylor." She glanced at Mark, who held the camera in his hand and was pointing to something on it, angling it for the customer to see. He'd turned a fraction and she had a glimpse of his face. It was the same, but different. His skin was pale, and she recognized the prison pallor. The young man spoke and drew her attention back. She peeked at his name-tag. Gary.

"Sure. You know Mark?"

She hesitated a beat. "Yes. It's been awhile though." Mark was still unaware of her presence, and looked like he was wrapping up a sale. He set the camera on a counter and put it back in the box, showing the customer some manuals before placing them in the box as well.

"*Oh, shit.*"

Startled, Jessie turned towards the manager. "Excuse me?"

The guy blushed, but he also had the oddest expression on his face. "Now I know where I'd seen Mark before. It was *him* in those pictures."

She raised her chin, giving him a hard look. "I think you're mistaken...Gary."

He shot a wide-eyed look at Mark then back to her. "But—"

Jessie narrowed her eyes and Gary broke off and gulped.

Mark's voice rose as the customer crossed the shop to the front door. "You have any problems or questions, don't hesitate to come back in. Have a nice day."

Gary backed away, and then turned towards Mark. "Hey, Mark. Someone wants to see you."

Jessie watched as Mark wrote something down on a pad of paper, and then glanced up. His initial expression of curiosity turned to frozen shock.

She approached him. "Hi."

He didn't speak until she had come to a halt, the glass counter separating them. "Jessie." He nodded.

"How are you doing, Mark?"

"I'm okay. You?"

She'd received warmer greetings from the people at the DMV. Jessie searched his face until he averted it; his fingers drumming a rhythm on the counter top. "I'm good, but I'd like to talk to you." She gestured to the store. "It might be better to go somewhere a little more private."

"I can't. I'm working now and I already had my break." He reacted as if she had asked him to rip his fingernails off one by one.

Jessie nodded. "Right. What about later? Tonight?"

He braced his hands on the edge of the counter, his head down. For a long moment, he remained in that posi-

236

tion, and then looked at her, his face calm. "Sure. I'll meet you at O'Leary's Pub. You know where that is?"

"Yeah. What time is good?" She wished he'd show some emotion, but his face, after the initial shock, was blank. Impassive.

"I'm off at six. I can be there by seven-thirty."

"Sounds perfect. I'll get there a little early to get a table." She began backing towards the door then stopped. "Mark. I missed you." Without waiting for his reaction, she turned and hurried out the door.

CHAPTER TWENTY

The rest of the workday passed in a blur, except for an odd conversation with Gary. The guy had been giving him strange looks ever since Jessie had left. After the third time he'd caught Gary staring at him, Mark threw his pen down on the counter. "What? Do I have something hanging out of my nose?"

"No, I'm sorry. It's just that…well, now I remember where I've seen you before." He turned away and began sorting through customer film envelopes.

Mark waited to see if Gary would clue him in. A minute later, he stalked over to his manager and tapped his shoulder. "And? Ya got me curious."

Gary straightened and his face was a deep red. It could have been from leaning over, but his expression hinted at more than that. "I shouldn't have said anything. What I see in photos developed here is private stuff." He stopped and scratched the back of his head. "I've seen plenty, but I don't talk about it. I mean, it's like a lawyer/client relationship, right? It should never go beyond these walls."

Puzzled and irritated at the long-winded reply, Mark leaned back against the counter and folded his arms across his chest. "What the hell are you yapping about?" It was probably the wrong tone of voice to aim at his boss, but the guy was rambling.

Shoulders hunched, Gary evaded Mark's look. "I saw those kinky pictures."

"Now you've completely lost me." It had been a mistake to ask. He had enough to think about without having to add concern that his boss was losing his mind.

Gary gave a covert glance around the shop as though expecting to see spies lurking in the corners. Mark didn't know whether to be amused or angry. He braced for a sophomoric comment from the guy, and had a smart comeback ready to jump off the tip of his tongue.

"The pictures where you were chained and had someone pour water on your face."

Mark sagged against the counter as if he'd been sucker punched. The shock changed back to anger. He straightened, grabbing Gary by the front of his shirt. "Who showed you those pictures? Where'd you get them?" He gave Gary a firm shake, but not as hard as he wanted. He ached to rattle the teeth right out of the guy's head.

Gary's eyes became round, and he shoved away. "From that woman who was here earlier. She came in a couple of times, said it was police business. Even had some government guy with her." He straightened his clothes. "Hey, Mark, I don't care what you do on your own time. Just as long as everyone is willing and nobody gets hurt."

"You sonofabitch…" Mark raised his arm to grab Gary again, but when the guy flinched, it felt like bucket of ice water washed over him, dousing his anger. He wouldn't become a crazy monster who made people fear him. He took a deep breath, easing it out and willed his muscles to relax. Instead of getting angry, he should find out who had shown Gary the pictures. As embarrassing as Gary's presumption that it was a sexual thing, it was a good cover. "Look, I'm sorry." He forced a smile. "I guess I got carried away."

Gary straightened his collar and said, "No problem. I'm sorry if I embarrassed you."

"Not a big deal." Mark sighed and scrubbed a hand down his face. "Who was the government guy?" That part totally confused him.

"The second time she came in with film, there was an uptight guy who flashed a badge at me and made me swear not to tell anyone about the photos. That it was a big secret." Gary ducked his head. "That made it even...odder."

"Second time?"

"Yeah. The first time, instead of water, it was when you were doing some kind of bondage thing." Gary's face turned brick red.

"It wasn't a bondage thing...I was just...bound. But not for reasons you're thinking. Anyway, what was Jessie doing with the pictures?"

Gary didn't look at him, just shrugged and sorted newly processed photos. "You'd have to ask her."

* * *

Mark paused outside O'Leary's as a wave of nausea hit him. It was just Jessie. He squared his shoulders and entered the dim interior. At least he'd picked a location where he felt comfortable. He and Bud had taken to watching ball games and shooting pool here a couple of times a week. Blinking as his eyes adjusted, it was a moment before he spotted Jessie sitting at a table towards the back. She hadn't seen him yet, and he took the opportunity to drink in the sight of her.

She wore her hair pulled back and twisted into some kind of clip that allowed a few strands to trail down and brush her shoulders. It was sophisticated, yet soft and inviting. At that moment, she turned and spotted him. Their eyes locked. His heart thundered like the hooves of a racehorse in the homestretch, and he couldn't move until a waitress crossed between them, breaking the connection.

"Hey." It was all he could manage as he slipped onto the bench opposite her.

"Hi, Mark." She handed him a menu. "I waited to order. I didn't know if you wanted to eat or just have a drink."

"Are you hungry?" Nerves had stolen his appetite, but he figured he should eat anyway. He studied the menu.

"I don't know if I'm hungry. I think I'm too keyed up to eat." She chuckled and he looked up from the menu in surprise.

"What's got you all nervous?" He could think of lots of possibilities and none were good. Was she going to tell him that she was married? Had a steady boyfriend? Thought he was guilty?

She spun a coaster in circles with her index finger and watched it as though fascinated. "I don't know." She shrugged and flashed an embarrassed smile at him. "I guess I don't know what to say to you."

Mark understood what she meant, but understanding didn't make it easier to respond. He crossed his arms on top of the table and leaned forward, and looked at the television screen over the bar. Should he ask her how she'd been the last year and a half?

The silence between them stretched. Finally, afraid she'd leave, he cleared his throat. "Listen, I...I've never been good at small talk, and I'm out of practice. What do you say we just order a pizza? We can talk about that."

Biting her lip, she nodded. "Sounds like a plan."

They decided on sausage and mushrooms and a pitcher of beer. Mark poured for both of them when the beer arrived. "I didn't know you liked mushrooms."

She sipped hers, and a tiny bit of foam clung to her upper lip. When her tongue darted out to catch it, he shifted in his seat and tried to keep from staring and hoping for a repeat performance.

"Yeah, I'm not picky. Mushrooms are good. I draw the line at green peppers though."

Feeling safe with the topic, Mark smiled. "Really? What do you have against peppers?" He took a sip of his beer. He'd never been a big drinker, but he'd missed having one now and again. Mostly, he'd missed the social aspect, being with friends and relaxing.

Jessie made a face and shuddered. "Ugh. I can't even stand the smell. It makes me want to puke." She grinned at him. "Consider yourself warned."

"Noted. I'll be sure never to eat green peppers before kissing—" He broke off when her eyes widened and met his. Heat flooded his face. "I'm sorry. I guess I was back in the past." He couldn't look at her as he lifted his beer and gulped.

She turned in her seat. "I wonder when that pizza will get here? I'm starved."

"Yeah, me too."

The TV screen was a blur as he stared at it. He hated this. He hated the awkwardness and the stilted conversation. He hated making her feel uncomfortable. Deciding he'd rather just rip off the bandage rather than tease it off bit by bit, Mark took a deep breath and plunged into the topic that was foremost in his mind. "I completely understand if you've moved on in your life, so you can tell me. I just have to know." He searched her face, unable to read what she was thinking.

She played with an earring, her eyes averted. He took her silence for an affirmative and tried to quell the pain that swept from his chest through his body down to the bones in his hands. He couldn't blame her.

"I just want you to know that I never had any involvement with terrorists." Sitting back, he blew out a deep breath. There — it was out. A burden lifted. He rubbed his hands together, studying his fingers because he couldn't look at her. "All this time, it killed me that you might think that I had something to do with it. I...I just wanted you to know. And for what it's worth, the government finally figured it out too."

The waitress arrived bearing the pizza. She chirped on about how hot it was, to be careful, and if there was anything more they needed to let her know. Mark might have thanked her, but he couldn't have sworn to it. All he wanted to do was escape.

Jessie sat with her hands clasped around her glass, her eyes on the pizza, but she made no move to take a slice. "I never really thought you had anything to do with it, Mark." She tilted her head, running the fingers of one hand through her hair and gave him a tight smile.

"You...you didn't?" He wanted to believe her so badly, but he recalled when he'd seen her in the cell. Fear and doubt had been written all over her face. He'd never forget that. "What about in the cell? You said I should tell them what I know even after I said I didn't know anything."

She shook her head. "I was confused. What was I supposed to think? You'd been taken away, had already been gone weeks. The newspapers were calling you a terrorist—"

Mark sat back hard. "It was in the papers?" So, everyone in country probably thought he was a terrorist. He rubbed the heels of his hands against his eyes.

"I'm sorry. I thought you knew."

"Yeah, I guess I did. My dad mentioned something, but I didn't think much about it at the time." There had been too many other revelations that night at his parents' kitchen table.

"I hated myself for believing the papers. Then a CIA agent came and questioned me after you had been gone awhile. I don't think I gave him the answers that he was looking for, but he made me think. I asked myself how could you possibly be guilty?" Her eyes never left his face and he held her gaze like a falling man clutched a lifeline. She tilted her head and twisted the earring again. "I remembered the pictures you'd shown me from your Afghanistan trip. Nobody who cared that much could hurt someone."

Mark's throat convulsed and he swallowed to ease the tightness.

"So, I tried to find out where you were, but I couldn't. It was like you fell off the face of the earth. Eventually, even the newspapers stopped covering it. Your release didn't get even a small mention that I could see." Her bitter tone at the last bit surprised him.

He wiped his hands on his thighs. Another thought hit him. The pictures. "Is that where the pictures came from? The newspapers?"

She gave a little shake of her head, her eyebrows knit in confusion. "What are you talking about?"

Throwing a quick glance over his shoulder, he leaned towards her. "Gary—my manager at the camera shop—told me that you had pictures of me in, um..." He shrugged, embarrassed. "Well, he said bondage, but I'm guessing they're from when I was in the brig."

Mark hadn't seen the pictures, but he could imagine them. He tried to stop his leg from jumping, but it rattled the table. Sitting back, he swiped the back of his arm across his forehead. How the hell could he be sweating when it was like a damn freezer in here?

Jessie's eyes hardened along with her tone. "Yeah. I do have pictures. It's one of the things I wanted to talk to you about, but Gary wasn't supposed to say anything." She finished off her beer and poured more.

His body tensed as he waited for her to continue. Even his leg stilled.

"I'm the only one with those pictures. They weren't in the papers."

He closed his eyes, relief washing over him, but then he thought of another question. "But if they weren't in the papers...?"

"I happened to go by your old building on the day you were evicted." She picked at the edge of the pizza, eyes downcast.

He tried to ignore his embarrassment, and encouraged her. "And...?"

"There were boxes of your belongings out on the front lawn. I took what I could, mostly photography equipment. I saved it for you at my apartment."

Mark straightened in surprise. "You have some of my stuff?" That was the best news he'd had since getting out.

She nodded, and then shrugged. "I wish I could have saved more, but I fit as much as I could in my car, took it home, and when I came back, there wasn't anything left."

Mark smiled. "No, that's fine. Anything is better than nothing, which is what I thought I had." He started to grab a slice of pizza, and then stopped. "But that doesn't explain the pictures."

"In one of the boxes was an old camera. I think it must have been overlooked or something. One day, I needed a camera to take pictures of my niece at a dance recital and I couldn't find mine. Yours was sitting right there, and I was in a hurry." She blushed. "I didn't think you'd mind, so I borrowed it."

He eased back against the seat, holding his breath.

"The pictures were fine, except for the last few. Those ones showed you chained." Her eyes flicked to his before sliding away.

Beer washed up in the back of his throat, and he stumbled out of the booth. "Excuse me." He rushed for the bathroom, and made it just in time to for the beer to hit the toilet bowl. When he stopped heaving, he used some toilet paper to wipe his face. Shaking, he staggered to the sink and washed his hands, leaned on the counter until the trembling subsided. He couldn't go back out there. Did she figure out what had happened? Is that why he'd had the dreams in the brig too? Mark grabbed some paper towels and wet them before running them over the back of his neck.

After a few moments, he tossed the paper towels in the trash and returned to the booth. Jessie had taken a slice of pizza, but hadn't bitten into it yet.

She angled her head so that he couldn't avoid looking at her. "Mark? You're pale. Are you okay?"

He nodded and grabbed some pizza and put it on his plate. "I'm fine. Guess I shouldn't drink on an empty stomach." He tried to smile, but it felt fake, and he was sure it didn't fool her.

"You only had one glass of beer." She took a bite of the pizza.

"Is it any good?" He ignored the remark and nodded towards the pizza.

She wiped her mouth with a napkin. "Yeah. Great."

He forced himself to take a bite. It was good, and he took another bite, washing it down with ice water. "So, how are you doing? Anything new going on with you?" Not only did he want to change the subject, he wanted small talk. He craved normal conversation.

As if sensing his need, Jessie began talking about her niece, Chicago politics and sports. They finished off the pizza and he felt better. Braving a second glass of beer, he took a sip. He didn't want the evening to end despite how hard it had been.

Jessie pushed her plate away and folded her arms on the table. "So, now I've seen first-hand the powers of your camera, which, by the way, I have right here." She reached down to the floor and retrieved the camera, setting it on the table.

Mark recoiled. "I don't want it. Why the hell would you think I'd want it back?"

Her eyes lit with excitement. "Yeah, it's scary, but it's also amazing. You, of all people, know how powerful this is. Now I know how you managed to get involved with all those crazy things." She fiddled with the lens. "I never had any dreams though."

He cleared his throat and said in a low voice, "That's because I did."

"You had the dreams?" Her eyes widened, and she said, "You dreamed what was in the pictures before it happened."

Speaking of it made the visions pop back into his head and he wasn't sure what was a memory of the dream, and what was the real thing. Not that it mattered. Both had been terrifying. He nodded, looking everywhere but at her.

"Oh, Mark. I'm so sorry. I didn't know."

He shrugged. "It's over now. I just want to forget it." He glanced over his shoulder.

"You expecting someone?"

"Huh?"

Jessie pointed down the aisle. "You seem to be looking for someone."

"No. Just thought I heard someone call my name." Mark tried to ignore the compulsion to check to see if anyone was listening.

"Okay." Her brow knit and she didn't look convinced. "After seeing those pictures, I worried even more about you. Did you tell your lawyer what they did to you? That they tortured you?"

His leg twitched. "Listen, I was treated just fine. I wasn't tortured." A sheen of sweat coated his palms and he wiped them on his thighs. "Can we just stop talking about it?"

Shock registered on her face. "I saw those pictures, Mark. Even Jim Sheridan didn't deny it when he saw the photos."

"Jim Sheridan? How the hell do you know him?" This second shock threatened to send him rushing to the bathroom again.

"He came to Chicago last summer and questioned me. I...I showed him the camera." She bit her lip.

"Shit." So, for months, Jim had known and hadn't revealed that information. No, instead he'd led at least a dozen more interrogations. The bastard.

"I'm sorry. I was trying to help. I figured if I showed him, proved to him that you had been telling the truth all along, that they'd set you free."

Sincerity was written all over her face and he couldn't be angry for her attempts on his behalf. "It's okay."

"But I still think you should get a lawyer." Her mouth set in a stubborn line.

"No! I can't talk about it. Don't ya understand?" His breathing quickened and he fought the urge to flee the bar. "I don't want to go back there."

Jessie cocked her head and reached across the table, taking one of his hands in hers. "Did they threaten you with that?"

Mark kept his mouth closed, feeling muscles in his jaw jump. He didn't answer but instead looked at their intertwined hands. Hers felt soft and warm and she rubbed one up his forearm. Clear nail polish coated the short neat nails. The contact felt wonderful, but, when he looked up, the pity in her eyes doused the feelings of warmth that had begun to stir.

"Listen, Mark. They won't lock you up again."

He pulled his hand free and crossed his arms. "You don't know that. They did it once, they can do it again."

She shook her head. "They made a mistake."

"Maybe, but it was a helluva mistake and took them over a year to fix it." Leaning forward, both hands braced on the table edge, he went on, in a low, harsh voice, "For all I know, this might all be some kind of trick. One of their sick twisted methods of control. I don't even know who I can trust anymore."

Jessie sat forward, mirroring his posture, her tone low but firm, "Now you're sounding paranoid, Mark."

He gave a short sarcastic chuckle and looked towards the door of the pub. Shaking his head, he tried to form a reply. In her mind, his fears probably seemed overblown. "Yeah, guess I do sound paranoid. But, I think I have a damn good reason to worry."

"I guess you do have good reason, but I don't see the government letting you go just to play a cruel trick."

Mark shrugged, still unable to look at her, and they fell into an uneasy silence.

"You trust me, don't you?"

He turned to her ready to say yes, but hesitated. Mohommad had been a friend. Someone he'd trusted. He'd trusted his country too. But this was Jessie.

Before he could answer, she said, "Is that why you didn't call me when you got out?" She sounded hurt.

This time he took her hand in his. "No...no. I do trust you, Jessie. And I did call you once, but I got your voice mail. I couldn't see leaving a message. For all I knew, you could have been married by now."

A soft smile dawned on her face. "Nope. Not married."

Even though he'd guessed she wasn't, a feeling of lightness fill him at her confirmation.

She looked at her watch. "I'm sorry. I have to get going. I have an early meeting scheduled in the morning."

Mark nodded and pulled out his wallet.

She waved him off when he attempted to look at the check. "No, my treat. I invited you."

"I've got money."

"Yes, but I know times are tough for you now."

"Listen, I don't need your damn charity or your pity." He pulled some bills out of his wallet and threw them on the table. "That should cover the tab." He rose, backing away from the booth, but stopped, unable to leave like this. Stepping up to the table, he leaned over and brushed his lips over hers in the briefest of kisses. "Sorry. I just had to do that. It's been good seeing you again, Jessie."

CHAPTER TWENTY-ONE

Mark stirred the scrambled eggs, scraping the cooked portions from the bottom of the pan. The toaster popped, and he snatched the slices and buttered them before they could cool.

The pan and the toaster had both been recent purchases at the thrift store. His kitchen was now stocked with a hodge-podge of plates, cups and silverware. Tilting the pan, he scooped the eggs onto a plate. In the brig, he had vowed to never eat scrambled eggs again, but eggs were cheap. Finances won out over aversions, and after the second or third time, they started tasting good again. As he added the toast to the plate, there was a knock on the door.

He glanced at the clock, figuring it must be Bud. He was the only person who ever stopped by, but he wondered what had made the landlord get out of bed before ten o'clock on a Saturday morning. Maybe Bud had another apartment that needed painting. Mark hoped so. His wallet could sure use some extra padding. He sucked a buttery crumb off his finger as he opened the door. "Hey Bu —"

"Hello, Mark."

"Jessie?" He wiped his fingers on his pants and stepped forward, pulling the door partially closed so that his body filled the threshold. "How'd you find me?"

She smiled. "I'm a detective, remember?" She held a box, and shifted her weight, hiking the box up to get a better grip.

"Yeah, but, I mean, why are you *here*?" Stunned, he blurted out the first thing that came to his mind. The hurt in her eyes made him cringe. "Sorry. I'm just surprised."

Jessie ducked her head and nodded. When she lifted it, her face had a pleasant, overly bright smile. "That's okay. I had a couple of reasons for stopping by. May I come in?"

The paint job and rug had helped make the room livable, but they couldn't work miracles and he felt heat creeping into his face. "Uh, sure." He moved back, allowing her to get past him. "Come on in."

Her smile warmed. "Thanks." She crossed to the sofa and set the box on it. Flexing her fingers as she glanced around, she nodded at the wall. "Nice shade of blue. And something smells wonderful."

"I just made some eggs...want some? There's plenty." He hated the note of eagerness that had crept into his voice. It made him sound needy, but he did have plenty of eggs.

"Oh no, I'm not hungry, but you go ahead and eat." A suspicious gurgle sounded loud in the room, and her hand flew to her stomach as her eyes went wide.

He grinned. "You sure you're not hungry?"

Her face turned crimson, but she laughed. "Guilty. I lied. I'm starving and it smells great in here."

"Have a seat." He gestured to the table just outside the kitchen. "I'll just stick some more bread in the toaster." He went to the kitchen before she changed her mind. After putting the toast down, he opened the fridge, and ducked his head in to see how much juice he had left. Satisfied there was enough to offer, he turned to ask if she wanted that or milk, but found her right behind him, her mouth level with his. All it would take was for him to lean forward just a fraction, and he could kiss her. He fought the impulse. She didn't need someone like him in her life.

Her face flushed, but she held ground for a second. Eyes wide, they flashed to his before she averted hers and stepped towards the sink. "I...I just wanted to wash my hands first." She spread her fingers and held them up.

He cleared his throat. "Right. Go ahead. I was just wondering what you wanted to drink. I have O.J. or milk."

"Orange juice sounds good." She dried her hands on a dishtowel, folded it, and set it neatly on the counter.

The toast popped while he was pouring two glasses. Before he could react, she reached over and began buttering the slices. The simple domestic act made him catch his breath. He shook it off. Long suppressed emotions bubbled inside, seeking exit, but he held on tight.

She looked around for somewhere to set the toast, and raised her eyes to his, questioning.

The cabinet where he kept his plates was right behind her, so he stepped close and reached over her head.

Her arm skimmed against his chest as she turned to see what he was doing. A shiver swept through him at the contact, and he almost dropped the plate.

She skirted around him, putting the toast on the plate as she went. "Sorry. I guess I'm in the way."

"No. You're fine."

After brushing her hands together, she shoved them in the front pockets of her jeans. The action pulled her blouse tight and he had to drag his eyes away.

Her quick retreat to the other side of the kitchen didn't escape his notice. Trying to recover his composure, he took the pan off the stove and added the rest of the eggs to the new plate. "Come on, let's go eat while it's still hot." His voice was gruffer than he intended.

Nodding, she took the plate he offered. He tore a couple of paper towels off the roll to use for napkins, grabbed the glasses of juice, and followed her around the corner to the table.

She took a bite. "This is good, Mark."

"Thanks." He shrugged. "It's just eggs." Pleasure surged through him at her compliment. It wasn't just about the food. It was how she glanced around the apartment with interest, and not a hint of condescension, or worse, pity. She might not want to be close to him, but at least she had stayed to eat with him.

Jessie sipped her juice. "So, to answer your earlier question, I came by with some of your stuff I told you about."

"My stuff?" He dropped his fork on the plate with a clatter and shot a look at the box. With all the things they had talked about that night at O'Leary's, he'd forgotten that she had mentioned rescuing some of his things.

"Most of it's there. There are a couple of lenses that were cracked. Since the box was full, I left them at my place. I can bring those by another time."

He didn't have money to repair cracked lenses so they could wait, but he'd grab at any excuse to get her to come by again, so he just nodded. "That would be great."

His leg bounced, jostling the juice and rattling his fork on the plate. It was all he could do to remain seated, so badly did he want to tear through the box right then and there. He took another bite of eggs, but he was no longer hungry. Instead, he felt like a kid on Christmas morning and couldn't keep from sneaking peeks at the box as they continued eating.

She laughed. "Go ahead and look. I won't be offended to be left finishing my meal alone." Another smile took any possible sting out of the comment.

"I'm sorry…it's just…well, it means a lot to me." How to explain to her that it was more than just some photo equipment? It was like getting a part of himself back.

Mark jumped up from the table and reached the sofa in two long strides. He lifted the box and set it on the floor as he sat on the edge of the couch. His heart raced and he had to wipe his hands on his thighs. With a deep breath, he tugged the top off. Several of his cameras lay inside. He held one. It was the camera he used most and he blew some dust off the lens. The weight of it in his hands felt wonderful. So familiar. So natural. The strap hung loose and he put it around his neck, feeling it settle into the usual spot.

A surge of emotion swept through him, catching him off guard. His hands shook and he clutched the camera in a death grip. He heard Jessie get up and approach, but he couldn't look beyond the camera in his hands. It was no more than a dark, watery shadow and his throat tightened. Blinking hard, he attempted to say thank you to her, but his voice failed him.

The couch creaked as she sat on the arm of it, and a second later, he felt her hand on his back. Without uttering a word, she rubbed slow circles, her hand warm even through his t-shirt. He pretended to work at some smudges with his thumb. After a few minutes, he lifted the camera from around his neck, set it on the table, and removed another. It was an older one he hadn't used often, but below that, wrapped in dish towels, were some of his lenses. He smiled. With them and his favorite camera, he could begin to take on a few photo jobs. It would be tough, with so many photographers switching to digital, but it was a start.

He cleared his throat, and this time, he was able to speak. "Thanks, Jessie." It was too soon to look at her yet. He didn't trust his emotions that much. "This is...it's fantastic."

"You're welcome." She squeezed his shoulder.

There were two more towel-wrapped bundles in the box. The first was his long lens. Excitement surged through him, and he grinned. Now he was truly in business. He had all the basics. As he picked up the last bundle, Jessie's hand tightened on his shoulder. Not a lot, but he felt her tension.

It was the camera. He knew it. Even wrapped in the cloth, the thrum of energy seeped into his hands. His brain screamed at him to drop it, but even as that command shot into his mind, his hands tore the towel off, as if seeking to get closer to the energy. "Damn it, Jessie!"

"Mark—"

Anger and fear gave his voice a hard edge as he cut her off. "I said I didn't want this one. Why the hell did you bring it?"

Revulsion battled with an overwhelming attraction and he couldn't let the camera go. Or wouldn't let go. He wasn't sure which. His fingers betrayed him and skimmed over the surface, tracing edges and flicking a speck of dirt off the steel rim around the lens.

"What was I supposed to do with it?"

"Get rid of it. Trash it. I don't care." He shrugged her hand off and stood, giving the camera a shake. "What am *I* supposed to do with it?"

Jessie crossed her arms. "I don't care, Mark. You can toss it in the garbage for all I care." She straightened, standing in front of him, her eyes boring into his. "I don't think I have the right to decide its fate."

"And you think I do?" He laughed, short and harsh. "You want to know about rights? I'll tell ya about rights. If I

256

use this damn thing again, I can kiss all my rights goodbye. Again."

"You don't know that."

"It doesn't matter. I can't take that chance."

She looked from the camera to him and shrugged. "I can't tell you what to do with it. It's just that the second you touched that thing, your whole body gave off a...a jolt of energy or something." She held his gaze. "It didn't do that for me."

Mark broke eye contact, hating that he thrilled at the rush of electricity shooting up his arm. "I feel it, but..." His body hummed, just like it had the first time he'd touched the camera. Eventually, he'd become used to the energy or had learned to control it. Overwhelmed and unsure, he sank onto the couch, and even as he cursed the camera, he cradled it against his stomach. "If I use this again, they could lock me up—just like before."

It surprised him to see tears on her face as she nodded. "Maybe. But maybe not."

"I can't risk it." He finally pried it out of his hand and set it in the box. "Do you know what it's like to lose every single right you ever had?"

She shook her head and sat beside him, her hand returning to his back. It felt good.

"Forget about liberty and the pursuit of happiness. That was history. Even the right to life was on pretty shaky ground." Mark gave a bitter laugh, then scrubbed his hands down his face, letting his arms drape across his knees.

Her arm reached towards his opposite shoulder, and she pulled him close in a quick sideways hug, her head resting on his shoulder.

He turned his face, catching the scent of her hair. Clean and fresh, the sun lit the strands. Her eyes were

257

closed, the dark lashes contrasting with her hair. When she opened them, she looked straight into his eyes, not moving her head.

Shifting, he twisted, one arm going behind her, resting on her waist. He brought his other hand up to stroke her face, looping her hair behind her ear. Her skin felt soft and warm, and he never wanted to stop touching it.

Her tongue darted out, wetting her lips, and when she dropped her gaze to his mouth, he was lost. He moved his hand up to cradle her head, tangling his fingers in her hair. He lowered his mouth to hers, tasting. So sweet.

Jessie returned the kiss, and he felt the heat of her hand on his jaw and groaned, pulling her closer. She drove him crazy as she slipped her hand under the back of his shirt. She reclined, pulling him along with her, their mouths losing contact, but he found new territory on her neck as he balanced one foot on the floor and his other leg straddled her, his knee buried behind the sofa cushions.

She arched her back, exposing her throat, and he followed the line of her collar, kissing a path down. She moved her hand from his back to his hair, sending delicious shivers coursing through him. He needed to touch more of her. Needed her skin against his. He skimmed his fingers down her throat, just under the edge of her blouse. Her clothing barred his way, and he touched the front of her shirt, fingers poised on the first button.

Her breath, ragged and fast, matched his own, and he stopped before undoing the button, searching her face for permission. She nodded and reached to pull him down, tugging his shirt over his head.

He had to pause to regain control when her hands traced his chest. Nothing had ever felt so good. Leaning forward, he caught her lips again, and then moved his mouth

258

up, trailing kisses over her cheek, to her forehead and hair, drinking in the taste and scent of her. She smelled of sunshine and oranges. She found a sensitive spot just below his ear and he shivered as her warm breath blew over the dampness left from her tongue.

Mark swallowed hard, and pulled away, before returning to nuzzle her neck, his hand working at the buttons on her shirt. Her bra had front closure and he smiled against her skin at his good fortune as he unsnapped it. She shuddered when he moved the cups out of the way.

He gave a growl of frustration when the back of the sofa got in the way of his attempt to remove her shirt completely. With a smile, she pushed him up, then stood and pulled her blouse off. With smile and a raised eyebrow, she reached for the quilt draped over the back of the sofa, and spread it over the carpet, and lay down on it.

The rest of the morning passed in a haze. After the first time, they lay panting, and he could have died right then and been happy. He might have dozed for a minute, but she shivered, waking him.

He rose on one elbow. "Are you cold?"

"Just a little."

He got up and retrieved his other blanket from the closet. They snuggled beneath it with him spooning her, his arm bent, and her head rested on the angle of his elbow. He rested his cheek on her shoulder.

"Your chin is scratching me."

"That's because I didn't shave this morning."

"Bum."

Mark chuckled. "Yeah, but if I'd have known you were going to come over and seduce me..."

"I didn't seduce you!"

She glared at him over her shoulder, but broke into a grin when he quirked his mouth and said, "If you say so. I was just minding my own business."

* * *

Jessie took a deep breath and stretched, her muscles protesting the hard floor beneath her. Mark still dozed, his breathing slow and even, one arm draped across his face, blocking out the bright sunlight. She curled against him and ran her hand up his belly, smoothed it over his warm skin, up over his ribcage. She scooted up to rest her head in the cradle of his shoulder, and turned her head, kissing his collarbone. He stirred, his arm falling to his side, but after a couple of deep breaths, he settled again.

She didn't know how he could sleep so soundly. Her left hip ached from the pressure of the floor and if she didn't get up soon, she'd be walking like a ninety-year old for a few days. Smiling, she nibbled a trail to the top of his shoulder. His skin smelled of soap, something clean and spring scented. She pressed into his side to kiss the side of his neck. Despite her complaint about his stubble, it looked sexy on him. The square jaw helped, she supposed.

She had never seen him this relaxed and took the moment to study his profile. His eyelashes were ridiculously long and thick. It wasn't fair. His nose straight, cheekbones to die for, and she glanced down to his chest, with a ripped body to boot. Nope. Some things were just not fair. Not that she was complaining. Grazing her fingers over his chest, she snickered when he squirmed in his sleep. His eyes fluttered open. Green. Definitely more green than brown.

His mouth curved as he gave her a lazy grin. "Hey." He arched his back, stretching. She swallowed at the play of muscles, enjoying the sight until he relaxed again with a contented sounding sigh, and turned to put his other arm over her.

"You okay?" He smoothed her hair back from her face, and she snuggled closer.

"I'm still hungry." Jessie let her hand drift down his abdomen, feeling his stomach tighten in response.

The concern in his eyes evaporated and the corners crinkled into an eye smile. "I think I can take care of that."

"Yeah? You think?"

"Absolutely."

He nuzzled her neck, and when he reached her ear, she couldn't take the exquisite torture anymore, and raised her shoulder, wriggling away with a gasp. "Aren't we...we confident." She tried to stifle another gasp he moved his hands down her body.

"Do you ever stop bickering?" His tone was playful and then his mouth moved lower, and Jessie did stop bickering.

* * *

Thirty minutes later, she pushed his shoulder. "Get up. This floor is killing me."

Mark turned onto his stomach with a groan.

Sitting, she rolled her shoulders. "Hey, I really am hungry."

Mark folded his arms, using them for a pillow, as he looked at her. "Yeah. I could use some food." He smiled. "I guess our breakfast is cold and rubbery by now."

Jessie stood, tugging the blanket off Mark to wrap it toga style around her. He didn't seem to notice that he was lying naked. Or didn't care. He watched her, an appreciative gleam in his eyes. Feeling shy, she lifted her chin and wrapped the blanket tighter. "What are you staring at?"

He just smiled and said, "You're amazing, know that?"

A blush heated its way up her face and to cover her mixture of embarrassment and pleasure at his words, she nudged him in the ribs with her toe. "Get up, lazy bones. We're going to get some lunch."

He popped up from the floor as if a firecracker had exploded beneath him, the smile stretching into a grin. He grabbed his clothes and began getting dressed. "Sounds great. I'm starving."

She had to laugh at his sudden change of demeanor, even as her face heated and she averted her eyes. "First, I need to go to the bathroom."

Her clothes lay scattered, and after gathering them, she left the room. A few seconds later, she heard the coffee table slide back into place, followed shortly by the clatter of dishes in the sink.

After taking care of business, Jessie dressed and ran her fingers through her hair. Her clip was long gone, probably under the sofa by now. Mark had a comb sitting on the vanity, and she reached for it, but hesitated. After what they had just shared, she was sure he wouldn't mind her using it, but she felt awkward. Should she ask first? What was he going to say? No?

After fixing her hair, she helped herself to his mouthwash. In for a dime, in for a dollar. She emerged to find him sitting on the sofa tying his shoes. He must have used the kitchen sink to freshen up because his hair was damp, like he'd run wet fingers through it.

"Ready to go?"

He stood. "Yeah." In the space of time it had taken them to get ready, his air of playfulness had dissipated, and he skimmed a hand through his hair, leaving a few strands sticking straight up before they fell back into place.

Jessie noted that his nerves seemed to match hers. What was next for them? She saw that the camera was on the couch. She took a deep breath and pointed her chin towards it. "How about we take that along?"

His eyes widened. "I—I don't think so." He shoved his hands in his pockets. "Not yet."

CHAPTER TWENTY-TWO

The next few weeks were the best of Mark's life. Every minute he and Jessie weren't working, they spent together. Mark didn't have a phone at his apartment, so Jessie began stopping by the camera shop on her lunch and they would make plans for the evening. More often than not, they ended up either at his apartment or hers. His sofa-bed wasn't very accommodating, and the floor lost its charm after the first few times. Before long, he was spending most nights at her place.

One evening, Jessie lay on the couch, watching television, and he sat down, lifting her feet onto his lap. "I was wondering...would you mind if I used the second bathroom as a darkroom once in a while? It already has a vent to the outside, and I'd buy all the stuff, of course. I want to be prepared, in case...in case..."

"You thinking of using the camera again?"

He stroked a hand up her calf absently, and shrugged. "Maybe."

"Sure. I guess so."

Mark nodded. "Thanks." He felt the weight of her gaze and pretended not to notice. Just because he wanted a place to develop the pictures didn't necessarily mean he was going to actually use it again. A commercial blared, and he reached for the remote and began flipping through the channels, not really paying attention to any that he stopped on.

"Have you thought about giving up your apartment?"

Mark paused in his channel surfing, surprised at the question. "And move in here?"

"It doesn't make sense for you to keep paying on that apartment and half the time, you're not there. Plus, well, the darkroom will be here." She turned towards the TV and pulled her feet off his lap.

He cursed his stupidity. Here she was offering her home to him and he'd acted like the thought had never occurred to him. He'd embarrassed her. "Jessie."

She blinked but kept her eyes riveted on the program.

"Jess...could you look at me?" He reached for her feet again, giving a toe a playful tweak.

Her face impassive, she turned her face to him. "Yeah?"

"I'd be honored."

* * *

"Done with that?" When Jessie nodded, Mark added her plate to the armful of dirty dishes, and carried them to the sink. The dark room was finished, and he'd returned his keys to Bud, who had acted sorry to see him go. Mark had promised to call to go out for a beer now and then and he meant it. He'd learned his lesson about losing touch with friends. As he rinsed the plates, he looked over his shoulder. "I got a couple of photography jobs."

"Really? That's wonderful!" She beamed at him over the rim of her coffee cup.

He shrugged, but couldn't quite smother the smile that tugged at the corners of his mouth. "They don't pay much, but it's a start. Gary suggested me when a woman came into the shop and mentioned looking for a photographer for a small wedding. "

"It's a great start. Soon, you'll be back to how you were before."

Mark wrung out the sponge, giving it a harder than needed twist. "Yeah. Maybe." Bending his head, he scrubbed the baking sheet. When would every mention of the past stop hurting?

A minute or so later, Jessie's hand reached into the sink and caught his. "Mark. Stop. You're going to ruin the finish on that."

He blinked. "Sorry. There was some chicken stuck to it."

She took the sponge out of his hand. "I'm sorry I said anything about the past, but we can't keep tiptoeing around it."

"Who asked you to?" Mark snatched the sponge and began wiping the counters. He heard her sigh, but ignored it. "You can talk all you want about the past. Hell, I can talk about it if you want."

"Right."

He glanced up at her skeptical tone. She leaned against the counter, arms crossed and eyebrow quirked. He flung the sponge into the sink. "What do you want to know?"

"What were the other inmates like?"

"I have no idea. I never saw any others."

Surprise showed on her face and she dropped the tough stance. "Ever?"

"Nope. It was just me and the guards." He grabbed the roll of paper towels, tore off a few and turned to dry the counters. "They weren't too chatty." His attempt at humor died as the remembered loneliness swept over him. "I saw a doctor occasionally, and a few times, a chaplain came by. He was nice." Ducking his head, he used his thumbnail to scrape a drop of barbecue sauce off the counter. "And Jim and Bill, of course. Saw them more than I wanted to." Lost in memories, he stopped scraping and stared at the slate gray stone beneath his hand.

"Mark, you don't have to say any more. I'm sorry." She'd lost the skeptical note.

He snapped back to the present and shrugged. "It's not a big deal." Wadding up the paper towels, he sought a change of subject, throwing out the first thing he could think of. "Getting back to photography, I was thinking of using my camera again. Just a few times."

Jessie stopped in the act of filling the soap dispenser in the dishwasher and straightened, box still poised. "Your special camera? Seriously?"

Mark nodded, not sure when he had made the decision to use the camera again, but the feeling had been building ever since he'd held it, and now that he'd said it out-loud, a surge of excitement shot through him. "Not every day. I have to work, but I have a few days off a week. If something comes up, maybe I can make a difference."

* * *

Mark slid out of bed, careful not to disturb Jessie. Today was the day. He stretched and rolled his shoulder, wincing as it popped. The dream to match the picture was still fresh in his mind. He'd wondered if the dreams would still come, but now he had his answer.

"Are you going?" Jessie scooted up in bed, the t-shirt she wore, one of his, slipping off her shoulder

He was tempted to say he hadn't dreamed any details and return to bed. After hiding the magic of the camera for two years, and then being punished for using it, his first instinct was to deny what he was planning on doing. But this was Jessie. She knew all his secrets.

"I figured I'd go. It couldn't hurt to at least see if I can change it." There. He'd committed.

She held his gaze until Mark had to shift his focus. They'd discussed it, and he knew she'd support him if he put the camera down forever, but he knew she wanted him to use it if he could.

He grabbed his clothes out of a drawer, setting them next to the camera. The thrill of using it yesterday still simmered inside of him, and he picked it up, shivering at the hum of energy that coursed up his arms. It felt odd, but pleasant, like a warm tickle in his muscles.

Jessie caught his eye in the mirror. "You want me to go with?"

Mark had thought about asking her to go with him. He'd love nothing more than to have her along to push him to use it, but he had to know if he could do it on his own so he shook his head. "No. I gotta do it myself." He set the camera down and rummaged for his socks.

The bedsprings creaked followed by the soft slap of Jessie's feet on the hardwood floor. She hugged him from behind and planted a kiss between his shoulder blades. "You'll be fine, but if you need anything, I'll be here."

He swallowed and his voice was rough when he said, "I know."

* * *

An hour later, he trotted down the EL platform steps and headed west. His photos had shown a warehouse engulfed in flames, but even worse, in his dream, he'd seen two people trapped inside the building. Two blocks later, he turned north. The area teemed with warehouses, but the one he sought sported a faded red logo on the side. It might have been a cardinal at one time, but the elements had turned it into nothing more than a faint outline. It was still easy to spot and he tried the front door. Locked. Of course.

The dream had omitted a key piece of information—where the fire would start. Without that, Mark could only guess. He circled to the back, skirting around an overflowing Dumpster. Pot holes filled with stagnant water dotted the pavement, and he swore when he stepped in one and flooded his shoe. Shaking his foot, he approached the deserted loading dock. Where the hell was everyone?

"Hello?" Silence. Mark swung up onto the cement block. There had to be somebody around. At least the two who were in his dream should be somewhere about. The large door was closed, so he tried a smaller one beside it. It opened, and Mark chalked one up in his favor as he stepped into the dim interior. His earlier jitters settled into a low hum of energy. The cavernous room was empty except for broken boxes and trash littering the floor. His footsteps echoed and dust motes clogged the air as he crossed to a door on the far side of the room.

Smoke. More than just dust filled the air—some of it was smoke. Tendrils licked around the base of the door. He touched the wood. It was warm, but not hot. This door had been in the dream and he was sure he could open it without facing flames. Still, he cringed when he pushed it open.

He coughed at the first blast of heat and smoke. His eyes watered and he crouched as he went left.

"Hey! Anybody in here?"

"Help!"

The cry came from directly behind him, and Mark spun. "Where are you?"

"We're stuck in here!"

The voice came from behind a heavy metal door. Mark tried the doorknob. "It's locked!"

He scanned the hall for anything he could use to pry open the door.

"We hid in here when the watchman came by this morning, now we're locked in. There's a crowbar behind the door by the loading dock. Hurry!" Coughing punctuated the instructions.

Mark raced back the way he'd come, looked behind the door and found the tool. When he reached the door, a fit of coughing overtook him and he crouched for a few seconds, hoping the clearer air close to the floor would ease his breathing.

Straightening, he jammed the flat end between the door and the jamb and pushed. He groaned with the strain. The door wouldn't budge.

Sweat ran into his eyes and he swiped his forearm across his forehead before bending to grab another lungful of air to try again. The latch broke with his second effort and he had to catch himself before he fell into the room.

The men rushed past him, and Mark staggered after them, but when they got outside, he didn't stop to chat, he just handed one the crowbar and kept walking. His throat burned and getting a drink of water was his second priority. His first was to use the pay phone up the block and call in the fire.

As he hung up the phone, he broke into a grin. He'd done it. He was back. A quick stop in a mini-mart for a bottle of water, and then he was up the steps to the "L". Fellow passengers wrinkled their noses at him as he walked through the car, but he didn't care. His heart raced with excess adrenaline and his hands still shook. It was the best feeling in the world. He thought of Jessie and amended his thought. It was the second best feeling in the world.

CHAPTER TWENTY-THREE

Mark examined the latest photos in the dim red light. What the hell? He looked at the whole batch and swore as he made sense of the images. Bodies and...blood? Bodies of men, women and children, teens and senior citizens — people who'd probably just been celebrating only moments before the photos were snapped — lay sprawled where they fell.

A white flag with a blue 'W' curled into the corner of the photo. He recognized that flag. Wrigley Field. Bile burned the back of his throat. Instead of one or two pictures depicting a tragedy, five photos had developed. Every one of them showed the same scenes, the only difference was the gate number over the exit tunnel.

This was big. Mark's hand shook as he hung the last photo to dry. How would he stop this? Who could do something so horrible? He shook his head. Stupid question. The real question was why?

He wasn't even sure what had killed the people. Leaning forward, he peered at the photos looking for clues. Other than the blood and bodies, there didn't seem to be much out of the ordinary. There was no debris or smoke, so a bomb wasn't likely. For so many to die or be injured, it had to have been something quick. Automatic gunfire?

As he studied the photos, he began seeing individuals. A blond woman still clutching a small child. Poking out from beneath a man was a tiny foot. A baby. Mark gagged and braced his hands on the counter, hanging his head. Several slow deep breaths later, he tried again, taking each photo down. They were dry enough.

He didn't want to see the faces, he only wanted to find clues, but his eye was drawn to the faces despite his attempts to look past them. It was no use. Everybody became a person. Every person became someone's child, someone's mother, someone's best friend.

Or someone's torturer. Mark snapped the fourth picture from the clip. *Shit!* Jim Sheridan. What the hell was he doing at a Cub's game? Not that it mattered. He was there in the picture. A victim just like the rest.

He couldn't look anymore. Not now.

What the hell was he supposed to do with these pictures? Mark yanked open the door of the dark room and stalked to the kitchen. He could throw them out. The trash was right there. He could pretend he had never seen them. His shoulders slumped. No he couldn't. As tempting as it was, the dream would come tonight no matter what. Tossing out the photos wouldn't change that.

What he needed was a shot of whiskey or a tumbler full of scotch, but he would have to make do with a lite beer.

Half the beer went down in one long guzzle, then he grabbed a second out of the fridge, tucked the pictures under his arm, and trudged to the sofa. He dropped the stack of pictures on the coffee table. In a corner of his mind, he had an idea that if he got plastered, maybe the dream that finished off the photos would never materialize.

He finished the beer and opened the second before flipping on the television, seeking distraction. His eyes kept straying to the pictures despite the baseball game playing on TV. Maybe because of it. The second beer went down almost as fast as the first, and he debated getting a third. Before he made up his mind, the phone rang, but he let it go three rings before he bothered to check the caller ID. It was Jessie. Part of him was glad, he hadn't had a chance to talk to her yet today as she'd had an early meeting, but right at the moment, he wasn't in the mood to talk.

"Yeah?" There was a gaping silence on the other end and Mark winced, picturing Jessie's surprise at his abrupt answer.

"Well, aren't you full of sunshine and light." She was pissed.

Mark closed his eyes and circled the heel of his hand on his forehead. "Sorry, Jess. I just developed my film."

Jessie's voice lost its sarcasm. "It's a bad one? What happens?"

He nodded to the first question even though she couldn't see it. "Yeah. Real bad. Something big. And...And there's something else..."

"Someone you know?"

Sheridan's final grimace, frozen on his face, shouldn't bother him so much. The bastard had it coming. "Yeah, I know him, that's for sure." He flipped the picture over. "It's Sheridan." Mark stood and paced to the window.

"Jim Sheridan?"

"Yep." That third beer called to him and he heeded the call. With the phone tucked between his chin and shoulder, he opened the fridge and retrieved two more bottles and returned to the sofa. "And hundreds of others."

"Shit."

"My thoughts exactly." He laughed, but the sound died in his throat. "What do I do?" It wasn't fair to ask her. It was his responsibility. He sucked in a breath. His responsibility. Had he answered his own question? Grabbing the third beer, he gave the top a savage twist.

Jessie's voice cut through his inner turmoil, "Listen, Mark. I'll be home soon, I'm just leaving work. We'll think of something. Have you eaten yet?"

Mark lifted the beer; despite the calories, it wouldn't count as food. "No, I'm having my own little cocktail party."

He heard her sigh. "I'll grab some takeout. Don't worry, we'll work this out."

Mark nodded again. "Okay."

* * *

Jessie juggled the bags of Chinese food as she opened the door. "Hey, I'm here."

Silence greeted her announcement. Puzzled, she set the bags down on the counter and went to the living room. Mark sat on the edge of the sofa, the fingertips of one hand resting on the mouth of a beer bottle. His other held a photo.

She walked to the back of the sofa and stopped behind him. Three empty bottles lined the right side of the coffee table. "Mark?"

Mark started and the bottle teetered, but he steadied it before it toppled. He looked over his shoulder. "I didn't hear you come in." His voice sounded wooden and his eyes were dull.

She leaned over and nuzzled his neck. "I brought food. Come and eat."

"Don't you want to see the pictures?"

"Not yet. I think we should eat first."

"Oh. Okay." He stood, swayed for a second, and then ambled out to the kitchen.

He sounded distant and he hadn't even asked what she had brought. "I got Chinese."

"Sounds good."

"I hope it tastes as good as it smells." She had a feeling she could have brought him a plate of dog food and he would have had the same reaction.

Mark loaded a plate with fried rice, cashew chicken, and egg rolls. Jessie filled a dish for herself as well, and poured glasses of ice water for the both of them. Mark didn't seem to notice when she took his beer and set it on the counter. He had brought the pictures in with him, and they lay face down on the table beside his plate.

"I wonder what he's doing at a Cub's game?"

Mark stared at the end of an egg roll. "Yeah, I can't picture him in that light." He shrugged and took a bite. After chewing for a few seconds, he said, "I guess he's a normal guy most of the time."

Jessie scooped up a forkful of fried rice. "Okay, so maybe we can get him to cancel his game plans."

Mark put the egg roll down. His mouth set in a hard line as he stared past her, his fingers drumming on the table. He didn't speak, but bent his head and took a deep breath. After a lengthy silence, he met her gaze, his expression defiant. "What if I don't *want* to save him?" He turned the pictures face up, and then pushed them across the table.

She winced at the images and set her plate aside, no longer hungry. Even though she knew what the guy had done to Mark; had even seen the pictures of it, she couldn't hate him. Jessie recalled the day she met Sheridan. Her first impression had been that he was cold, but then she saw something else. A dedication that she understood, and she couldn't help admiring his attempt to seek the truth.

Jessie searched his eyes, knowing that she had to word this just right. "I know that Sheridan isn't high on your list of favorite people." Ignoring his 'ya think' expression, she continued, "but he still doesn't deserve to die." She swal-

276

lowed hard, shooting another glance at the picture. "None of these people deserve to die."

"Maybe it's karma." Mark pulled the picture in front of him and his arms rested on either side of it, his fingers still drumming. The table jiggled rhythmically and Jessie knew without looking that Mark's leg would be bouncing.

It would be so easy to agree. Jessie squared her shoulders. Easy was never the best option. "It probably is karma or payback or whatever the hell you want to call it, but there's a reason you get these photos and dreams, Mark. You have this...gift—this power, to see the future." He cringed at that, but Jessie forged on, "I don't think you are supposed to pick and choose who you'll save."

Mark glared at her before shoving away from the table. He snagged his beer off the counter and stormed into the living room.

Jessie sighed, resting her forehead in her hands. What a mess. She stood and began to put the food away, deciding to let Mark settle down a bit before approaching him again. Refilling her water glass, she took it out to the living room.

Mark leaned a shoulder against the window frame, his back to Jessie as he stared out the window. Every so often, he tipped the bottle and took a swig.

"I should hate the guy." He sounded weary.

Jessie muted the ball game.

Mark tilted the bottle, draining it. He absently picked at the label, peeling it back. "The things he did to me..." He sighed, then crossed to the sofa and sat beside her. "I should have felt glad when I saw him in the picture." He raised one shoulder in a half-shrug as he pulled the label completely off the bottle. "But I didn't. All I felt was sick."

"Sick at what happens to him? Or..." She left unsaid the other option, that he felt sick that he would have to save Sheridan.

"I've been thinking...what if he interrogates someone and they have information. Real information. Not...not like what I had." His voice dropped and it sounded like he almost swallowed the last words. Mark set the bottle down on the coffee table and smoothed the label flat. He turned to look at her. "What if he learned something that would save other people's lives?"

Jessie hadn't considered that, but now that he mentioned it, it made sense. "And if you don't save him, then that information remains unknown." The idea was mind boggling.

Mark nodded. "Yeah. It would mean that, maybe, there was a purpose for...for everything."

"Like that was the reason you were locked up?"

"Ya know, when I was gone, I thought about the camera a lot." Mark slouched back against the arm of the couch, his legs splayed at an angle under the coffee table. "There wasn't much else to do, and I must have gone over every picture that ever came out of it...and every dream I had." He paused as though organizing his thoughts, his gaze flicking to hers. "I realized that I had a connection with at least one person in every single photo."

Jessie pulled her leg up under her and leaned against the other arm, facing him. "What do you mean? What kind of connection?"

He took in a deep breath and let it out with a sigh. "I didn't know it at the time, but in hindsight, I found connections in at least eighty percent of them, and I'm sure if I researched it, I could find some for the other twenty percent." Mark sat up, his pose mirroring hers. "Some were people

I've passed on the street in the neighborhood, or relatives of people I know...someone from college. Things like that."

"And you never realized this before?" She reached for her water and took a sip.

Mark shook his head. "Nope. I guess I should have, but I didn't. I mean, I realized some of them were familiar." He lost the smile. "But most photos weren't so obvious."

"I don't understand how you could have all those pictures, and dreams, yet not know that you knew the people in them?"

He stood and ran a hand through his hair. "Yeah, I sound stupid, but think about it. How many people are you acquainted with? You know, faces you nod to as you pass them in the supermarket, or at the bank. When you see them out of context, you don't know where you know them from. Hasn't that ever happened to you?"

Jessie pursed her lips. How many people did she come into contact with every day whose faces were a blur to her? Too many. "I see your point. You said most of your photos take place right around here, right?"

Mark nodded and began pacing behind the couch. "So, Sheridan—he came to Chicago, right? If he hadn't met me, the camera wouldn't have produced his photo."

Jessie stared at the silver label lying crinkled on the table as she thought things through. She still had questions. "So...what about nine-eleven?"

"What do you mean?" Mark stopped mid-pace, his brows knit in confusion.

"It took place a thousand miles from here."

He nodded and bent his head for a moment. When he raised it, his eyes had a haunted expression. "Yeah. That occurred to me too, but I have a feeling I must've had a connection to someone who died that day."

279

"You knew someone who was in one of the Towers?"

Mark shrugged. "Maybe, or maybe one of the planes. I don't know for sure. For days afterwards, I avoided all the coverage. I—I couldn't even look at a newspaper."

Jessie imagined that it would have been torture for Mark to watch all of that when he had tried to stop it. It had been hard for her, and she didn't have the guilt factor. "I'll bet you did know someone. I think just about everyone in the country knows someone who knows someone who died that day."

He was right. She felt it in her gut. "There were a lot of people from the Chicago-area killed." There had been lists in the Chicago papers and she had recognized a few names. Nobody she knew personally, but she had felt saddened by even the small connection.

She became lost in her thoughts and barely noticed when Mark wandered to the windows again. A woman she had gone to school with had lost her husband on one of the planes. And a guy from her precinct had lost a brother who had been a New York police officer caught when the towers collapsed.

"So, I guess I had to meet Jim Sheridan so that I could save him."

CHAPTER TWENTY-FOUR

Jim scrolled through his newest memos. In the last month, intelligence chatter had picked up clues to something big, but details were sketchy. The only intelligence they had said the plan was going to happen soon, and the code name for the operation was 'Cracker Jack'. He skimmed the memos again, jotting down anything that might be of importance.

On the top of the legal pad, he'd written Cracker Jack, and then listed questions he wanted answered. Timing, location and target. He closed the memos and opened another file with older memos. Maybe there was something in them that didn't mean anything at the time he'd read them, but might point to something now. He pulled up the notes from current investigations. A gun dealer in the suburbs had reported a couple of men trying to buy ammunition for automatic weapons. When told that wasn't possible, they'd asked if the owner knew how they could get it. He'd declined to help them. Security tapes had provided pictures of the men, but without names, it didn't help much.

"Damn it." He rolled his chair away from the desk and put his hands behind his head, elbows out as he searched his mind. If he were a terrorist, what would be an inviting target? It would have to be somewhere with lots of people, so that they could instill terror. That's where the terror in terrorist originated. Blowing up a government warehouse out in the desert didn't strike fear into the heart of the average person. Terrorists' goal was to create fear in hopes that citizens of a country would blame their own government for whatever policies that the terrorist groups had issues with.

Grabbing his pencil, he scooted up to the desk again. It was July but past the fourth, which would have been a likely date. He clicked through his calendar to see if anything stood out. Nothing major until the air show in mid-August. That was still a few weeks away. The Taste of Chicago had already passed. There were always music festivals and concerts. Other likely targets included important buildings, but measures taken in the last few years had made it more difficult to destroy them. Jim hoped that the newer security rules at airports and around likely targets made them less desirable. Trains and subways had been targets in the past, and hard to secure. The possibilities were endless. He glanced at his watch. Almost noon. He'd been in the office since seven, and had worked sixteen hours a day for the two weeks. His team had done the same. To show his gratitude, he'd bought tickets to tonight's Cub game for all of them. They all needed a little break to clear their heads.

"Excuse me, Jim?"

He glanced at the door to his office. "Yes, Beth?"

His administrative assistant leaned into the room. "There's a guy on line two who's called a few times for you while you were at your meeting earlier. I offered to transfer him to another analyst, but he insisted on talking to you. He wouldn't leave a message or a number. Said he was calling from a pay-phone."

Curious, Jim nodded. "Okay. Thanks." He reached for the phone. "Sheridan speaking."

He could hear someone breathing rather hard and he almost made a smart comment about how unwise it was to prank phone call the FBI. He decided to give them the benefit of the doubt. Perhaps the person hadn't heard him answer, so he tried again. "Hello? Is anyone there?"

The person on the other end cleared their throat. "Uh, yeah, I'm here."

The voice tugged at his memory but he couldn't place it. "Who am I speaking with?" He put his hand over his other ear to block out the noise from some colleagues trooping past his door.

"It's...it's Mark Taylor."

Jim's grip on the phone slipped as the shock hit him. He recovered quickly. "Taylor. What can I do for you?"

"I have to talk to you, Sir. It's urgent."

"I'm listening, so talk."

"Not on the phone. It's gotta be in person."

Suspicion piqued but so did his curiosity. "Why can't you tell me now?"

"I can't take the chance. I know this call is probably recorded."

Taylor didn't have to say anything more about recorded phone calls. Jim remembered that detail as the lynchpin of their case against him. "Okay. Fine. I'll meet you, but it has to be somewhere public." It wouldn't be wise to meet the guy in a back alley; that was for sure. Taylor probably wanted nothing more than to stick a blade in him.

"Yeah, okay. You know where O'Leary's Pub is. Can you meet me there in an hour?"

It was on the tip of his tongue to ask how Taylor was sure that he knew where that pub was, but then he recalled seeing Jessie Bishop at the establishment. It wasn't hard to put two and two together. It might not be a bad idea to request her presence at the meeting. "I'll talk with you on the condition that Detective Bishop is present. I think she's someone we both trust." He hadn't thought of it before, but he did trust her. She was a straight shooter.

Taylor didn't answer for a moment and Jim wondered if the guy even knew that he and Jessie Bishop had met last summer. It had only been a couple of months since he'd seen Bishop at that pub. At that time, she hadn't seen Taylor yet.

"I'll ask her. I can't promise though. She's working."

"Okay, well, if I walk in and don't see her, I'll just turn around."

"Listen, I know you hate my guts, and I feel the same about you, but what I have to say has nothing to do with either of us. That's all I can tell you now."

He could picture the other man's face flushing with anger. Against his better judgment, he gave in. "Okay. One hour."

* * *

Jessie sounded stressed. "I'll be there. I've been going crazy knowing what's going to happen. I've tried to get more security at the game, but without something concrete, the brass won't go for it."

"I know the feeling." Mark circled the heel of his hand against his forehead, grimacing at the dull ache behind his eyes. He sat in his boss's office and glanced out to the store when the bell above the door jingled. "Look, I gotta go, a customer just came in. See ya in a little bit." For the next thirty minutes, he tried to remain patient as he showed the customer several of the digital cameras. Gary had said he'd be back from lunch by one o'clock, but it was already twenty after. O'Leary's wasn't far, but he'd have to leave soon to make it on time. He rang up the camera, amazed that the guy bought it in spite of Mark's distracted sales pitch.

The bell sounded again and Mark heaved a sigh of relief when Gary entered.

"Sorry, Mark. I started talking to this hot waitress. I got her number and everything." He grinned and didn't look the least bit sorry about being late.

Resisting the urge to roll his eyes, Mark shrugged. "That's great, but listen, I'm going to have to run, I have an errand I wanted to do on my lunch hour. I just sold a Nikon. I didn't get a chance to file the paperwork."

Gary bounced behind the counter. "No problem. I got it."

Before leaving, he retrieved the brown paper bag containing his camera and the prints of the horrific attack from the back room. This time, he had proof.

Mark jogged the four blocks to the pub and stopped at the entrance to catch his breath. His shirt clung to him and he cursed Gary for being late and forcing him to run. He already felt his stomach knotting at the prospect of seeing Jim. Last thing he wanted to do was look as nervous as he felt, and having sweat dripping didn't make for a calm appearance.

The interior was dim after the bright sunshine, and he paused to scan the room. Tugging his shirt away from his chest, he was grateful for the blast of air conditioning from the vent above the entrance. Sheridan and Jessie at a table in the corner. *Damn.* He'd hoped to get here first and get the upper hand, have some control. Jim sat with his back to the corner and had a view of the whole room. Their eyes met and Mark had to fight the impulse to flee. The door opened behind him as a group of women entered. The flash of sunlight reminded him that he wasn't trapped anymore. He could leave whenever he wanted. That thought propelled him forward.

Jim gave a short nod, but Mark ignored it as he wound his way past other tables and customers. He couldn't help noticing that Jessie didn't look at all uncomfortable with the guy. She even smiled at something he said. A trace of a smile lurked around Jim's mouth. Were they talking about him? Jessie turned and the smile slipped from her face when she saw him. Her brows knit as she glanced at the bag in his hand.

He was about to tell her what it contained when Jim jumped to his feet and shot around the table. "Hold on. What's in the bag, Taylor?"

Mark halted. As much as he wanted to push past Jim without answering, he couldn't. A year of conditioning to obey the man's orders had left their mark. He dropped his gaze. "It's just a camera." It took everything in him, but he raised his head and said, "The one I told you about. Over and over."

Jim's eyes narrowed and he held out his hand. Mark gripped the rolled top of the bag tighter for a second, the muscles in his arm rigid. The tension grew with Jim's eyes never leaving Mark's, his hand still waiting expectantly. Finally, Mark shoved the bag at Jim, but couldn't keep from balling his hands into fists as rage boiled inside of him.

Jessie stood and took Mark's elbow with one hand, the other going to his back. The reassurance she offered with her touch and smile helped. "Come on and have a seat. We ordered a pizza already."

Mark acquiesced, but looked at her blankly, his mind still on the camera in the bag. Pizza? Did she think that they were actually going to sit and eat like they were old friends?

He pulled his arm from her grasp and ground out, "I'm not hungry."

It had been his plan to simply divulge the pictures, relate the details that he recalled from his dream, and get the hell out of there. Socializing hadn't played a part in it. The crinkle of the bag drew his attention back to Jim. The man had returned to his seat and without asking, opened the bag and withdrew the contents.

Jim gave the camera a cursory look, but when he shuffled through the photos, his mouth set in a hard line, the only sign that the pictures registered. He went through them twice before he glared at Mark and slapped the prints down on the table. "What did you do this time?"

The accusation in the words hit Mark like a punch and his jaw clenched so hard he thought he'd crack a molar. *The bastard!*

Jessie pushed a glass of water towards him. "Here. You look hot from your walk here." Her eyes flashed a warning to him. While he gulped the cool liquid, she slid the pictures in front of her and flipped through them. "Mark didn't do anything. He got these pictures the same place I got those ones last year. You were there, Jim. Don't act surprised." She raised an eyebrow at him.

Jim shot a look at Jessie. "Come on. That was a set-up and you know it. I still haven't figured out how you pulled it off, or who the leak was, but I'm not going to fall for it a second time."

Mark set the glass down, sloshing water over the side and swiped the back of his hand over his mouth. Well, that was that. He reached out, grabbed the bag on the table and swept the camera into it then snatched up the prints. "Don't say I didn't try to warn you." He pushed his chair back and stood.

Jessie grabbed his hand and gave a tug. "Mark—"

"You're not leaving until I find out where the hell you got these photos." Jim rose, cutting off Jessie's plea. Eyes hard, he held Mark immobile with his look.

Mark refused to back down as he and Jim glared at each other like two alpha dogs. He was determined to win this time. Jessie had come to stand beside him and said something, but he heard only his own blood pounding in his ears. Without warning, images from last night's dream shot through his mind, overwhelming him with their intensity. Like a flashback, he was there again, just as vividly as he'd been in his dream. He locked his knees to keep them from buckling, and grit his teeth as he tried to maintain his rage. It was no use. Screams of the children ricocheted through his head. A shudder swept over his body.

His anger died when he realized the truth. This meeting wasn't about him. It was about saving people-regular folks just out enjoying a game. About saving them from crazed gunmen who thought killing innocents earned them a place of honor in the afterlife. What he had been through in prison paled in comparison to the fate that awaited hundreds of people leaving the ballgame tonight.

Mark had to convince Jim that the pictures were real. Or would be real. It was the only chance anyone in the photos had. If he couldn't control his anger, he'd fail. Again. It might not have been his fault on September 11th, but it would be today.

To stop this, he needed help and Jim had the resources to get the bad guys. He took a deep breath and forced his shoulders to relax. "Can we start over?"

Jim blinked. His stance softened and after a beat, he stuck out his hand. "Jim Sheridan."

He stared at the hand. His plea was meant to erase the last few minutes, not their whole past. Mark wasn't ready to forget those fifteen months, but he'd go along for now. He'd do whatever it took to fix this if it meant not having another tragedy hanging around his neck. Swallowing hard, he clasped the other man's hand. "Mark Taylor."

The handshake introduction did more than calm the waters. With a shake of his hand, Jim gave Mark back something he'd been missing since being arrested. His dignity.

They returned to their chairs as the waitress arrived with their pizza. She paused in puzzlement as if sensing the residual tension in the air. "Um, cheese and sausage, right?"

Eyes burning, Mark avoided eye contact with everyone and covered his emotion by putting the photos back in the bag before the waitress saw them.

Jessie moved the water glasses out of the way so the waitress could put the hot pizza in the center of the table. "Yes, that's correct. It looks great."

* * *

What the hell had just happened? One minute Jim was sure Taylor was going to attack him, but the next, anguish flashed in the man's eyes followed by something else. Resolve? Jim took the spatula and lifted a slice of pizza onto Jessie's plate. He slid the utensil under another and raised his eyebrows in a silent question as he nodded towards Taylor's plate. The guy looked wrung out, but he accepted the pizza and poured water for all of them while Jim served up the food.

"This is good pizza." Jessica dabbed at her mouth.

Taylor glanced at her but didn't react to the statement. He looked distracted and hardly touched his food.

"Yeah. It is. I'll have to remember to come here more often. Who'd have thought an Irish pub would have decent pizza?" Jim took a sip of water and wished it was beer.

She glanced at Taylor briefly, and apparently communicated something to him because he nodded and took a bite. Turning back to Jim, she shrugged. "No kidding. But hey, it's Chicago. We love our pizza."

Jim took another slice. The pub was busy, and background noise covered the uneasy silence that hung over the group as they ate. Taylor's leg bounced under the table, occasionally it bumped into the bottom. It was something that seemed beyond Taylor's control. Every time they'd interrogated him, the leg would jump. At first, Jim had taken it for a sign that the guy was lying, but later, realized it was stress related. The fact it was going like a piston now meant the guy was extremely keyed up. When it seemed the other two were finished, Jim balled up his napkin and tossed it on his plate. "It's time to get down to business. Level with me. What's this all about?" He gestured to the paper bag on the fourth chair.

Taylor sighed and reached for the bag. "I have no reason to lie to you, and every reason to keep this to myself." His mouth twisted and he gave a shake of his head. "I hope I don't regret it." He withdrew the photos and went to put them on the table, but the pizza pan was in the way, so he stood and came around next to Jim's chair. "Forget about the camera for a minute. Just look at the pictures. Really look."

"Okay, fine." He'd go along with him. When he'd first looked, all he'd noticed were bodies and blood, but this time he took note of the setting. It looked familiar. He picked up one photo and angled it towards the light. It appeared to be a gangway. The victims were every age and race, but he saw a theme, a commonality. Most were wearing Cubs gear—T-shirts, jerseys or hats.

Taylor pointed in the upper left corner of the photo. "See the white flag? The one with the 'W' on it?"

Jim squinted. It was hard to make out but he could just see it. "Yeah."

"Well, the good news is, the Cubs win tonight. The bad news is, nobody's going to care."

"Okay, so you did some photo editing. It's a damn fine job too, Taylor. You might think about doing something useful with your talents." Jim glanced at his watch. He had a meeting in thirty minutes.

"Goddamn it! Would ya listen to me? Why would I go to all this trouble? Huh? To take another chance that you'd lock me up?" Taylor turned away, his hands on his hips, the muscle in his jaw flexing. He waved a hand at Jim. "*Shit.* Whatever." He snatched up the photos and returned to his seat.

Jessica folded her arms and leaned on the table. "Mark's telling the truth. I've seen it. I'm the most skeptical person you'll ever meet, but sometimes we have to admit that we don't have the answer, do we? There are still mysteries in the world." She waved a hand towards the photos. "Do you think I want to risk my career? Hell no. I've worked too hard to get where I am. But, this is real."

Jim shrugged. "What do you want me to say?"

She shook her head and darted a look at Taylor, who was sorting through the pictures before returning her focus to Jim. "Look, even if you don't believe us, could you at least arrange for tighter security at Wrigley Field tonight? Tell them you got information from a source you can't reveal. You've been doing this a long time. They'll believe you."

He almost considered her suggestion. If nothing else, it'd be a good training exercise, but training exercises took planning and cost money. There were channels to go through, he couldn't just announce one on a whim.

Mark leaned across the table and spun a picture in front of Jim, stabbing a finger on it. "Before you go accusing me of having anything to do with what's going to happen in about eight hours, I suggest you take one more look at photo four."

Jim leaned forward and glanced at it. It was more of the same but from a different angle. There was no flag in the corner. "You forgot to add the flag to this one." He smirked at Taylor. Busted.

"You're a real son of a bitch aren't you?" Taylor jumped to his feet, his fists clenched, and arms akimbo.

Jim tried not to flinch, sure that the other man was about to round the table and slug him. He'd been expecting it. It's what he'd have done if the tables had been turned, only he wouldn't have made up a crazy story to get Taylor here. No, he'd have just found the guy and let him have it.

Taylor sucked in a deep breath, and blew it out, his shoulders and hands relaxing as though he'd commanded his body to relax. "I'm sorry, Jessie. I tried. I shouldn't have even shown him that last one. It's not like he doesn't deserve his fate."

Jessica jumped up and circled to Taylor, taking his arm and leading him a few steps away. She spoke in a low voice, but Jim heard her. "You don't mean that, Mark. I saw you agonizing over this. You know it's the right thing to do."

Taylor looked away from her, off to the right, his mouth set in a hard line. The muscles in his neck and jaw flexed. He turned and looked at her for several seconds before finally nodding. Jessica's fingers tightened on his arm, briefly before Taylor returned to the table. He tapped a finger on the photo. "See anyone you recognize in there? The one lying in a pool of blood behind the old lady?"

Jim sighed but examined the photo yet again. He bent to take a closer look. Cold washed over him and the hairs on his arms stood on end. "That's me."

In the picture, his eyes were wide, but the way he laid, and the bullet hole in his forehead indicated that he was dead. He'd seen enough dead bodies in pictures to recognize one... even when it was his own. "How'd you do that?"

Taylor moved to the chair beside him. "I don't do anything. The camera does. But, I have dreams." He pulled a folded piece of paper out of his back pocket and set it in front of Jim. "I wrote down all the details I could remember." He sat leaning forward expectantly, elbows resting on his knees, hands clasped. His eyes, wide with hope, darted from Jim to the pictures. "I've got no reason to make this up, and I sure as hell have no part in what's going to happen if we don't act." His gaze met Jim's. "I swear to God."

It was crazy, but Jim believed him. Years of training had made it instinctive for him to study body language, tone of voice and subtle expressions to decipher when a suspect was being truthful. Not only did he read the truth in the man's face, but the truth, incredibly, made more sense. The details on the paper filled both sides of the page, and staging a photo shoot of that magnitude would cost a fortune. Logistically, Taylor wouldn't be able to pull it off.

The guy was right about one thing. It made no sense for him to go to all the trouble to stage a photo shoot like this and then write it all down. There was no payoff as far as Jim could tell. He flipped through the prints again. The photos showed dozens of bodies, with more strewn farther up the concourse. Faking something like this would cost a fortune.

The site was definitely Wrigley Field and if it had been used for some elaborate photo shoot, the media would have reported it. Jim rubbed his hand over his mouth and sighed. Hell, the guy was lucky to have a couple of dimes left to rub together. The fact that he was partially responsible for Taylor's financial straits didn't elude him. That made this even more puzzling. He laid the pictures side by side on the table, and spread his hands wide. "I don't get it."

Taylor straightened, his expression once again blank. "What?"

"According to these, I'm going to be a victim here too."

Taylor shifted forward again, and glanced at Jessica, who had resumed her seat. "Yeah. It looks that way."

"So, why'd you tell me?"

Guilt stole over Taylor's features and he cleared his throat. "Honestly, it's probably the hardest damn decision I've ever had to make."

Jessica nodded. "We discussed it last night. Of course he wanted to stop this, but, he's taking a huge risk here. You realize that, right?" Her eyes narrowed as she continued, "After what he went through the last time he tried to prevent something like this, who could blame him for ignoring these pictures?" She picked up number four. "And even though he didn't say it, I'm sure it crossed his mind that *you* being a victim wouldn't be a bad thing."

Jim felt heat climb his face, and Taylor stared at the floor. She was right. He couldn't blame Taylor. He shrugged. "I understand. So...we have a lot of work to do if we're going to prevent this." Another thought hit him. Cracker Jack. Baseball. It made sense and he mentally kicked himself for not making a connection sooner.

Taylor's head snapped up. "You believe me?"

Standing, Jim stacked the photos, trying not to look at the one with his own image. "Do I have a choice?"

CHAPTER TWENTY-FIVE

Over a year's worth of shame and humiliation exploded out with a single breath. Mark bent forward, elbows on his knees, hands clasped behind his head as he absorbed the fact that Jim believed him. His throat convulsed, and embarrassed, he closed his eyes. He sensed motion in front of him, and lifted his head to meet Jessie's gaze. No words were necessary, and then he broke the eye contact and stood, suddenly restless.

The lunch crowd had dwindled in the mid-afternoon, and he was glad for that. Their section only had one other table and with a couple of older guys who weren't paying any attention to them. Jessie took her purse off the back of her chair and he grabbed the bag. Together, they followed Jim to the front of the pub. The waitress prattled about the weather as she rung up the meal. When Mark pulled out his wallet, Jim waved him off and paid with a credit card. Ten minutes ago, Mark would have protested, and fought for the right to pay for his own meal.

Energy pumped through him and, not knowing where to focus it, Mark went outside to wait for the other two. Pacing in front of the pub, he felt ready to burst as emotions tumbled one over the other. Elation and satisfaction at finally being vindicated bubbled inside. The bubble of joy burst when a guy wearing a shirt emblazoned with a Cub's logo passed him. Time was running out. What was taking them so long? Just as he thought that, the door opened and both exited, cell phones pressed to their ears.

Jim glanced at Mark, but spoke into the phone, "I need everyone on this. A level one alert...that's right. Wrigley Field." He approached a dark blue sedan with government plates parked along the curb. Still barking orders into the phone, he leaned against the car.

Mark turned to Jessie, about to ask what was next, but she held her hand up, her head bent to her phone.

"Sir, just giving you a heads up. The FBI is now involved and advises we get all available manpower on the Wrigley Field case." She brushed past Mark and stopped, a finger in one ear as she spoke to what sounded like her boss.

Confused, and unable to make eye contact with either, Mark resumed pacing. Did this mean they didn't need him? It sounded like they had called in the cavalry. His lunch hour was over and if he wanted to keep his job, he'd need to get back. Aimlessly, he wandered up and down the street, checking every few seconds to see if the other two were done with their conversations. Lacking direction, and feeling unneeded, he turned and headed for the El. He'd gone half a block when Jim caught up to him and grabbed his arm.

"Mark! Wait, where are you going?"

He whirled at the contact, yanking his arm out of Jim's grasp, and walking backwards. Just because they had called a truce didn't mean he felt comfortable being touched by the other man. "I figured I'd head back to work. You don't need me."

"Like hell we don't!" Jim motioned him back towards the sedan. "Come on. We need to pick your brain to find out any more details."

"Pick my brain?" A chill washed over him and he halted. "What do you mean?" Visions of chains and a stark white room rose in his mind.

His fears must have shown because Jim's eyes widened and then he put up both hands. "No, it's not what you're thinking. I mean just see if there are any more details you can recall. Maybe something that didn't seem important when you first wrote down your notes." His phone rang then, and as he answered it, he inclined his head back towards the car, his hand resting on Mark's shoulder.

Jim and Jessie exchanged cell numbers, and he and Jim left her to work things from her end. Mark climbed into the car and tried not to think about how surreal it was to be voluntarily in the passenger seat of his tormentor's car. The short trip could have been awkward, but Jim kept his eyes on the road and his ear to his phone as he continued to direct operations. Jim concluded the conversation and dropped the phone into a center compartment between the seats, then cast a look at Mark. "Do you need to call your work and let them know you won't be back in today?"

Mark reached for the phone. "Yeah, if you don't mind." Mark explained that his errand was taking longer than he thought, and if it was okay for him to take the rest of the afternoon off and make up the time the next day. Gary was fine with it, didn't even ask many questions, and instead, acted thrilled that he'd have the next evening off to take out the waitress. Mark hung up, a smile lingering at the excitement in the younger guy's voice.

When they arrived at the FBI building, Jim whisked him through security, telling the personnel that he was bringing Mark in for questioning.

In the elevator, Mark wiped his hands on his thighs, and then shoved them in his pockets and leveled a look at Jim "I'm not in any trouble, am I?" He had to ask. He had to be sure. The guy had only spoken a few words on the ride over and even now, Jim stared at the lit numbers on the panel. He might have been alone in the elevator for all the attention he paid Mark. The lack of communication was nerve wracking.

Jim's brow furrowed and he gave a little shake of his head, before turning to Mark. "No. Why would you be in trouble?"

"I don't know...it's just you told security that you were taking me up for questioning." Mark shrugged and allowed a touch of sarcasm to flavor the next sentence. "I can't imagine why that would make me nervous."

The doors slid open and Jim put his hand on Mark's shoulder again as he guided Mark around the corner. "Listen, right now, you're what we call an asset. You have info I want. Sorry I'm not getting that across to you. I have about a million things going through my mind right now. I've got to get all the different agencies on board, coordinate efforts, make sure we're all talking to each other, and-well, more than you probably want to know. Regardless, I should have been more sensitive in my wording. Sorry about that."

Mark hadn't been looking for an apology, just reassurance, but he was pleasantly surprised and accepted it. "No problem."

They came to what looked like a conference room with computers on tables along the walls and a long table in the middle. "Here we are. I'm going to get you started looking at some photos of suspects." Jim yanked out a chair in front of a computer, his fingers flying over the keyboard. In seconds, the screen was full of photos. He showed Mark how to go to the next screen when he needed to, and then he clapped him on the shoulder. "Okay, I'm going to go let the others know I'm back. This room is going to get crowded soon. You feel comfortable with this?"

Mark smiled, appreciating Jim's attempt to be less intimidating. "Sure. I'm good."

Jim left, but within a few minutes, more people trickled in. Some sat at the conference table behind Mark, others took spots at other computer terminals and soon the clacking of keys filled the air. Some of the pictures he studied were mug shots, but others were obviously surveillance photos. A few times, Mark stopped and closed his eyes, allowing the dream to replay in his head. Nobody bothered him except for one woman who asked if he'd like something to drink. He accepted a cup of coffee.

While Mark plowed through the pages of suspects, Jim returned and began issuing instructions to some of the others in the room, who then left, presumably to carry out those instructions. As soon as one person exited, another entered. The atmosphere crackled with tension and Mark had a hard time concentrating on the photos.

"I got CPD on line two."

"Jim, DHS is holding on three."

"What about DOD? Anybody call them yet?"

"Right. I want all your manpower available…No, we can't do that…It would create panic."

Mark put his hands over his ears and concentrated on the computer screen. He knew some people had photographic memories, but he wasn't one of them, except when it came to the dreams. For days after having one, he could call it up at will, like it was stored in a computer file in his brain. He put that ability to full use over the next thirty minutes.

"Uh, Jim…?' He turned in his seat, and waved his hand. Jim broke off the conversation he was having with another agent. He strode across the room and Mark pointed at the screen. "This looks like one of them." The pic appeared to be taken with a security camera. It was grainy, but he recognized the man from the shape of his face. He had a long jaw that, even with the dark beard, made it seem to jut out.

Jim leaned over Mark's shoulder, and pulled up a file on the suspect. Finger poised over the print button, he looked back at Mark. "You sure about him?"

Mark hesitated. Was he sure? If he was wrong, nobody knew better than he the horrible price this guy would pay. Was he ready to consign someone to that fate based on a grainy photo and the image in his brain? If he said no, and it turned out that the guy was one of the terrorists, and people died, how could he live with that?

Jim straightened, then twisted, leaned a hip on the table and faced Mark. "It's your call, but you have to be sure." He crossed his arms and waited, but there was an air of urgency in the room. They couldn't wait all day.

"Yeah, I know." Mark closed his eyes, calling up the guy in the dream, and tried to ignore the image he'd seen already. What if what he'd seen had influenced what he saw in his head now? Could he take that chance? He looked again. It was the guy in his dream. It was a match. "It's him."

Jim nodded and then rattled off orders to someone behind Mark. Something about finding that man. Mark bent forward, his fingers massaging the bridge of his nose. He felt sick.

"You okay?"

Mark sat back and blew out a breath. "Yeah…just a little overwhelmed is all."

"That's okay. It's a lot of responsibility." His tone conveyed understanding and that he was no stranger to the stress involved.

"Guess I should keep looking." Mark scrubbed his hands down his face before taking a gulp of coffee.

Jim stood and slapped him on the back as he walked past. "Good job."

An hour later, Mark had identified three more and teams were sent off to find the men. As luck would have it, one of the suspects was already under surveillance. He and Jim went over Mark's dream notes sentence by sentence to see if there was a scrap more they could glean from the information. Of the two men that hadn't been identified, he was able to recall that one had waved to a little boy who had held his father's hand as they exited the gate a minute or so before the shooting began.

"Okay, so, if you're willing, we'll station you with the team at that gate. If you can spot that little boy and father, it could give us an extra minute to find the guys in the crowd."

"Yeah, sure. I'll be there."

Jim set his pen down on the pad of paper. "Mark, I want to make certain you fully comprehend what you're getting into. This has the potential to be extremely dangerous. You weren't in the photos originally, so there's no to reason think you would have been killed in this. If you go tonight, you could change that. Do you understand?"

Mark nodded, amazed at Jim's understanding of how the future could change based on actions they would take prior to the incident. "I'm well aware of the possible outcome."

"Nobody will think less of you if you opt to remain at a distance." His gaze was sincere and that alone steeled Mark's resolve. He'd see this through to the end.

"I'm a bit out of practice, but it won't be the first time I've been in bad situations. I know what the deal is." His leg bounced and he stood to cover the reaction. "Besides, I can't shake the feeling that I need to be there."

Jim gathered the notes and rose. "Okay then. We'll see if we can dig up a vest for you."

Time simultaneously flew by and dragged. His part done for now, Mark paced the hallway, tried on a Kevlar vest, and finally, sat in a chair in Jim's office while the other man was off doing whatever it was that still needed to be done.

He noted the lack of personal touches in the office. There were no pictures on the desk, no homemade looking paperweights like those that a child or grandchild might make. Even the mouse pad was generic. Did the guy's life completely revolve around CIA or FBI? Mark had never wondered about Jim's life before. For all he cared, the guy could have caught fire and Mark wouldn't have spared the saliva to spit on him. Now, he was sitting in the guy's office wondering if the guy had a life. He even felt a little sorry for him.

"All right. We were able to track down two of the guys." Jim breezed into the office. "And guess what? Their car was loaded with weapons and enough ammo to mow down the whole bleacher section."

Mark sagged in relief. This was concrete proof. No matter what else happened, lives had been saved and he had helped. Nobody would be able to deny it.

"What's the matter? I thought you'd be thrilled." Jim threw a puzzled look in Mark's direction before rummaging around in his desk

"I am…it's just that…well, I'm relieved that there's proof now. It's not just based on my dream and photos."

Jim pulled out a bottle of ibuprofen and shook out a couple. He tilted the bottle towards Mark, his eyebrows raised. "I buy these in bulk."

Mark smiled at the dry humor and took the bottle. His head pounded too. He washed down two of the pain relievers with the last dregs of his now cold coffee and made a face. It had been his third cup and the caffeine overload hadn't helped ease the stress.

"While the two suspects in custody are questioned, we're going to head over to the park and start scouting around. You ready to go?"

* * *

"Have you heard from Jessie?" Since they'd parted ways at the pub, Mark hadn't spoken to her, and wondered what was going on.

Jim pulled up in front of the stadium. "Yes, she's helping one of our teams track down a suspect who's still at large. CPD knows the city better than we do, so having their cooperation is vital."

He wasn't thrilled with the idea that Jessie was out there hunting down a terrorist. She'd be pissed if she knew he was worrying. It was her job and she was good at it.

Jim pulled into the lot just outside the fenced in players' lot. A security guard tried waving him off, but when the man approached the window, Jim flashed his badge and the guard's demeanor changed. He directed them to a spot close to the entrance. It was still over two hours until game time, but already, the sidewalks teemed with fans. Vendors mingled, hawking banners, bobble-heads and scorecards. Down the street, sports bars overflowed with fans getting a head-start on the fun. The scent of grilled onions, hot dogs and baking pavement melded together and stirred up memories of past good times.

Mark had been to countless games and had always loved the atmosphere outside the field. He'd usually taken the El. It stopped right behind right field and it was just a short walk up Addison to the front of the park. He remembered the old donut shop that had been where a McDonald's now stood. Winchell's Donuts. When had that disappeared? He couldn't recall the last time he'd seen it.

When he was a kid, his dad had brought him down to a game at least once every summer. They'd leave Madison at dawn and arrive just as the players were arriving. His dad would go buy a bag of donuts while Mark would beg autographs from the players.

"Mark...hello?" Jim waved a hand in front of Mark's face.

Shaking his head, Mark took a step back, embarrassed to realize he'd stopped walking, and was instead, standing and daydreaming. "Sorry. I was just thinking about when I'd come here as a kid with my dad."

"All the way from Madison?"

"Yeah. How'd you kn—" Mark broke off, remembering that this guy knew everything about him. He shoved his hands in his pockets and glanced at Jim, surprised to see the other man's face redden.

"This is awkward." Jim crossed his arms.

Mark kicked at a stone in the parking lot, and then winced when it went further than he'd anticipated, and pinged against the undercarriage of a car. "Yeah." He shrugged. "Anyway, even though we were in the middle of Wisconsin, we could pick up WGN on our antenna."

"So, when was the last time you and your dad went to a game?"

Jim began walking and Mark ambled along beside him. "I can't remember. It's been a long time. Before college,

I guess. When I dropped out, we were too angry at each other to spend much time together."

"Angry?"

"Yeah. I was supposed to be a doctor, like him. At least, that was his plan." They skirted a large group of teens. Once on the other side of the group, Mark sighed. "Guess things would have turned out a lot differently if I had become a doctor. I should've listened to him."

"Hmmm...You never know. You're not doing too bad at your chosen profession."

Mark stopped walking and stared at Jim. "You've gotta be kidding me."

Jim shrugged, but evaded Mark's eyes. "Hey, I went through your financial records, you were doing well. Add to that, your other talent..."

"Talent?" Mark gave a harsh laugh. "Curse is more like it."

"Is that what your dad thinks of it?"

Mark stopped when they came to Waveland Avenue. He crossed his arms and scanned the street. "My dad...he thinks I'm crazy."

"He doesn't believe you?" Jim stood at his shoulder.

Unable to speak, Mark simply shook his head.

"Here's your chance to prove it to him." Jim held out his cell-phone.

"What's that for?"

"Call him. Tell him what's going to happen. Even if we stop this right now, the media will get a hold of something and you'll have proof."

"You think I should just call him?" Mark wiped his hands on his thighs. "Just blurt it out?"

"Well, do it quietly. You don't want to create a panic here." Jim's mouth quirked in a wry smile, then he grew serious. "I mean it, Mark. Take it. Call your folks. We don't know how this is going to turn out."

He had only spoken to his dad once since he'd left, and it was a brief happy birthday wish. A handful of other times, he'd talked to his mother, but she always managed to make him feel guilty. Not intentionally, but he knew she hated the rift between them.

The images in the photos pushed to the front of his mind. Jim was right. If something happened to him, he didn't want his parents thinking the worst of him. He wanted a chance at good-bye. He remembered the regret at not having that chance when he'd been arrested. "Yeah. Okay."

Jim wandered a short distance away, his back turned, and Mark appreciated the privacy. He dialed the number and smiled when his mom answered. "Hey, Mom." It was a minute before he could get a word in edgewise, then he laughed. "Hold on, a sec. I'm fine. Sorry I haven't called more often. I mean that. I don't have a lot of time, but I just wanted to tell you that I love you, and I promise to call more often."

His mother's voice took on an edge of panic. "Something's wrong. What is it?"

"No, nothing's wrong. In fact, for once, everything is going well. Is Dad around?"

She didn't sound convinced, but said, "I love you too, hon. Here's your father."

"Yes?" His dad spoke in a gruff tone, as though expecting the worst.

"Hi, Dad." Mark pressed the phone to his ear as a noisy group passed.

"Where the hell are you?"

"I'm right outside Wrigley Field. As a matter of fact, I'm here with the FBI."

"Why? What did you do now?"

His jaw clenched. "Nothing. I didn't do anything, Dad. I'm helping them, as a matter of fact."

"Helping them?"

"Yes. I used my camera, the one I told you about. It's a long story, but I got the camera back, and the FBI believes me about some pictures and the corresponding dream I had."

"You've got to be kidding." He sounded less skeptical.

"It's true. Watch the news tonight or the next few days. Hopefully, it won't be anything big. Not if we're successful." The reality of what was going to happen if they failed tempered Mark's pleasure that he had proof and that his dad sounded like he might believe him.

"What are you doing to help?"

"I'm going to try to identify some people. They couldn't get an ID on one guy from the photos, the picture wasn't clear. I hope I'll see him."

"Is it safe?"

That he asked touched Mark, and he had to clear his throat before speaking, "As safe as they can make it."

Jim approached.

"I gotta go, but Dad...I love you."

Silence greeted the declaration, and then his dad coughed. After a beat, he spoke, his voice hoarse, "Be careful, Mark."

"I will. Bye." Mark clicked the phone shut and handed it back to Jim. "Thanks."

Jim nodded, then dialed a number and put the phone to his ear and walked off a little way.

Mark took a deep, ragged breath. His dad hadn't said it, but it was there, in his voice. His father cared about him. No matter what happened now, there'd be nothing left unfinished. Despite the circumstances, he felt light, energized. He scanned the crowd, wondering if the terrorists were already about. Jim motioned for Mark to walk with him. Mark jogged to catch up, tugging at the vest beneath his polo shirt. It was only an hour since he'd put it on, and already, he hated the thing.

"Here's the plan. We've put spotters on top of surrounding buildings, have undercover agents in the stadium, some posing as security, others as fans, and we've set up a command center in that van over there."

Mark looked towards where Jim pointed. A white box truck, no different than hundreds on the streets of Chicago, was in a fenced off parking lot beside a small firestation just behind the left field wall.

"Okay."

Jim spent a few minutes introducing Mark to the agents in the van. The back of the van looked like a small communication center. Computers, wires, and video monitors filled every spare inch, watched over by four agents.

One of the men watching a video, pointed to the monitors. "We've already placed some cameras at optimal points around the park, so we'll have some extra eyes out there. With the video, a screen capture can then be compared to images already in our database." He went on to explain the capabilities of some of the other equipment.

Mark whistled softly. "Pretty impressive."

The agent grinned. "Yeah, and this baby is armored." He picked up a small ear-piece. "We got a present for you."

In a few minutes, they had Mark wired so he could send and receive audio.

"You can speak directly to Officer Sheridan, but we'll hear everything as well. You can turn it off with that little button there so we aren't subjected to every word of your conversation, but when the time comes near, you need to remember to turn it back on. I'll be listening in and relaying information to other teams, in addition to giving you updates."

Feeling in over his head, Mark licked his lips. "Got it."

Jim thanked the men for the quick rundown, and poked a finger in Mark's chest. "If we can't stop this, and things get hot, I expect you to high-tail it to that van. This vest you're wearing," He prodded it again. "it's only good against certain kinds of weapons."

"What about you?" After his initial reaction to seeing himself a victim in the photo, Jim hadn't mentioned anything about it. If the man was nervous or scared, he kept it hidden well. Mark had to admire him for that.

"Never mind about me. This is my job, not yours. You just give me your word that you'll get your ass out of harm's way."

"I don't have a death wish—I'll get back." Mark shuffled his feet and rubbed the back of his neck. He might not have a death wish, but he also had no intention of scuttling off to safety while the bad guys were killing people.

Eyes narrowed, Jim studied him, but his cell-phone rang, and with a last hard look, Jim answered the phone.

A surge of fans headed into the stadium in the next hour leading up to the first pitch. Once the game began, the crowd thinned out. By the second inning, the lights came on, casting a warm glow above the stands. He and Jim made several circuits around the stadium and Mark noted the abundance of Chicago police officers. A contingent of mounted police and several officers with dogs patrolled the sidewalks. As they passed a group of young people, Mark

310

heard one comment on the police presence. He had to bite his tongue not to tell the kid to get away from the park. Jim had explained that if there was a public announcement concerning this, it would do little more than create panic. If the terrorists were deterred, either by the warning or if the game were canceled, they'd likely just go to ground and strike somewhere else. Not only that, but creating panic and disrupting the normal activities of Americans was half the goal.

Jim left Mark outside the left field gate while he went to double-check something. This was where he'd seen the father and son exiting just prior to the shooting. If he could spot them exiting, it was the best chance he had of preventing the annihilation at this gate.

While Mark understood, and even agreed with the rationale, he couldn't help feeling guilty and wondering if every fan he passed was someone who would be a victim later. The game progressed and when some celebrity led the crowd in singing "Take me Out to the Ballgame", Mark's jaw clenched and he took a deep breath. The clock was ticking.

He closed his eyes and pulled the dream up again. The gunmen had worn dark hooded sweatshirts with a large Cubs' logo emblazoned on the left side of the chest. They'd used the baggy sweatshirts to conceal their weapons. Mark had seen them at gates K, D and F, but wasn't sure if any had been stationed at gate N leading out of the bleachers. Jim had teams there. He focused on anything that had been in the vicinity of the gunmen. Cars, vendors, a person who stood out from the crowd. Anything. The terrorists had taken up positions flanking the gate, partially hiding behind the great white doors chained open at the end of the game. When they began firing, their stream of fire crossed. As panic set in, the crowd had fallen back, racing in the other direction. At least half the dead had been trampled in the ensuing panic, many on the ramp that wound down from the lower grandstands. With the same scenario playing out at three of the four gates, the death count had to be in the hundreds if not thousands. Countless more would be injured.

A hand clapped him on the shoulder and Mark whirled. "Hey!"

Jessie jumped back, her hands up. "Whoa! Take it easy."

Heart hammering, Mark bent, hands on his knees. Slowly, he straightened. "Damn it, Jess."

She cocked her head, one eyebrow raised. "You're a bit jumpy. You sure you're up to this?" She wore a Chicago PD navy t-shirt, and he could make out her Kevlar vest beneath it. That gave him some peace of mind.

"Yeah, I'm up to it. I was just going over the dream in my mind when you startled me is all."

"Sorry." She took a quick peek around, then reached up and stroked his cheek. "I hope I didn't cause you to miss something important."

Seeing nobody paying any attention to them, Mark ran his hand from her shoulder up to the back of her neck, pushing his fingers up through the soft warm strands at the nape. He pulled her in for a brief kiss. "I hope I don't get you fired, but I had to do that."

She remained close and grinned. "Nah, nobody's looking. Besides, you kissed me, and it's not like they can fire you. I could press charges for interfering with an officer in the line of duty." Her arms crossed, and she brought a hand up to her chin, head cocked. "Or maybe...assault."

Mark smiled. "It would never stick."

Jessie laughed. "You're probably right." She took one of his hands in his, her lighthearted mood evaporating. She searched his eyes. "I know this is bigger than what you've

312

done before, but do you think there's a chance we can stop this?"

Mark took in the extra security around the park, thought of all the teams in place and what he knew of the plan. "Jim's got everything covered, as far as I can tell. It's just a matter of spotting the gunmen before they start shooting." He sighed and added, "I hope."

A tiny smile returned to Jessie's face. "You're pretty remarkable, you know that?"

Surprised, Mark stepped back. "What makes you say that? I'm shaking in my boots here."

"No, not about that. I think we're all wound pretty tight right now. I mean that you not only are working with Jim, but you're even praising him."

Mark opened his mouth, but closed it without saying anything. What could he say? That holding a grudge would be pointless at the moment? Maybe later, when everyone was safe, he could resurrect the anger, but not now. Not when so many depended on their cooperation. He stuck his hands in his pockets and kicked at a pebble, sending it skittering across the street. The crowd roared, and he turned towards the field. "It's almost time."

Jessie nodded. "Yeah, I have to get back to my post." Without a glance to see who was looking, she stood on her toes and kissed him. "Be careful."

CHAPTER TWENTY-SIX

Jim returned along with four other agents. All wore varying types of Cub's apparel, and he knew that each agent had a small arsenal on his body. It eased Mark's mind somewhat. The game had progressed to the top of the ninth and the first out by the Milwaukee Brewers brought a huge cheer from the stands along with a trickle of fans exiting. With the Cub's in the lead, Mark noted most of the fans leaving were Brewer fans. A thunderous cheer rose, and along with it, Mark's heart rate. Two outs. Just one more to go and the game would be over. He glanced at his watch. Ten-fifteen. The sound of the crowd increased, and he could picture the fans all standing to 'help' the pitcher get the final out.

"You ready?" Jim put his phone in his pocket. "Better switch on your mic."

"I guess so." Mark found the button hidden in his collar and clicked it. Adrenaline flooded him, heightening his senses and he was sure that his heart thumped loud enough that the agents on the other end of the audio could hear it.

The trickle of fans became a steady stream, making it harder to pick out a man and small boy. He moved closer to the gate, aware of Jim trailing a short distance behind him. Not only was Mark trying to find the father and son, he was scanning for the terrorists as well. Without the luxury of closing his eyes to pull up their image in his head, he tried to concentrate just on the men in the age range of the father and the terrorist. He headed towards the west end of the gate, taking up one of the positions a terrorist had in his dream. If they weren't there already, they soon would be.

He leaned against the edge of the exit, trying to look like he was waiting for someone. Jim mingled in the crowd, just a few feet away, his gait uneven as he pretended to be inebriated. He had a wide grin on his face and every few seconds, let out a whoop, as though celebrating the Cub's win. With so many people, Mark lost track of the other four agents. He hoped they hadn't gone far. Along the street, officers from the Chicago P.D. stood guard. The gate was really two gates separated by a brick column. Large white double doors secured the gates when closed, but now both sets were open wide.

A burst of people passed, and Mark strained to see back into the crowded concourse for the man and boy while darting looks near the gate for the gunman who would wave. A group of rowdy teens crossed in front of him and he almost missed the father and son. Just as the group jostled past, he saw the boy grin and wave at someone. He followed the child's gaze and saw a man wearing a dark blue Cub's hoodie standing a few feet outside the gate. The man wiggled his fingers and broke into a smile. Mark shivered at the gleam in the man's eye and he forgot about the microphone in his collar. His sharp intake of breath must have registered with the agent on the other end because a voice in his ear asked him if he had something. He kept his eyes glued to the man. "Yeah. I have one. He's just a few feet away."

"Hold your position and keep him in sight. We have help coming your way."

Jim was beside Mark in seconds. "Which one?"

Mark pointed with his chin. "The guy with the hoodie moving towards the far opening there."

As though feeling eyes upon him, the man scanned the crowd, and zeroed in on Mark and Jim.

For the space of one breath, Mark froze, unable to look away. An instant later, all hell broke loose.

The suspect reached beneath his sweatshirt, Jim bolted towards him. Light glinted off metal. Shouts went up and bodies rushed past Mark as two agents, and a Chicago police officer joined Jim in swarming the man.

The suspect shouted in another language as he tried to break free. A voice from the left side of the gate yelled back in the same language. Mark followed the sound. "*Shit. There's the other guy!*"

The second man was standing behind the other door at Mark's gate. He'd already pulled out his weapon. The images from his dream mingled with real time, giving the moment a surreal quality. Shoving people aside, Mark cut through the people, his eyes never leaving the gun.

"Taylor, get back!"

The shout blasted through his ear-piece and he staggered, clutching his ear. He yanked the device out and flung it away. People had already noticed the commotion and added to it with screams and shouts. Mark hesitated, unsure what to do. The distance was short, but the crowd cutting between made trying to cover the distance akin to fording a fast moving river.

He elbowed people aside and shouted, "I need some help on the far side of gate K!"

Without the ear-piece, he had no way of knowing if anyone had heard him. A thick swarm of fans emerged, and Mark tripped on a stroller, his hand scraping on the ground as he fought to keep his balance. Only a few people remained between him and the gunman. The man glanced at Mark, and leveled his gun. Instead of aiming into the stadium, or even at Mark, he swept it towards the left, where his fellow terrorist wrestled with Jim and the other agents. The image of Jim in the photo flashed through Mark's mind.

A portly woman stepped in front of Mark just before he reached the gunman, and with a curse, Mark snagged her by the shoulder and flung her forward. With a leap, he launched himself at the terrorist. He tried to grab the barrel of the rifle, but the impact sent them both crashing into the brick column. Dazed at the impact, Mark blinked a few times to clear his vision. The suspect had landed flat on his back and must have been stunned too, but only momentarily. In an instant, he was rolling to his side. Mark ignored the darkness cutting off his peripheral vision and lunged to straddle the terrorist. The gunman twisted in an attempt to get away and reach his rifle. His eyes shone with hatred and he spat some words at Mark as he struggled.

Mark reached for the gun, fighting for control of it, grunting when an elbow connected with his cheek. The other man held the barrel and levered the butt at Mark, catching him on the left temple. Mark sagged as stars exploded in his head and his vision wavered. His grip on the barrel loosened, but he blinked and fended off the darkness. The suspect tried to hammer him with the butt again, but Mark blocked it and shoved the barrel away. Using his leverage and the other man's momentum, he drove the barrel into the cement where it scraped a white line in an arc on the pavement.

The gun ripped through Mark's hands and he lunged in a desperate attempt to get it back before he realized it was Jim who had taken it. His frozen moment of surprise was broken as a sharp pain burned across his left bicep. Mark gasped as his attention snapped back to the terrorist. The man clutched a knife as he shifted for another attempt.

What the hell? Where had that come from? There had been no damn knife in his dream. Mark threw his body to the right. With Jim controlling the gun, he just wanted to get out of the way. Hand clamped to his arm, Mark staggered to his feet and stumbled a short distance into the stadium, just outside the men's room.

Turning back, he saw Jim and three other agents wrestle the gunman into submission. The whole fight lasted less than a minute. It was over. Relief that the gunmen were caught mixed with anxiety of the outcome at the other gates. He scanned the faces of those exiting, looking for signs of panic.

The crowd churned through the concourse, hardly pausing to take in the scene. He supposed that most thought it was just a drunken fight. A slew of Chicago police flooded the area and the gun was nowhere to be seen. That was probably a good thing.

As the adrenaline ebbed, the pain in his arm and head skyrocketed. He groaned and bent at the waist. Blood welled through his fingers and dripped onto the pavement.

A hand was on his back. "Can you sit?"

It sounded like Jim, but feeling dizzy and light-headed, Mark didn't dare look up, but closed his eyes instead. "Yeah." He folded a leg and sank down, swallowing hard at the sudden nausea the movement caused.

"Stay here. I'll be right back with some help."

That sounded like a great plan to Mark. "I'm not going anywhere."

Beyond the gate, out on the sidewalk, traffic cops directed the crowd. Their orange batons twirled, keeping the people moving. Music blasted from the speakers, and the jubilant mood of the crowd hadn't diminished despite the drama played out just a few minutes ago. It was hard to believe.

Mark bent his head, swiping the blood out of his eye with his shoulder. He looked up the concourse. There were no bodies, just smiling people, happy about the win. A few cast curious glances his way as they passed, but most ignored him.

Paramedics rolled a stretcher up beside him. "Somebody call for a medic?" The one who'd spoken took one look at Mark and answered his own question, "I guess that would be you."

"You guessed right." Mark thought for a second. There had been some initial panic and there was a possibility that someone had been trampled. "I think, anyway. There could be injured farther up the concourse."

The paramedic shook his head. "I don't think so, but others will be checking to make sure. So far, you're it."

"Really?" Mark tried to stand to get a better look, but the other medic put a hand on his shoulder.

"Hold on, pal."

"But I gotta see—"

"There's nothing to see," Jim broke in, striding up to Mark.

Mark craned his neck, wincing as the lights hit his eyes. "What about the other gates?"

"It's all good. The other teams apprehended four more terrorists without a single shot being fired." He pointed at Mark. "You, my friend, were the only one injured." It sounded like an accusation, but the corners of his eyes crinkled.

Sinking back, Mark rested his injured arm atop his bent knees and allowed the medic to take the other one to check a pulse. "Jessie?"

"She's fine." Jim glanced to his left, towards the gate. "Speak of the devil…"

Jessie rushed around the corner and stopped in her tracks, her mouth dropping open. "Are you okay, Mark?" Without waiting for an answer, she turned to Jim. "What the hell happened to him?"

She squatted beside Mark and glanced at his arm before running her fingertips over his cheek. He winced and recalled the blow from the elbow. "It's nothing." The paramedic wrapped a blood pressure cuff around his uninjured bicep, and Mark watched the needle bounce up on the dial as the cuff tightened.

Eyebrow raised in disbelief, Jessie gently grasped his chin and angled his face to see the spot where the butt of the weapon had connected. His head pounded and his stomach churned, but he couldn't admit it in front of her.

"He's fine." Jim shrugged. "He can take a lot more than that."

Mark lifted his head at the tone of voice. Jim met his gaze, a hint of a smile playing around his mouth as his eyes lit with respect.

After a moment, Jim gave a short nod. "I have to get going. I have a ton of paperwork to do." Despite his words, he made no move to leave.

"Sure." Mark would have said more, but the paramedic shone a light in his eyes. The wave of nausea rose to tsunami level, and he put his good arm down as he pivoted to face away from everyone. He lost his lunch and dinner, and almost his consciousness. He focused on Jessie telling him it was okay while the medic told him to take deep breaths.

He spat the bitterness out of his mouth. Someone pressed a wet cloth into his hand.

"Here. You can wipe your mouth with this." It was the paramedic.

"Thanks." Mark blew out a shaky breath and slowly turned back.

Fans still exited, but now it was down to the stragglers—the hard core fans who stayed to celebrate until ushers urged them out. Their whooping and hollering sliced into his brain.

"Dude!" A trio of fans who appeared to be just old enough to drink legally, stopped beside Jim and stared at Mark. "Whoa. Looks like you had real good time!" The guy who spoke appeared to have had a great time himself. His friends laughed.

The speaker raised a plastic cup with an inch of beer left in it. His companions raised empty cups. "To the home team! We won!" He downed the drink, bumped a fist against his chest, and...burped.

Jim threw a glance at Mark and grinned. "Yeah, we did." Then he put an arm out, rounding up the trio. "Time to move along, fellas."

The End

Author Note

I would really appreciate, if you have a moment, if you could please leave a review for this book on Amazon. Many readers enjoy browsing reviews before selecting a book to read.

While this is a work of fiction, a lot of time was investing in researching the three actual Americans who are/were held as enemy combatants. I am not voicing an opinion on whether the real enemy combatants are terrorists or not—I only used the information, and creative license to make my story as realistic as possible—aside from the magical camera. I researched memos to someone at that very brig which discussed issues with the prisoner. At the time I read the memos, they had only recently been declassified and were heavily redacted, making it impossible to determine who the memos were addressed to, or even which prisoner they were discussing. However, there was enough information to build a picture of what life might have been like for those prisoners. There is no acknowledgement by the government of waterboarding or any other methods of enhanced interrogation of these prisoners.

If you have a moment, please leave a review. Many readers love to read reviews before selecting a book to read. For more information on the research, please visit my blog, linked in the next section.

Acknowledgements

I wouldn't have been able to finish this book without the help of so many people. First and foremost, I would like to thank Jessica Tate. For about four years now, we've been pushing each other to write via our online writing sessions. I'm not sure what I would do without that push.

Without my amazing beta reader, this book would have been a complete mess, so a special thank you to Dianna Morris.

And last, but not least, a huge thank you to my 'forumily'. You all know who you are. I love that there is a place I can go to get support, feedback, vent, or just get a much needed laugh. You are all awesome!

About the Author

I know a lot of these are written in third person, but that just feels too unnatural for me so I'm going to be a rebel and write this in first person. I'm M.P. McDonald, and I live in a small town in Wisconsin with my family, just a stone's throw from a beautiful lake, and literally spitting distance to a river on the other side. We love the peace and quiet and being able to go down to the beach on a hot summer day for a quick swim. Chicago and Milwaukee are just an hour's drive away in either direction, so we are never far from the excitement of a big city.

When I'm not writing, I work as a respiratory therapist at a small hospital that is part of a large hospital system in eastern Wisconsin. I enjoy my work and since it's completely different from writing, it keeps things interesting.

I love to hear from readers. No, I mean it. I love to hear from readers, even if it's not all good. Without feedback from readers, I might never have undertaken these books. I hadn't planned on writing a series for Mark Taylor, but readers kept asking, so I was happy to deliver.

CONTACT ME

Here are some ways you can reach me (and I always write back.):

Find the next books in the Mark Taylor Series here: <u>The Mark Taylor Series</u> (available in print and audio book)

My Blog/Website: www.mpmcdonald.com

Email: <u>mmcdonald64@gmail.com</u>

Twitter: @MarkTaylorBooks

Pinterest: <u>http://pinterist.com/mpmcdonald</u>

Made in the USA
San Bernardino, CA
17 January 2016